Something in the ceiling screamed, an incredibly high-pitched, inhuman sound. Vriess could hear it scrambling away from him, letting him know he'd only winged it. Whatever it was. Vriess's eyes tried to track the progress of the creature as it scuttled over the ceiling.

His attention drawn, he didn't see the drop of alien blood suspended from the ceiling right over his leg.

He didn't become aware of it until he smelled his smoking flesh and clothing and glanced down to see parts of his leg melting away. Confused, horrified, Vriess slapped at it. Some of the stuff eating away at his leg got on his fingers and started burning like hell. He swung his hand, then nearly put it in his mouth before realizing what would happen. The whole while he struggled with the pain.

Then it was back; he could hear it—or could it be a different one? This one was more aggressive, not just scrabbling around on the ceiling, but trying to get through it. Suddenly, it broke a corner of the tiling free and shoved its head through.

And it was all head . . .

ALIEN™
RESURRECTION

novelization by
**A. C. CRISPIN
& KATHLEEN O'MALLEY**

based on the
motion picture written by
JOSS WHEDON

ASPECT®

WARNER BOOKS

A Time Warner Company

WARNER BOOKS EDITION

™ and Copyright © 1997 by Twentieth Century Fox Film Corporation
All rights reserved.

Aspect is a registered trademark of Warner Books, Inc.

Cover design by Tony Russo and Don Puckey
Front cover photo courtesy of Twentieth Century Fox
Back cover photos by Suzanne Tenner. © 1997 Twentieth Century Fox. All rights reserved.

Warner Books, Inc.
1271 Avenue of the Americas
New York, NY 10020

Visit our Web site at
http://warnerbooks.com

W A Time Warner Company

Printed in the United States of America

First Printing: December, 1997

10 9 8 7 6 5 4 3 2 1

This book is dedicated to
Sigourney Weaver.
Thank you for creating a
female action/adventure hero
we can all look up to.
After all, the first *"Hero"* was a woman.

SIGOURNEY WEAVER   WINONA RYDER

ALIEN

R E S U R R E C T I O N

TWENTIETH CENTURY FOX presents A BRANDYWINE production SIGOURNEY WEAVER WINONA RYDER "ALIEN RESURRECTION" RON PERLMAN DAN HEDAYA
J.E. FREEMAN BRAD DOURIF and MICHAEL WINCOTT music JOHN FRIZZELL special effects ALEC GILLIS and TOM WOODRUFF, JR. editor HERVE SCHNEID, a.c.e. costumes NIGEL PHELPS
photography DARIUS KHONDJI, a.f.c. produced GORDON CARROLL DAVID GILER WALTER HILL and BILL BADALATO based DAN O'BANNON and RONALD SHUSETT
written JOSS WHEDON directed JEAN-PIERRE JEUNET
www.alien-resurrection.com

PROLOGUE

That's an alien!

Vincent Distephano jerked back involuntarily at the realization. *How the hell did it get down here in the aft command capsule?* He made himself stop moving as he stared in surprise at the creature's grotesque appearance.

The alien's eyes seemed huge, totally disproportionate to the rest of its elongated, misshapen head. The narrow, elliptical iris appeared to curve around the lens, marking it as something other-worldly, non-Terran. It blinked, its translucent lids moving so rapidly, Vinnie couldn't say if the blink started at the top, the bottom, or even from the sides. In fact, the lids, when not in motion, could not be seen at all. It blinked again, rapidly, two, three times, then turned its head.

Was it aware of him?

Oh, shit!

The creature's jaws opened threateningly, thin ropes of clear, thick drool forming between thin lips, dripping slowly down dangerously pointed teeth. So many teeth! The lips drew back in a fierce, but silent snarl and the creature moved forward slowly.

Vinnie forced himself to remain motionless as the thing's maw opened and closed slowly, dripping strands of thick, sticky saliva.

If one of those things got down here, he thought, *there could be more of them. Maybe a whole damned swarm! Where'd they come from anyway? How'd they get aboard?*

Did it matter? This one was here, right now, with him, and that was the bottom line. The alien scuttled forward and stopped, its movement rapid, insectile, its tail bobbing like a sensor. Could it see him? Was it even aware of him here in the command capsule? Were the huge eyes functional, or had they evolved to detect food or prey by some light-source or sensation undetectable to humans? Could it, perhaps, be more sensitive to motion or scent than vision?

The alien's grotesque, elongated head swiveled as though the creature were trying to evaluate the entire scene. The many blinking lights and active, multicolored screens of the command console must be distracting it. Maybe all the command console activity would keep it from discovering Vinnie. He sincerely hoped so. He swallowed.

Just then, one of the observation screens flickered, changing images so rapidly that the alien pivoted to face it. The planet Pluto, sitting silently beneath the ship, was suddenly featured in a startling close-up as one of its few small geysers erupted, spewing liquid nitrogen into space. The brightness of Pluto's frost bands, even with the random dark reddish areas, was a shocking contrast with the total blackness of the space around it. The creature moved its head from side to side, observing the planetary activity. The geyser activity crested, the silent spewing reaching its zenith. The screen brought the activity into clearer focus, zooming in. In response, the alien turned completely away from Vinnie and suddenly darted toward the screen, as mobile as a spider.

Now! Quick! While it isn't looking! Move it! With the sharp reflexes of the trained soldier he was, Vinnie's hand darted out, his trigger finger extending, flexing—

WHAM!

Gotcha, sucker!

He lifted his hand, examining the crushed remains of the dead alien insect stuck to the end of his finger. *Wonder what the hell it was?* He shook his head in disgust. General Perez would have a shit fit if he heard that there was an alien bug aboard the pristine perfection of his vessel, the *Auriga*, never mind right in the command capsule. Was this one the only one, or were there others? It only took two to make a thousand. Hell, with some alien species, it only took **one.**

Still examining the squashed bug, the young soldier took a last slurp from his milk shake, swallowing the dregs. *He'd have just as big a shit fit about your eating on duty, boy.* Vinnie smiled. Yeah, General Perez was strictly by-the-book, but Vinnie had missed breakfast and he wouldn't make it to lunch without something to tide him over. Sitting in the command capsule was about the most boring thing to do on the enormous ship. The only thing worse would be to be stuck here with a growling stomach.

He crushed the flimsy cup and stowed it in a pocket, then took the straw from his drink and poked at the remnants of the bug with it. He could still see the elongated head, the tiny, but vicious teeth.

Ugh! You are one ugly mutha. So, how did **you** *crawl on board? You must be from one of the general's "unofficial" cargo deliveries from some obscure colony beyond the fringes of the frontier. Not that I would know, or would wanna know!* When you were a soldier working on a top-secret installation drifting around the gravitational center of Pluto and Charon—*in other words, the middle of bum-fuck nowhere!*—you learned not to ask, not to tell **anything.**

The only thing Vinnie had learned in his seemingly endless one-year tour of duty aboard the *Auriga* was that an assignment to a top-secret installation had to be the most **boring** job any soldier could be cursed with. Nothing ever happened here, nothing! And General Perez made sure of it, with his constant inspections, his spit-and-polish routine. Every piece of equipment, every computer chip, every installation aboard the *Auriga* was top of the line, new, shiny, polished, and maintained to perfection. There weren't even any mechanical crises to relieve the boredom.

Well, in three months, Vinnie would be out of here. And having successfully completed a top-secret tour, he'd have his pick of assignments.

Better believe my next one will have more action than this did. Maybe the outpost on Rigel. Shit happens there. It's cutting edge. Not like this spook-fest.

He inspected the insect again, picking the pieces apart with his straw. The *Auriga*'s losing war with bugs was at least humorous in a ludicrous way. Vinnie wasn't used to seeing insects in space. Of course, the military was notorious for transporting vermin anywhere it traveled, from rats and fleas in cargo and food stores aboard ancient wooden ships, to the introduction of the brown tree snake around the South Pacific Islands in cargo, food, and weaponry crates that caused the extinction of entire bird species in the twentieth century, to a nearly debilitating infestation of common cockroaches from supposedly sterilized, vacuum-sealed dehydrated food delivered to the first Mars colony in the early days of space colonization. But the conditions of most cargo holds usually eliminated the little bastards, so these days the problem was minimized.

Except for the *Auriga*. Between the mosquitoes that had escaped from some early lab experiment and kept popping up in the strangest places, to the spiders that had appeared suddenly after one of Perez's unofficial cargo drops, to the occasional alien bug like the one he'd just squashed, the huge spaceship seemed like a giant bug collector! It was as if the galaxy's lowest life-forms had made it their business to show General Perez that no matter how important he was to the military, no matter how critical his hush-hush operations were out here on the edge of the solar system, he still couldn't control Mother Nature. Vinnie smiled.

Scraping the remnants of the bug, still dripping blood and drool, into the plastic straw, Vinnie considered reporting the "sighting." That was the general's rule. It drove the Old Man crazy to have any uninvited guests aboard his pristine vessel. He always wanted the bugs caught, alive if possible, for "classification" so they could track down its origins. Vinnie thought about the paperwork involved, the investigation, thought about all that ridiculous hassle over a bug. He looked at the end of the straw.

Screw that!

Pointing the straw toward the immaculate viewport of the command capsule, he blew hard into it, ejecting the crushed insect. It impacted against the clear port, splattering, sticking to the transparent material just like a bug on the windshield of a land speeder. Vinnie laughed.

And that, son, is the high point of this interminable shift!

He glanced over the command console and the multiple screens. Everything was quiet. Calm. Boring as death. Even the geyser had stopped erupting. The soldier sighed, scratched his nearly shaven head, and tried not to watch the clock counting down the seconds left in his shift.

Maybe another bug would show up to distract him. He could always look forward to that.

1

Dr. Mason Wren moved briskly along the neutral-colored corridors toward his main lab. General Perez had summoned him for an unexpected briefing while he was in the middle of breakfast, and the twenty-three minutes he'd lost in that meeting were now playing havoc with the scientist's schedule. Fortunately, Wren could rely on his staff to be on time, to start all the morning programs, check all the results of the night shift's work, and be ready to apprise him of the experiment's current status. He strode along, checking his lapel pager out of habit. No messages. *Father*—or rather, the artificial male voice of the massive state-of-the-art computer system that maintained life-support, research functions, and all other critical systems of the gigantic *Auriga*—would tell him if there were any messages.

No news is good news.

When Perez had first called him, he'd anticipated trouble, some problem in the new construct, but no. It'd just been some work details the Old Man wanted him to be aware of, so he could be sure his chief scientist was up to date. It'd been two weeks without any middle-of-the-night summons to the lab, and Wren had been gratified at the sudden burst of progress they'd been making. Maybe, at last, they'd finally turned the corner.

The slender, balding scientist approached the lab doors at his usual quick clip, barely noticing the two fully armed soldiers standing guard. They were invisible to him, part of the scenery, like furniture or the rivets on the pneumatic doors. He was aware on some level that the soldiers themselves changed every four hours, but to Wren they all looked identical—square-jawed, eyes locked ahead, olive-drab body armor, massive weaponry held at ready, ever on alert. Black, white, brown, male, female—they all looked the same to Wren. They were soldiers. Grunts. Joes.

He and his staff were *doctors*. They were *scientists*. From the least experienced tech to himself, his staff served a higher purpose; the expansion of knowledge, the advancement of humanity, the improvement of the human condition. The soldiers had one purpose to Wren, to make sure he and his staff could accomplish their goals. They were all—both soldiers and scientists—military, but the demarcation of value was clear in Wren's mind.

As he continued his approach, the doors opened soundlessly, admitting him to the main lab. As he passed the two guards, he noted distantly, with some amusement, that not only did they *look* identical, they even chewed their gum in the same rhythm. Like robots. No, not like robots. Robots had actually been pretty individualistic . . . when they'd still existed.

Behind him, the doors closed as soundlessly as they'd opened, and now the soldiers were forgotten. As he'd expected, his staff was all here, everyone fully engaged, doing their jobs, the work of science. And this lab was the perfect place to do that job. Every piece of equipment, every program, every person in here was the best. And their results would prove their value.

Wren came up on the first workstation, glancing at the myriad screens there. He noted the rapidly shifting data patterns, recording in his mind the progress they indicated. He looked sideways at Dr. Carlyn Williamson, and she gave him a small smile.

"We're still on the money, Dr. Wren," she told him, pleased.

He smiled back. "Nice way to start the morning, Carlyn."

He moved to the next station, nodding at Drs. Matt Kinloch, Yoshi Watanabe, Brian Clauss, Dan Sprague, and their graduate student, Trish Fontaine. Kinloch gave him a thumbs-up, which Wren knew was a positive reference to a battery of tests they'd begun last night. Wren returned the gesture and kept moving. One part of his mind noted the similarity of garb of himself and his staff—scrubs or military drabs covered by identical ubiquitous lab coats—and wondered if Perez had as much trouble telling his people apart as Wren did the general's soldiers.

After he'd toured the area once, and been satisfied that everything was exactly the way he wanted it—a situation that seemed almost too good to be true—Dr. Wren finally allowed himself to approach the incubator.

Dr. Jonathan Gediman, his young, dark-haired, eager associate, was waiting for him, his body so tense with anticipation, Wren half expected him to start dancing from foot to foot. Wren really couldn't blame his protégé. Everything he'd seen this morning told him things were still progressing beautifully. But after all the failures they'd endured so far, Wren wanted to postpone any sense of satisfaction. There was still plenty that could go wrong.

"You waited for me," Wren said to his associate. "I appreciate that."

Gediman nodded. "I had enough to keep me busy. Are you ready to view her now?"

Wren repressed a frown. He didn't like the tendency Gediman had to personalize the specimen. It didn't seem professional. But Gediman was such a good worker, so committed to the experiment, and so creative, that Wren tried to overlook such foibles.

"Sure," Wren told Gediman, "let's look at the specimen."

Gediman tapped the controls in the proper sequence, and they both watched data stream across the small screen at the top of the incubator. The tall metal cylinder adjusted its own temperature, as cold vapors wafted off the exterior. Slowly, mechanically, the external metal housing rotated, then rose, moving up until it touched the ceiling, where it halted. The metal housing opened automatically, revealing a smallish cryogenic tube about a meter long and a half meter in diameter.

Wren stared up at the data. The length and progress of incubation, components of the chemical growing medium, electrical stimulation of cells, and so on, moved across the screen in a constantly updated pattern.

"There she is!" Gediman's voice murmured softly.

His tone made Wren glance at him. Gediman's eyes were wide, his expression as hopeful as a father seeing his newborn infant for the first time. It pleased Wren. In many ways, this *was* Gediman's offspring. Gediman, Wren, Kinloch, Clauss, Williamson—every person in this lab was the specimen's parent, and Wren encouraged them to feel proprietary about it. That kind of possessive pride encouraged greater effort, more creative thinking, a devotion to the cause that no salary could compensate for. Wren had to smile.

"Look at her face!" Gediman said with that same proud awe.

Wren looked, as the specimen floated into view

through the opaque gel that surrounded it, nurtured it, urged it to develop. At first, the specimen seemed little more than a vague mass. Curled in a classic fetal position—*and that alone marks a miracle of scientific achievement*—it floated closer to the glass, allowing Wren to see what Gediman had noted.

It was the face of a child, a lovely human girl, and Wren found himself swept up in the same excitement that had captured Gediman. The features had developed to the point where they were recognizable, not just as human, but as an *individual*. Tiny wisps of baby-fine brown hair floated around the perfectly shaped head, giving the specimen an ethereal appearance, like some kind of mer-child. Wren blinked, pulling his mind out of fantasy. His trained eye examined the various tubes, cables, and readout sensors attached to the tiny specimen. Everything was right where it was supposed to be, doing its job, feeding the specimen, nurturing it, stimulating it to grow and develop far faster than nature ever intended.

But then Wren had no patience for nature—not for its slowness, not for its errors, and certainly not for its random surprises. He was not the least bit interested in nature's surprises. His job was to anticipate nature and mold it to his needs. It was beginning to look as if he'd finally done that. He smiled, his fingers grazing the incubator's sides almost caressingly.

"She's beautiful, isn't she?" Gediman said quietly.

Wren opened his mouth then closed it, only nodding. *It's certainly developing far better than we had any right to hope.* As the specimen floated away from him, he thought he saw the developing eyes roll under their lids. He wondered if it could yet detect differences in light and dark. He wondered what, if anything, it could sense.

*   *   *

Suddenly, it was bright and she recoiled. You could be seen in the light. It was harder to hide in the light. Her body curled around itself. The warm wetness surrounding her said safety, but the bright light made her fear. Chaotic dream images flickered across her faltering consciousness.

The cold comfort of cryo-sleep.

The driving need to protect her young.

The strength and companionship of her own kind.

The power of her own rage.

The warmth and safety of the steaming crèche.

The images were meaningless and meaningful at the same time. She recognized them on a level far beyond consciousness, far beyond learning. They were part of her, part of who she'd been, what she'd been. And now they were part of what she was becoming.

She floated in the gelatinous, comforting warmth, trying to hide from the light. And the sounds. Murmuring, distant sounds that were outside of her. Inside of her. They came and went, the sounds, meaning nothing, meaning everything.

She heard the inside sounds again, one so much stronger than the others. The one she always listened to. The one she tried so hard to remember. She heard it whisper—

My mommy always said there were no monsters—no real ones. But there are.

If only she knew what it meant. Perhaps someday. . . .

For just a moment, Wren let himself hope, let himself anticipate. There would be papers. Books. Publications. Awards. This was just the beginning.

The fetus floated, turning in the gel-filled incubator, and Wren had to admit that Gediman was right. It was beautiful. A perfect specimen. . . .

Its back was to him now and the curved spine bumped the glass. He saw it then, something that had not been there before.

"Did you notice that?" he asked Gediman matter-of-factly, keeping his voice even.

"What . . . ?" Gediman muttered, then spied the specimen's back.

"There." Wren pointed to the four buds on either side of the spine. "These. Four of them. Right where the dorsal horns should be."

Gediman frowned, seeing them. "You think she'll start developing abnormalities?"

Wren shook his head. "We'll watch them. They could mark the beginning of embryonic failure."

"No . . . !" Gediman sighed.

"Let's not anticipate trouble. If we get lucky, they may just be vestigial growths. In that case, they could be removed."

Gediman looked worried, some of his earlier joy dissipating.

Wren patted his back. "It's still far superior to any specimen we've grown to date. I'm hopeful. You should be, too."

His associate smiled again. "We've come so far, and she's doing so well. I hope you're right, Dr. Wren."

So do I, Wren thought, watching the specimen. He hoped this was not yet another of nature's little jokes at his expense.

One month later, Wren and Gediman once again stood before the incubator. This unit was much larger than that first one had been, nearly three meters in height and a meter around. The child-size specimen that had floated like a small cork in that early incubator had grown and flourished until it nearly filled this current chamber.

The atmosphere in the lab was one of high anticipation. Wren couldn't help but notice how often his staff members wandered close to the incubator, just to look at it, marveling at what they'd accomplished.

So much from so little. Ancient blood samples. Bits of tissue from the marrow, the spleen, the spinal fluid. Scattered, shattered DNA. Infected cells. From all that, this.

The specimen turned, its shoulder-length, wavy brown hair floating loosely around its face, occasionally obscuring the attractive, recognizably human features. Its hand curled into a fist, then relaxed. The eyes beneath the closed lids moved back and forth.

Dreaming? What kind of dreams does it have? Whose dreams does it have?

Wren looked up at the incubator's readouts. The first screen showed the specimen's ECG—its heartbeat, steady, rhythmic, its sinus arrhythmia completely normal. Good. Very good.

He turned to the second screen. Where the first screen was labeled to identify the adult-size female specimen—the designation "HOST" appearing in prominent letters—the second screen was labeled "SUBJECT." Across it registered a second ECG. This heartbeat moved much faster than the host's, with a wave pattern that was tachycardic. Still, it was just as strong as the host. It was sound.

Wren smiled. He looked again into the face of the host specimen. It was frowning. If he were more of a romantic, like Gediman, he would think it looked unhappy.

Whose dreams are you having? Your own? Or those of your symbiont? I would love to know. . . .

Dr. Jonathan Gediman couldn't believe his luck. Dr. Wren was actually going to allow *him* to do the operation. Standing in the chilly sterile room, in sterile clothing, with his body completely scrubbed and ready, he fumbled with the surgical visor as he manipulated it into place. Beside him Dr. Wren stood ready, gowned, expectant, anxious. Dr. Dan Sprague was there, too. Dan had congratulated him when Wren made the announcement, his sincere good wishes helping a little to ease Gediman's jitters. Some of them anyway.

The visor focused wildly, and he touched the controls. The apparatus would allow him to automatically enjoy whatever range of vision he needed, from far-seeing binocular vision to a microscopic ability that would let him examine tissue right down to the cellular level. Taking a deep breath, he tried to steady his nerves. He nearly jumped when Sprague reached over with sterile gauze and mopped his brow.

"Take it easy there, bud," Dan teased. "You're sweatin' like a dog."

Gediman nodded, thinking distractedly, *Dogs don't sweat.* He blinked, and focused his mind. If only Wren weren't standing so *close.* Even without the visor, Wren would spot the tiniest screwup, the smallest error. For that matter, so would Sprague.

Cool it, Gediman, he told himself. *It's not like this is your first surgery! This is a simple procedure. You've done similar ones a million times.*

Yeah, but not here. Not on this specimen.

Not on Ripley.

Specimen was Wren's word, but Gediman had stopped thinking of her that way when she was just a microscopic bundle of eight perfectly formed cells.

He turned his head and let himself look at her, really *look.* Behind the thick transparency of the enclosed surgical chamber that separated her from the medical staff, she was breathing normally, slowly, in anesthetized sleep. She looked relaxed there on the table, her eyes unmoving, her strong jaw slack in sleep, her lips slightly parted. Except for the multiple catheters and sensors decorating her body under the diaphanous, shroudlike surgical drapes, she looked as attractive as Sleeping Beauty must have waiting for her prince's kiss. Gediman wet his lips.

She looks normal. A tall, attractive young woman. Even the clinging amniotic gel and the blue tinge to her skin doesn't change that.

He was so proud of her.

She'd come through so much, accomplished so much already. And this would be her proudest moment—if he didn't screw it up.

He walked up to the instrument panel, slipping his gloved arms into the surgeon's controls past the elbows. Wren and Sprague flanked him, watching. Around the encased surgical theater, behind protective transparencies, milled the rest of their team. Every one of them had an investment here.

He slid his fingers into the sensitive glovelike controls, felt them mold around his hands and arms, and gently wiggled them to get the contact right. Carefully, he manipulated the controls, watching the various robot arms in the surgical chamber come alive in response.

"I'm ready," he said to the room, glancing at his readouts. Everything looked good. Brain activity. Respiration. Heart rate.

He moved the laser saw into position over her sternum.

"Remember," Wren said softly, nearly in his ear, "take it slow. Just one step at a time. I'm right beside you." He'd meant that to give Gediman confidence but it had just the opposite effect.

He initiated contact with the laser, drawing a bright, straight line so the incision would proceed caudally from midsternum to just above the umbilicus. He glanced at Ripley's readouts. She wasn't under that deep, and he wanted to be sure she couldn't feel this.

"I've got it," Sprague said quietly beside him, mopping his brow again. It was Dan's job to keep track of her anesthesia. Gediman trusted him, but. . . .

The initial incision was done. He manipulated the robot clamps, attached them to the skin, had them retract just enough. Then the laser again, to carefully cut between the muscles on the fascia, right on the *Linia alba*. Then, after that, the peritoneum. In moments, he was through. Bleeding was minimized as the laser cauterized as it cut. The incision looked good.

"Excellent," Wren breathed. "Okay, now, move the tank in place. Careful. . . . Get ready with the amnio. . . ."

Gediman was ahead of him. He'd already signaled for the small incubator full of amniotic fluid to be delivered. He watched as it slid into place mechanically beside Ripley's supine body, nestling near her ribs and hip. The surgeon could feel the anxiety in the room climb as the tiny chamber silently traveled to its destination, halted, then slowly raised its lid.

"Good," said Wren. "Good. We're ready."

Gediman bit his lip. His right hand flexed in the control glove.

A specially padded robot clamp moved into position at his urging, and cautiously snaked its way into the incision site, disappearing inside Ripley. Gediman turned back to the readout screens, following the clamp's progress inside his patient. He manipulated the clamp carefully, skillfully.

A bead of sweat tracked down his forehead, sliding toward the visor, but Sprague was there, mopping him, trying to control the profuse, nerve-induced sweating that had broken out all over the surgeon, in spite of the cold room.

He watched the clamp and the color-enhanced images of the interior of his patient the biosensors provided. He smiled.

"There she is," he murmured delightedly.

The prize. The goal of all their work.

He tightened the clamp carefully, even as Wren whispered unnecessarily, "Easy! Easy!"

"I've got her," Gediman purred, as he slowly extracted the clamp from Ripley's body.

Every eye was focused on the incision site as the clamps drew out of Ripley's abdomen.

Cradled in the padded vise curled a tiny, red-stained, embryolike creature, its features blurred by the blood and connective tissue of its mother.

"Readouts are good," Wren told him, as he studied the parasite's bio-scan.

"Same here," Dan agreed, reporting on Ripley's.

Dimly, Gediman was aware of the rest of the crew drawing closer to the glass, peering to see for themselves. No one spoke. All eyes focused on that one small bundle. . . .

"I'm severing the connections," Gediman announced.

"Go ahead," Wren agreed.

He moved another device around the creature, one that would cut and cauterize each of the six thin umbilical-like structures that tied the tiny Alien to its host. He moved the cutting clamp quickly, expertly, decisively. . . . Four, five, six! It was free.

The creature suddenly writhed and uncoiled, as if being severed from its mother had told it it was time to begin its own independent life. Time to breathe. Time to grow. Time to move.

It squirmed, twisted in the padded clamp, lashing its tail, and finally opened its small jaw in a silent scream.

"Damn!" Sprague swore at the tiny bundle's raging protest.

"Careful!" Wren ordered, all business. "Don't release it. Get it in the tank."

Gediman nodded tersely. He knew he had the thing

secure as it fought and twisted impotently in the clamp's grasp. He slipped it into the amnio tank, not releasing it until the cover was nearly secure. He released the creature and extracted the clamp in one swift move that left the tiny Alien encased safely in the protective incubator.

"Beautiful!" Wren exclaimed. "Beautiful work, Gediman." He grasped Gediman's shoulder in congratulations.

The surgeon released the breath he was holding, as Sprague mopped his brow again. He felt his whole body relax and only then realized how tense he'd been. "Thank you, Dr. Wren."

They all watched as the small incubator tank—with the now frantically swimming creature searching for escape—disappeared from the surgical chamber the same way it had been delivered. Kinloch and Fontaine would accompany it on its journey to the growing chamber, and monitor it until it was out of danger.

Gediman looked across at the observation deck, saw the rest of the team smiling at him, Kinloch giving him a thumbs-up. He smiled in return. Then, finally, he turned back to Ripley.

Pulling off his visor, he hesitantly glanced at Wren. "Well . . . ?" He indicated Ripley, still sleeping in the chamber.

"The host?" Wren asked, not looking at her.

Gediman glanced at the readouts. "Her ECG is normal. . . . She's doing fine." He stopped himself, as he realized he was arguing *for* her. Wren already thought his interest in this *specimen* was unprofessional. He had to watch what he said; Wren hadn't made up his mind about her fate. Gediman waited tensely.

Wren looked over the screens, then took a second to gaze at Ripley. Finally, he said, "Sew her back up."

Gediman had to stop himself from blurting out, *Thank you!* He knew it was well within Wren's right as chief scientist to terminate her. For some reason, Gediman couldn't accept that. It was such a *waste*! Especially after all their work.

"Dan," Wren was saying to their associate, "close up here, will you? I think Gediman's had enough excitement for one day."

Gediman smiled, and nodded at Dan.

"Sure thing," Sprague agreed. "Be happy to."

Gediman glanced over the readouts automatically one more time. Anesthesia, respiration, heart rate, all looked good. He let Wren pull him aside.

"Well," Gediman said, letting the excitement creep into his voice, "that went as well as could be expected."

"Oh, better than that, Doctor," Wren said respectfully. "Far better than that."

Something told her to wake. She ignored it. Once she woke, the dreams would all come real. Once she woke she would exist again, and there had been peace, finally, in nonexistence. She was sorry that it might be over.

Something told her to wake. She resisted.

Slowly, she registered a dim sensation. Something outside of herself. Something happening to her self. Something taken from her.

Something she wanted taken?

She couldn't remember.

In spite of the cold, in spite of the brightness, she opened her eyes.

She could see everything happening all around her, see it perfectly. But she could understand none of it. Strange metallic and plastic armatures moved rapidly around her, pulling closed a gaping wound in her chest, even as a different armature moved to seal the wound closed. She registered the sensation, some slight pain that was easy to ignore. Her eyes moved around as she gathered information.

Then she realized. It was gone. They'd taken it from her. Her young. Part of her felt enormous relief. Another part of her felt tremendous rage. She vacillated between the feelings, understanding neither, merely experiencing the emotional swings as she lay perfectly still, watching the surgical arms.

Two of the mechanical arms, she realized, were somehow connected physically to one of the creatures looking into the strange, clear egg case she was trapped in. She was ringed by these creatures, all of them looking down at her while they presumed her helpless. The arms swung and moved, performing their work, completing tasks she had neither asked for nor wanted nor understood.

She watched the creature manipulating the arms, watched it watching her so intently. With neither rage nor relief, she reached up quickly, snatched the forearm of the creature shielded from her behind the sealed egg case. With detached curiosity, she gripped the arm with a modicum of strength and twisted it just to see what would happen.

It was interesting. The creature instantly stopped hurting her. That was good. She twisted more, and there was a strange cracking, grinding feel to the part of the being caught inside the artificial arm. Even more interesting was the reaction of all the creatures outside the clear egg case. The one attached to the arm was flailing wildly, pounding on the case with its free arm, its mouth opening hugely as if to bite her. How funny. She wondered if it were making sounds. The strange egg case she lay in seemed to prevent any sound from passing through, because all she could hear was her own breathing.

She blinked and twisted the arm again. More flailing, more writhing. And now more and more creatures *racing around the one she'd caught, grabbing him, moving their tiny, ineffectual mouths open and closed, waving their arms. So much excitement.*

One of the creatures pushed the others aside, looking down at her in the case. He stared at her wildly, his tiny eyes opened as wide as they would go. He slapped at devices on his side of the case, manipulated things she couldn't see, and suddenly, she felt her eyes grow heavy.

She was sorry. She didn't want to sleep. She wanted to watch the creatures. Learn from them if she could. And more than that, she wanted to get out of here. . . . But sleep stole over her before she could worry about it further.

In seconds, the gleaming, sterile surgical theater had gone from exultant success to chaos. Wren could hear the horrible snap and crunch of Dan Sprague's bones from ten feet away where he and Gediman had been discussing the Alien embryo. Dan's screams could be heard throughout the entire station.

The sterile chamber had instantly filled with every available team member, soldiers, and other observers, all of them violating every protocol they'd been rigidly trained to follow. And none of them could free Sprague from the host specimen's grip.

It was unprecedented. It was unexpected. It was exciting!

Wren shoved his way to the front where he could see the host and her victim, and get control of the situation. Everyone was shouting conflicting orders, while Dan just kept screaming . . .

. . . and she just lay there under her drapes, her wound only partially sealed, her face as impassive as a sphinx as she deliberately twisted.

Wren pounced on the anesthesia controls, increasing the dosage radically.

Gediman was beside him, frantic for his pet. "Don't kill her, Doctor Wren, **please don't kill her!**"

Don't beg, Gediman, Wren thought at him in disgust. *It's unprofessional.*

The host blinked lazily, still not releasing Dr. Sprague. Her eyes moved, seemed to latch onto Wren's. She looked straight at him, into him, through him. He felt a chill. Then her lids closed slowly, and in seconds her grip relaxed.

Clauss and Watanabe had Dan on a stretcher in seconds, Watanabe quickly, efficiently examining the badly broken arm. Bones pierced the skin and sterile gown in several places. The arm was mangled so badly the hand was facing in a completely unnatural direction. Blood pulsed from Dan's arm, flowed over the immaculate sterile gown, splatted onto the floor. In the sterile room painted in gleaming whites and neutral tones, the blood's brilliant red was all the more shocking.

At least he was sterile, Wren thought clinically. *We should be able to avoid infection, in spite of all these people violating the sterility of the room.* He was pleased to see Watanabe taking charge. He'd specialized in orthopedics before coming here.

The young doctor looked up from his writhing patient. "Dr. Wren, I'd like to take Dan into surgical room C and prep him immediately."

"Go right ahead, Yoshi," Wren approved. "Brian and Carlyn can assist. Will you need anyone else?"

"No, that should be fine," Watanabe assured him, then signaled to the soldiers to take Sprague's stretcher out of the room. Everyone but Gediman filed out with it.

Gediman had moved back to the robot controls, efficiently closing up the host's wound, in spite of the disorder around him. Wren approved.

But Gediman looked twitchy. Wren wondered if the

sudden shocking violence of the host's attack had been
more than he could handle.

"You okay?" Wren asked. The theater was once
again quiet, restored to its normal sterile ambiance.
Only an abstract pattern of blood spatters marked the
accident.

Gediman nodded abruptly. He finished the closure,
withdrew the instruments. The host slept on, as its surgical chamber was automatically removed to a secured
recovery cell.

"I'm fine," Gediman insisted, in spite of his shaky
voice. "And . . . and I'm grateful, Doctor. I appreciate
your not euthanizing her. I think this was just an unfortunate incident. . . ."

Wren pulled his attention away from the host and
back to his protégé. "There was nothing unfortunate
about it, Gediman. Dan will recover. And now we
know something about the host we didn't know before.
Something we couldn't have anticipated. An unexpected . . . benefit."

He smiled at Gediman, knowing his excitement
about this unexpected development was obvious, and
watched as his associate slowly realized Wren's attitude about the host had changed radically. Suddenly,
Gediman realized Wren no longer saw the host as a
liability but as an advantage. Gediman had long argued
against terminating the specimen, but Wren was only
interested in the wealth of information that could be
gleaned from a cadaver. But now Wren was his ally,
not his opponent, in determining the host's fate.

Gediman relaxed with a sigh and grinned back at
Wren.

"We'll know more in the next few days," Wren said,
"both about the host, and the subject. They should be
very interesting days for us, don't you think, Gediman?"

The associate grinned. "Oh yes, Doctor, I certainly
do."

2

She crouched in the dark, making herself small, and assessed her environment. At least she was finally awake enough to do so. The light was at a minimum, but that did not hamper her. She could see everything she needed to. The space holding her was large enough to stand and stretch in, even walk around, but she did none of those things. She wouldn't, either, until she knew more. She breathed slowly, quietly, and remained folded tight, assessing.

The cell was empty, holding only herself. There was no water, no clothing, no furniture, nothing that she could use to cause harm to herself or others. She was covered with a flimsy, white drapery, left over from the surgery.

There was a small viewport in the ceiling above her cell, and suddenly a shadow crossed it, making her tense. She didn't move, didn't breathe, but paid close attention to the owner of the shadow. Boots appeared, stood over the viewport for several seconds, then quietly moved on. So, she was being watched. That was good to know.

Long minutes later, when she was sure the booted feet were not about to return, she began to assess herself. Her mind was still sluggish from her long sleep, from the surgery.

Surgery. Why did I have surgery? Have I been sick?

She pushed the questions away. They only confused her. She would wait and hope to learn.

Her face itched. She touched it, scratching lightly. Her skin, still wet and tender, peeled off in large flakes. The skin beneath the peelings felt stronger, drier. She scratched herself cautiously, peeling her skin in long, slippery strips that she discarded. It felt good.

While busy peeling herself, she discovered again the scar running along her chest. Her fingers traced the smooth, perfect line. It was sensitive, but not terribly so. Lifting the drape, she peered at the wound. It troubled her, but she couldn't say why.

As she traced the line with a fingernail, she became distracted by her own hand, and pulled it out from under the drape. There was something odd about the hand, something unfamiliar. She peered at the tapered, elegant fingers—only five!—and finally, the fingernails. They were long, strong, extremely sharp. They looked strange, but they were her own nails. Yet, she'd felt as if she'd never seen them before. As if they didn't belong there.

Troubled for reasons she couldn't define, she put one in her mouth and chewed, trying to shorten them, bite them off. But they wouldn't yield, at least not to teeth.

As she bit at her nail, she spotted something dark on the inside of her forearm, near the elbow. She instantly forgot about her nails, and stretched her right arm out to inspect it. There on the skin was a mark. She frowned, trying to remember.

It's a number. The number eight.

She touched it, then pulled her hand away. What

could that mean? Instinctively, she knew it was not her name, nor was it long enough to be her identification.

The number eight.

As she stared at it, trying to make sense of it, she heard a faint buzzing. A tiny, flying organism suddenly circled her head, distracting her. She watched it, fascinated, as it studied her, even as she studied it.

Moving lower, the organism settled on her inner arm, right near the tattoo. She watched patiently, curiously. What was this? What might it do?

Carefully, she lifted her arm for a better view.

The tiny organism had long delicate legs, elegant tiny wings, and a long stinger. A name came back to her.

Mosquito!

She almost smiled at the memory, it was so clear. This was an insect. A mosquito. She watched as it balanced like a dancer on her arm.

Slowly, it inserted its stinger into the flesh of her arm, doing it so delicately she felt nothing. The process amazed her, and she watched with the morbid fascination of a child. The creature's abdomen began to fill

with my blood! It's sucking my blood.

Long forgotten information about the insect began registering in her mind as she watched the creature drink its fill.

Then, in seconds, the insect began to change. Its swollen abdomen began to shrivel, the translucent wings began to curl, the delicate dancer's legs fold up, as if melting from the inside out. In seconds, it was a dried-up black husk.

She blinked, finding the transformation interesting, but only for the moment. Blowing on her arm, she disposed of the corpse, then thought no more about it. Glancing up at the viewport, she waited for the next reappearance of the booted feet.

3

"**N**ame?" the purser asked, checking her register.

"Purvis," the man responded automatically. "Larry. I.D. code twelve, seven, forty-nine." He handed her his computer chip.

She took it, inserted it into her handheld, waited for the information to come up on the screen. She smiled and nodded at him pleasantly. "You're cleared. Welcome aboard, Mr. Purvis."

The short, slender man smiled back at her. *Mr. Purvis.* He liked that. The Xarem corporation touted itself as a top-flight organization, and so far it seemed to be so. The purser waved him into the ship so she could register the woman standing behind him, so he moved along, following the signs for the cryo-units. The ship was small, only used for transport, and even the crew would be going to sleep once they were on course and out of the solar system.

Well, Purvis didn't care if there weren't any amenities on board. According to the literature that had convinced him to sign on to this outfit, they'd all be waiting for him at the nickel refinery on Xarem. The whole damned planet was named for the company. Prior to their mining claim, it'd been nothing but a number. A couple of months nap time, and he'd be there. New career. Starting over. Not bad for a middle-aged guy.

He wouldn't think about the life he was leaving behind him here on the Moon. He'd spent two years trying to patch things up with his wife, all for nothing. His kids were grown and on their own—it was time to move on himself. And it wasn't like he was joining the French Foreign Legion! Conditions on Xarem were supposed to be the best.

Suddenly, a twist of loneliness surprised him, hitting him hard. He shook his head. Time to get over it. Time to move on. This would work. It was a new beginning. A new future.

He'd get to do things on Xarem he'd never have a chance at doing on the Moon. See new things. Experience new experiences. Maybe he could even fall in love again. He was young enough . . . he might even start another family.

Focusing on that hopeful thought, he climbed into the cryotube that had his name printed on the label. A steward was moving among the horizontal sleeping boxes, checking out the tubes, the drug mixtures, the computer setups. Nice and thorough. Purvis liked that.

He stowed his bag in the compartment inside the tube, and settled against the comfortable cushions. Soft music was piped into the tube to relax him, while a gentle, feminine voice told him what was awaiting him in his new career on Xarem. He smiled, closing his eyes, waiting for the cool chill of cryosleep to take him.

This was just the beginning of the biggest adventure of his life.

* * *

Gediman finished the auscultation as Ripley sat quietly on the exam table. Since they'd taken her out of the recovery cell, she'd been the picture of placid cooperation. Because she was being a model patient, Gediman had sent away the armed guard who'd been looming over her, so Ripley could have privacy during the exam. Of course, there were still two guards armed and ready stationed right outside.

Even though there'd been no sign of the violent nature she'd shown during yesterday's surgery, Dan Sprague, recuperating in his quarters, had declined Gediman's invitation to meet her up-close-and-personal this morning. The rest of the staff had shown a similar reaction when they'd learned she would be brought here ambulatory and conscious and had made themselves scarce. That was fine. They all had other critical duties to attend anyway. And besides, Gediman wasn't afraid of her. He was *fascinated* by her. He was grateful for the time he might spend alone with her, studying her, discovering her abilities, her capacities.

You're just a modern Dr. Frankenstein, aren't you, Gediman? And this is your bride. . . .

Walking around behind her, he eased the patient gown apart where it was split up the back, and examined the four diagonal scars on either side of her spine. They were neat, clean incisions, the remnants of the deformed dorsal horns her body had tried to grow. Removing them had been Wren's work, and excellent work it was. Fortunately, they had been merely vestigial, totally useless, and removing them had not compromised her development.

He came around front, aware that she'd never stopped watching him, even when he was behind her. He had the impression that she was ever alert, completely ready . . . for something. He wanted to ease her concerns, whatever they might be.

"Ripley," he said quietly, in the same "doctor-voice" he'd once used on children subjects in another experiment, "I'm going to take some blood from you. The needle will sting a little, but otherwise it won't cause you any harm."

She watched him, giving no reaction. He moved slowly, making sure she could see everything, making sure he didn't startle her.

It's more like working with a big jungle cat than a child. Only her eyes move. Her body stays still, coiled. I almost wish she had a tail she could lash that would at least indicate her mood.

He slowly applied a tourniquet, then picked up the specially designed syringe, needle, and blood-collection tube. They were made from an ancient design but with ultramodern space-age materials. Carefully, he inserted the needle, then moved the collection device over it before even a drop of her blood could escape. The clear tube filled quickly with dark red frothing liquid. She never flinched, watching the procedure with the same dispassionate calm she'd shown all morning.

Just as he finished removing the tube, then the needle, from her arm, he heard Wren's voice.

"Well, how's our number Eight today?" the senior scientist asked, looking at the computer pad that held her complete record. Had any living organism ever been charted so thoroughly? Gediman doubted it.

"Appears to be in good health. . . ." Gediman assured him, labeling the tube and putting it in a special rack.

"How good?" Wren asked.

Gediman couldn't help but grin. "Extraordinary! As in . . . completely off our projected charts!" He glanced at Ripley, wondering how she'd view Wren, but her expression and attitude never changed, though her attention now was on the senior scientist. She peered at him, unblinking, through slitted, emotionless eyes.

Still moving carefully, respectfully, Gediman adjusted the gown, dropping the front below her breasts so Wren could see. "Look at the scar tissue! See the recession?"

Wren stared. Like the doctor he was, he did not notice her lovely, bare female breasts, but instead the incision line that nestled between them. He seemed incredulous. "This is from . . . ?"

"Yesterday!" Gediman said, almost gleeful.

"This is good," Wren admitted, looking pleased. "This is very good."

Gediman nodded like a kid. He knew damned well Wren had never seen tissue regeneration like that in his whole life.

Wren took a step toward the unmoving woman as Gediman lifted the gown back up, tying it behind her neck, restoring her modesty. Wren was smiling at Ripley, as if trying to reassure her. Gediman could tell by his demeanor, though, that he'd never had to work with patients, experimental or otherwise.

"Well, well, well," Wren said patronizingly, "it looks like you're going to make us all very proud—"

Ripley struck, her arm darting out with the speed of a snake as she latched onto the doctor's throat. Wren's voice was cut off in midword.

Before Gediman could even register what was happening, she was off the table, marching the flailing doctor across the room, shoving him roughly against the wall. Wren's face was bright red; he couldn't draw air at all. Gediman gaped, wild-eyed, as the woman who'd sat like a mannequin through an entire physical exam erupted into sudden violence. Grasping Wren's throat with one hand, she lifted the senior scientist a foot off the floor with minimal effort. Gediman was frozen with horror as Wren turned blue, his lips drawn back in a grinning rictus, his heels kicking ineffectually against the wall. Ripley was throttling him with both hands now, as he grasped and clawed at her wrists, fighting, struggling, his efforts useless.

Ripley's eyes weren't passive slits anymore. They were wide, all-seeing, enraged, burning. Gediman could only stare as she uttered her very first word.

"*Why?*" she demanded of the doctor she was killing.

"Oh, my god . . . !" Gediman gasped, every bit as panicked as the choking Wren.

DO SOMETHING! his brain shrilled, and he spun, searching, trying to remember—*THE EMERGENCY ALARM!* He slammed his hand against the red button on the opposite wall.

The sound seemed to activate Wren; he struggled desperately, finally breaking her hold. He fell hard and scrambled to get away but Ripley pounced on him like a cat toying with a mouse already slated for dinner. Her long legs scissored around Wren, squeezing the air from his lungs, as she pinned his shoulders to the floor. Wren clawed the floor in a feeble attempt to escape. Klaxons blared, lights flashed, but Ripley never noticed, just kept strangling the life out of her victim. Single-minded. Predatory.

Pneumatic doors swished open; guards raced in. One of them, with *Distephano* stamped on his helmet, ran up to the woman and aimed his gun at her. "**Let him go!**" Distephano roared at her, his gun held ready, rock-steady. "**Release him or I'll shoot!**"

At point-blank range! Gediman thought, terrified. *He's got that thing on full charge. It's powerful enough to stun a rhino. It'll kill her . . . !* He looked between Ripley and the blue-faced Wren, back and forth. *She has to be stopped, but . . . !* Wren's kicks were growing more feeble.

"**I said let him go!**" Distephano yelled, his voice firm, controlled. The second soldier who'd entered with him acted in perfect consort with her associate, clearly intending to back up his action.

Ripley looked over her shoulder at the armed man and his partner, her expression glazing over, changing back to the dispassionate mannequin. For half a second no one moved, as Distephano's trigger finger tightened imperceptibly. Then the woman opened her hands almost casually, as if she'd just lost interest in Wren, and dismounted from his back. The scientist collapsed against the floor and struggled for air.

Gediman glanced at his senior officer, wanting to go to him, offer first aid, make sure she hadn't crushed his larynx or broken his ribs, but he was afraid to move, afraid any motion on his part would set Ripley off again, or draw the fire of the two soldiers.

Wren suddenly drew in a ragged, harsh breath, his color quickly going from blue to red again. He sucked in air desperately, gratefully.

Distephano moved forward boldly, shoving Ripley, who was standing once more, to the middle of the room. "On the floor! On your face! Now!" he ordered, still shouting, still in cold command.

She stood her ground, every bit as tall as he, and met his gaze defiantly, eye to eye.

He shot her where she stood, the electrical charge slamming into her, sending her hurtling into equipment and specimens.

"NO!" Gediman heard himself scream, his voice high-pitched, shrill—hysterical. Had that stupid grunt killed her?

Both soldiers closed in on the prone woman where she lay sprawled, her limbs twisted, useless. They were ready for another shot—a killing shot.

Before Gediman could do anything, Wren struggled to his knees, waved at the soldiers. His voice was ragged as he called out, "No! No! I'm not hurt! Back off. . . ."

It's too late! Gediman thought, wanting to cry. *Too late! All that work. Now, she's dead. Dead or so badly damaged. . . .*

Ripley groaned, rolled slowly onto her back, panting, looking around the room as if she'd never seen it before. Somehow, her eyes found Gediman, held him. He stared back, amazed. She was still functioning! Her mind still worked! After taking a charge like that!

She stared unflinchingly at Gediman, finally murmuring one word. "Why . . . ?"

Across the room, Gediman heard her quiet question, and felt a stirring of fear. What would happen when she found out?

Surreptitiously, *she tested the restraints again. They held solidly, unyielding. She relaxed. The man sitting in front of her, talking, never noticed, never realized what she was doing even though she was only one good stride away from him. Neither did the armed, alert guard behind her. They were dull, these humans. Dull, and soft, and slow. But they could build effective devices, devices that gave them advantages in spite of their dullness, their softness, their slow speed. Like the device that contained her now. It was comfortable, and stronger than it appeared. Once forced to sit in it, she could not leave. She could not free her body, her arms. When she was locked inside it, they could move her around at will, take her anywhere, do whatever they wanted.*

And all she could do was sit. Sit and wait. She was good at waiting. Better at it, she suspected, than these humans.

The man before her was talking. Talking, talking, talking. He'd been talking for so long she would've happily crushed his throat just to shut him up. He was trying to get her to speak, now that they knew she could. He was trying to get her to recognize simple images and repeat their names. They'd been at this for almost an hour. She was bored to death.

He held up a simple drawing of a building and

spelled out its name. "H-O-U-S-E." She didn't answer, so he spelled it again with infinite patience, his voice gentle, modulated. "H-O-U-S-E." She stared straight at him and said nothing, just to make him uncomfortable. He spelled it again.

The name on his white garment read "Kinloch." The name on the guard's helmet said "Vehrenberg." The sign over the mechanism that opened the door read, "You must summon the guard on duty before the door will be opened." It said the same thing in six other languages including Arabic and Japanese. She knew that because she could read those languages. She didn't question how she could do those things, any more than she questioned how she could breathe, or think, or eliminate. She just did them.

Kinloch held up another drawing. "B-O-A-T."

She wondered if his bones were as brittle as those of the man behind the glass, the man who'd been working on her with the robot arms. Those thoughts entertained her through several more spellings. The fifth time he spelled the same word, she decided she'd had enough. Wearily, she muttered, "Boat."

The man's expression was so pleased, she instantly regretted it. He showed her another picture. This time she repeated the word instantly, just to curtail the repetition. "Dog."

The drawings all had associations in her mind, but none that triggered specific memories. They were things that had names, easy names, names she knew. It was a pointless exercise. She glanced at the pile of drawings Kinloch had in front of him and nearly groaned. It was such a thick pile!

In the experimental lab, General Martin Allahandro Carlos Perez stood ramrod straight, arms crossed across his broad chest as he stared at the video monitor that displayed the woman's testing session. He watched, but he was not sure he approved. Maintaining the host after the subject had been retrieved had never been part of the original plan. It had never even been considered. When the two scientists, Wren and Gediman, and the two soldiers, Distephano and Calabrese, had made their individual reports after the host's attack on Wren, Perez had hauled the two doctors into his office for a good old-fashioned chewing out. But, in spite of the fact that they were military, just like he was, they weren't really soldiers. In spite of their training, they were still *doctors*. While science required the same kind of rigid disciplines that military service did, historically, doctors were always the least conventional of soldiers, forever defying orders and creating havoc during their service. Perez knew it was because their first fealty was to the pursuit of knowledge, while a true soldier's was to his commander, and his unit, and the twin gods of discipline and order. Science and martial order were often incompatible masters, and this host—this *woman*—was proof of that.

*She took a full charge at point-blank range and it merely stunned her. What the **hell** is she? And what the hell do these two want with her?* Perez knew one thing. He didn't like the idea of her staying on his ship. No, he didn't like that, not at all.

The two scientists, still trying to appease him after being forced to admit that they'd maintained the host's life without officially notifying him of their intent to do so—never mind securing his permission—hovered around like a pair of nervous moths looking for a safe place to land. Perez frowned, remembering that they'd found grain moths in the mess stores today. How the tenacious little bastards survived processing he'd never understand.

"It's unprecedented," Wren interjected, as the woman routinely identified the images on the child's flashcards.

"Totally!" his pet doctor, Gediman, parroted right after him. "She's operating at a completely adult capacity!"

The two scientists exchanged eye contact as if they had some sort of telepathic rapport.

Perez frowned. "And her memories?"

A look passed between them. "There are gaps," Wren said finally, reluctantly. "And there's some degree of cognitive dissonance."

Perez wondered if Wren really *knew*, or if he were guessing. Or if *she* were pulling the wool over his eyes. She'd already caught them off guard with two unprovoked acts of violence—*if a predator's attack can ever be considered unprovoked*. What else might she be capable of? Perez was responsible for every person on this ship, even these two damned fools. Could he justify keeping this . . . this . . . *What the hell is she anyway?* Did he dare keep her alive and endanger *everything*, just because she gave these two overgrown kids some extra time to play doctor?

Wren was clearly uncomfortable with Perez's lack of enthusiasm. He wiped a bit of dirt off the video screen, as the doctor working with the host held up the picture of a big orange cat. She looked at it, hesitated, then looked away, frowning, as if searching her memory.

That's interesting, Perez thought, wondering why that particular image—

"She's freaked!" Gediman decided.

Wren glared at him disapprovingly. Perez knew he had no patience for that sort of unprofessional subjective language. It amused Perez to see the frayed edges of their alliance. *No discipline. No loyalty. No focus. Just curiosity. Maybe that's what killed that cat she didn't want to look at.*

Wren spoke decisively. " 'It' has some connective difficulties. A kind of low-level emotional autism. Certain reactions. . . ."

Perez tuned him out. Wren had a tendency to remind him of a politician—his vocabulary might be more complicated, but it was just as empty. He kept his focus on the woman. Whatever she was, she was still that. At least outwardly. He didn't really approve of Wren's attempts to deny that. Whether they decided to terminate her or not, labeling her with a lot of scientific jargon wouldn't eliminate her individuality, her will to survive.

The scientist in the room with Ripley gave up on the cat picture, and pulled up a different one. It was a simple cartoon-like drawing of a little girl with blond hair.

The restrained woman's body suddenly stiffened. The bored expression vanished, and her face changed, grew attentive. She stared at the picture, clearly surprised. Then her brow furrowed, her eyes softened. For a moment, it almost looked as if she might cry. The change was startling, and revealed, for a moment, her true humanity. Even the scientist in the room was taken aback and sat silent, no longer prodding her with the spelling of the word he wanted. For a moment, none of them said anything. None of them could.

The cartoonish picture of the child wavered before her eyes as her body jerked upright in the restraints. *Her child! Her young! No, not hers . . . . Yes, mine! My young!* The picture meant everything and nothing all at the same time. Her mind swam with tumbled, chaotic scenes and memories she could not sort out.

The steaming warmth of the crèche. The strength and safety of her own kind. The aloneness of individuality. And the driving need to find—

Small, strong arms wrapped around her neck, small, strong legs wrapped around her waist. There was chaos, and she was that chaos. The warriors screamed and died. There was fire.

I knew you would come.

The sweeping pain of loss—sickening, irretrievable loss—flooded her mind, her entire body. Her eyes filled with liquid until she could not see, then emptied, clearing her vision, then filled again. It meant nothing—it meant everything.

Mommy! Mommy!

She searched for the connection to her own kind, she searched to find the strength and safety of the crèche, but it was not there. And in its place was nothing but this pain, this terrible loss. She was hollow. Empty. As she would ever be.

She looked at the doctor holding the picture and longed to ask him the question she had asked the others. The question she knew they would not answer.

Why? Why?

Someday, she would have her answer. If not here and now, then soon. As the echoes of her young's voice ricocheted around her brain, she determined she would have the answer. She would take it from them. In spite of their guns, in spite of their restraints. She would take it by force.

On the video screen, the woman blinked rapidly, and in spite of himself, Perez felt moved. *She remembers the child, the little girl she saved. How is that possible?*

"But 'it' remembers," he murmured to Wren, conceding, if reluctantly, to his scientist's language. Then he looked straight at the doctor. "Why?"

Wren was surprised as well. He couldn't hide it. He turned away from the video screen and fumbled for an explanation. "Well, I'm guessing . . . collective memory. Passed down generationally, at a genetic level, by the Aliens. Almost like a highly evolved form of instinct. Perhaps it's a survival mechanism to keep them unified, keep their species intact, regardless of the differing characteristics they might have to adopt from their varied hosts." He mustered a tight smile. "An unexpected benefit of the genetic drift."

Does he think I'm as big an ass as he is? Perez stared at him unflinching, one wolf challenging another. The scientist dropped his eyes.

Perez snorted mockingly. " 'Benefit' . . . ?"

He stared at the tortured expression on the woman's face one last time. *I've seen enough!* Turning smartly on his heel, he left the room.

Marching out of the lab and down the hallway, the two doctors trailed in his wake, still trying to win him over, placate him.

"You're not thinking termination . . . ?" Gediman asked timorously.

"Oh, boy, am I thinking termination!" Perez blurted. Gediman's pained expression pleased him in a perverse way.

Wren interjected quickly, assertively, trying to reassert his status as chief scientist. "We don't perceive this as a problem. The host . . . . It . . . ."

Perez halted, and turned to face Wren, moving right into his personal space. The two men stood toe to toe. "*Ellen Ripley died* trying to wipe this species out of existence, and for all intents and purposes she *succeeded.*" He jabbed a finger into Wren's sternum. "I'm not anxious to see her picking up her old hobbies." *Especially not if she's been the recipient of the "unexpected benefits of genetic drift!"*

To Perez's surprise, Wren didn't flinch, but stood his ground. "It won't happen."

Gediman, that little gnat, had to interject in a conversation between two *men*. Grinning, he babbled, "Comes down to a fight, I'm not sure whose side she'd be on!"

Perez spun on him, scowling. "And I'm supposed to take comfort in *that*?" The scientist took two steps back and schooled his expression.

Perez continued down the hall, the two close behind him, conferring, muttering with each other, exchanging those *looks* like two schoolboys getting ready to raid the girls' dorm. Perez fumed.

There were so many *other* things happening here that were so much more important. Had they completely forgotten their goals? The entire reason for this operation?

Save me from scientists! They can't keep this station insect-free, but they can find all kinds of time to waste work hours and money on the one individual that could endanger this entire project.

Finally, he stopped in front of a secured door. Punching in a code from memory, he paused while the computer digested it, then extended a breath analyzer toward him. He exhaled into the gauge. It would not only use the specific molecules of his breath to determine his unique identity, and would prevent anyone without the proper clearance to enter, it would forbid entry to anyone with approved clearance if they were under the influence of drugs or alcohol, something that retinal analysis couldn't detect.

Irritably, he sensed the two doctors still muttering behind him. In spite of his displeasure, they seemed amused, as if they knew he'd end up giving in, if only on a day-to-day basis. He shook his head slightly as the doors parted, admitting them to the inner observation area. It was dark in the small booth, and abnormally quiet. The men themselves grew still as if this place called for stillness. Two fully armed guards stood at complete attention, arms at the ready, as they flanked a large observation port. The general did not acknowledge the soldiers or tell them to be at ease. As long as they stood at this station, they would not be at ease. Not here.

Perez stepped up to the observation port. He stared into another chamber, that one even darker than this one, and waited for his eyes to adjust to the dimness.

"Bottom line is," he finally said softly to the two doctors, "she looks at me funny and I put her to sleep. The way I see it, number Eight is a meat by-product." It irked him to concede that much, knowing they would see it as their victory. But that was because they didn't understand him, understand the way he thought. It didn't matter how long Ripley lived on board his ship, if she crossed the line he had drawn, no appeals from her fan club would save her. He would do—had already done—everything necessary to make this project a success. He wasn't about to let one woman change that.

Perez narrowed his eyes, seeing something move in the shadows of the other chamber. He smiled tightly. "This girl *here* is the money." *Oh, Ripley, if you could see your little girl now.*

The shadows shifted, moved, turned in their direction—drew closer to the glass.

"How soon before she's producing?" Perez asked the scientists.

"Days," said Wren, his tone just as quiet as the general's. "Less, maybe." His voice dropped even lower. "We'll need the cargo. . . ."

"It's on its way," Perez said abruptly, annoyed that the doctor had mentioned that in front of the soldiers on guard. Had the man *no* sense? Did he even understand what *classified* meant?

He squinted, straining to see into the darkened chamber, to see the real prize of all their work. *There. There she is! Yes, that's my girl!*

Like a nightmare shadow, *Regina horribilis*—the Queen Alien—stepped into the light just enough to be seen.

Surreptitiously, she tested the confined space again, but it held solidly, unyielding. It was an Alien environment of unnatural smoothness with one transparent wall that

*permitted her to see out. But all she could see was an-
other environment just like this one. There were two
humans always in place on the other side of the transparency, two humans and their pain-inducing devices.
They never made sounds, never turned to look at her,
merely stood there. At regular intervals that she could
measure they were replaced with two others that were
so identical she could not tell them from the originals.
She could not smell them through the transparency,
though certain scents did come to her from the air sup-
ply system.*

*Now, three other humans stood at the transparency,
viewing her. Two of them she recognized. They had
been present at her bizarre birth. She somehow sensed
they were responsible for it—that, and her entrapment.*

*She examined and tested the environment again, but
the humans watching her never noticed, never realized
what she was doing even though she was only one good
stride away from them. Neither did the two guards
standing with their backs to her. They were dull, these
humans. Dull, and soft, and slow. But they could build
effective devices, devices that gave them advantages in
spite of their dullness, their softness, their slow speed.
Like the device that contained her now. It was comfortable, and stronger than it appeared. Once forced inside it, she could not leave. When she was locked inside
it, they could move her around at will, take her anywhere, do whatever they wanted.*

*And all she could do was wait. She was good at
waiting. Better at it, she suspected, than these humans.*

*One of the humans was talking to the others. That's
all the humans seemed to do, stand and view her and
talk with one another. She didn't understand them, but
then, she didn't need to. She knew the colony had faced
them before. There had been victories, there had been
defeats. There would be victory again. She could wait.
She was good at waiting, even if, right now, she was
bored to death.*

The name on one of the observers' garment read "Perez." The names on the other two read "Gediman," and "Wren." The sign over the mechanism that opened the door they had entered through read, YOU MUST SUMMON THE GUARD ON DUTY BEFORE THE DOOR WILL BE OPENED. *It said the same thing in six other languages and she could read those languages. She didn't question how she could do those things, any more than she questioned how she could breathe, or think, or eliminate. She just did them.*

The humans continued talking with one another.

She wondered if their bones were as brittle as those of the man who'd freed her from her host. She wondered if their blood was as warm as that of her host, tasted as sweet, ran as freely when they were torn apart. Those thoughts entertained her through her boredom.

Soon, it would be time for her to reproduce. This tiny, Alien environment would be too small to contain her magnificent ovipositor, too small to contain the wealth of her brood. Too small, too cold, too hostile.

She longed for the steaming warmth of the crèche. The strength and safety of her own kind. She was burdened with the aloneness of her special individuality. And the driving need to reproduce—

Soon there would be warriors enough to protect her, and to construct the perfect crèche. And these humans, these pitiful, soft humans, would be food for her young, and host to the new brood. It would happen.

But there were memories. Of unexpected chaos. Warriors screaming and dying. And fire. And one human, standing firm, holding her own young in her arms. Causing death and destruction to the crèche.

She blinked, confused, her mind a sudden shambles of fragments, memories, instincts she could not sort out.

The sweeping pain of loss—sickening, irretrievable

loss—flooded her mind, her entire body. It meant nothing—it meant everything.

She searched for the connection to her own kind, she searched to find the strength and safety of the crèche, but it was not there. And in its place was nothing but this pain, this terrible loss. She was hollow. Empty.

But she would not always be. Her body knew. There would be another crèche. There was always another crèche. She would build it herself. She and her children. In spite of their guns, in spite of their restraints, the humans would fall to them. They would feed her, and she would give birth to her young. She would take this place by force. As she always had. As she always would.

Our structural perfection is matched only by our hostility. Even the humans admire our purity. We are survivors unclouded by conscience, remorse, or delusions of morality.

The perfect organism . . . .

4

Gediman sat across from Ripley at the mess table, but several seats away. He wanted to give her space, even if it was only the illusion of privacy. It was quiet in the combination mess hall/recreation complex, and they were the only two eating. There were two guards posted at the door, but they were such a part of the scenery aboard the *Auriga* that Gediman barely noticed them. He doubted Ripley did anymore, either.

She was still in restraints, but in the last few days they'd been loosened to permit her more mobility. Ever since they'd shown her the picture of the little girl, she'd been strangely passive and introspective. She'd offered no resistance to anything, and had shown no more tendency to violence. Wren thought the picture of the child had triggered enough of her human memories to allow her to assume some of her old personality. She'd been a ship's officer, Wren said. She knew how to obey, to follow orders. Gediman wondered.

The relaxed restraints allowed her to feed herself for the first time. Gediman was pleased about that. Force-feeding her had been unpleasant, and he didn't believe they'd been getting enough nutrition into her. However, now that she had the chance to feed herself, she didn't seem terribly interested. She'd eaten some, but mostly she'd just moved the stuff around on her plate. It was typical ship's fare—processed, dehydrated, and reprocessed enough to barely resemble any recognizable food—but she showed little appetite. Gediman was worried about depression. Wren had shrugged off his concerns.

Gediman was almost done with his breakfast when he noticed her examining her fork, showing much more interest in it than she ever had the food. He wiped his mouth.

"Fork," he said to her helpfully. He wanted so badly to communicate with her, establish a basis of understanding. If he could do that, he could find out what was going on in her mind, the one aspect of her they couldn't really study. What did she remember? What did she know? Gediman was consumed with finding out.

Ripley eyed him sideways through slitted lids. She always avoided direct eye contact. She parroted the word softly, but incorrectly. "Fuck."

He was embarrassed for her and was glad no one else was present to hear. He corrected her gently. "Fork."

Her expression changed. He almost thought she'd smiled, but then it was gone. She startled him with a question. "How did you . . . ?"

It seemed such an effort for her to speak, he anticipated the rest. "How did we get you? Hard work. Blood samples. Tissue samples, taken on Fiorina 161, on ice in the infirmary there."

Such a simple explanation for such a complicated job. It was unprecedented work. The samples were varied enough, and there were plenty of cells, but the DNA was in chaos. It had been an amazing discovery to find that the embryonic Alien that had already infected Ripley's body when the blood and tissues were taken had not stopped its invasion there. Like a virus, the embryo had actually invaded the host's living cells—every last one of them—and forced them to change to accommodate its growth and development. It was a major breakthrough in adaptive evolution. It was a way to guarantee that any host, any host at all, would provide whatever it was the developing embryo needed, even when the host's own body was inadequate.

The infusion of Alien DNA into Ripley's own had been how they'd managed to incubate her *and* her embryo. But it hadn't been easy. They'd had to separate out the DNA right down to the RNA, reconstruct it, try to get it functioning. . . . It had been work, incredibly hard and frustrating work, and it had taken years.

But now she sat here, like any other human being, eating food like any other human being.

And her terrible child, even now—

"Fiorina 161. . . ." Ripley said quietly, as if tasting the word, fitting it into her mouth. *"Fury . . . ?"*

"Does that ring a bell?" Gediman asked, pushing. If she would only *talk* to him. "What are you remembering?"

She didn't answer the question, just gave him that same sideways glance. "Does 'it' . . . grow?"

Gediman blinked, surprised. "If 'it' . . ." *She's asking about the embryo we took from her? Yes, she must be!* "Yeah, 'it' grows. Very fast."

"It's a Queen," she said decisively, putting down the fork. She pushed the plate away.

She was under anesthesia. How . . . ? "How did you know?"

"It'll breed," she said, tonelessly. For the first time, she looked him straight in the eye. "You'll all **die**. Everyone in the . . . ," she glanced at the fork,

". . . **fucking** . . . company will die." She continued to stare at the fork.

"Company?" *What was she talking about?*

"Weyland-Yutani," Wren explained. He'd entered the mess hall and come around behind Ripley, but Gediman had been so absorbed in his conversation with her, he'd never noticed.

Wren still wore that patronizing little smile on his face, the same expression he always wore when he was dealing with Ripley. It was odd that he should, Gediman thought, considering that the marks she'd left on his throat were still visible.

The chief scientist boldly sat next to the woman. He had no interest in giving her personal space. Instead, he seemed intent on invading it, as if pushing her, as if he wanted to see whether she'd strike out at him again. Gediman didn't like it, but there was nothing he could do. It wasn't as if Wren ever listened to **him.**

As Ripley glanced at him from the corners of her eyes, Wren brazenly picked food off her discarded plate, the way a parent might eat from his child's meal.

"Weyland-Yutani," Wren explained to Gediman, "were Ripley's former employers. They were a Terran Growth conglom; had some defense contracts under the military. Long before your time, Gediman. They went under decades ago, bought out by Wal-Mart. Fortunes of war." He turned his attention back to the woman, gave her a cool smile. "You'll find things have changed a good deal since your time."

There was that fleeting change of expression on her face again, Gediman noted. Almost a smile. "I doubt that," she said.

Wren didn't pretend to misunderstand her comment. "We're not flying blind here, you know. This is the United Systems military, not some greedy corporation."

Like he wouldn't work for a 'greedy corporation' if

they'd let him do this kind of science, Gediman thought, but kept it to himself.

Ripley only stared at her plate. Her words were lifeless. "It won't make any difference." The sentence seemed to trigger some memory in her, making her frown and consider. Then she continued, "You're still gonna die."

Wren clasped his hands in front of him, in full "doctor" mode. "And how do you feel about that?"

She shrugged. "It's your funeral, not mine."

Wren didn't like that answer. His impatience started to show. For once, he dropped the pedantic child-speak he usually inflicted on her. "I wish you could understand what we're trying to do here. The potential benefits of this race go way beyond urban pacification. New alloys, new vaccines . . . ! There's nothing like this on any world we've seen." He stopped, as if realizing he was revealing too much about himself.

Gediman could see the frustration in Wren's expression. But Gediman knew Ripley couldn't possibly understand or appreciate their plans. They were, after all, the kind of dreams only scientists could value. But Wren was right—the potential was boundless. It might take decades to determine the genetic complexities of the creatures and how the unique genetic code that could grow acid blood and silicon carapaces could be adapted to different lifeforms. Learning how the parasitic symbiont genetically and chemically modified its host would advance biochemistry and biomechanics into the next century. The work they'd done to simply produce Ripley and her Alien offspring had set cloning techniques ahead a hundred years!

Wren's patronizing tone returned. "You should be very proud."

She actually laughed. It was a bitter, ugly sound. "Oh, I am."

Now Wren tried to reassure her. "And the animal

itself is **wondrous.** They'll be invaluable once we've tamed them."

Ripley turned that laserlike stare on Wren, who drew back before it. "It's a **cancer.** You can't teach it **tricks.**"

Wren had nothing to say to that, much to Gediman's surprise.

Ripley toyed with the fork again, drawing inward, thinking. Gediman ached to know what. But all she said was the simple word, "**Them.**"

Distephano watched the small private ship on an approach vector to the *Auriga.* Up till now, this had just been another boring shift, killing time in the command capsule. He noted the approach of the small ship in the log, then sent an official notification to the general. He'd never seen a private vessel out here before. Not this close to the *Auriga.* Granted, this was nowhere near as exciting as the incident last week with that test-tube female in the lab. But how often was something like *that* going to happen?

Officially, he'd been told nothing about the incident after making his report, but unofficially he'd heard the charge he'd given the female had certainly straightened her attitude out. She'd been meek as a lamb ever since. In fact, he'd heard they'd taken her completely out of restraints yesterday. They were even giving her a little "walking around" space. Sounded okay to him, since there were always two guards on her. And after they heard about his action, the others knew to pay attention. It was the most exciting gig around here, guarding the test-tube lady. What a weird assignment!

Almost instantly, he received a reply to his report.

"Approaching vessel has General Perez's approval to dock," *Father* said, the masculine computer voice eerie in the confines of the small bubble. "Authorization code six-niner-niner-three. Security on full alert."

Interesting, Distephano thought. Private vessels rarely, if ever, brought cargo or supplies to the *Auriga.* This was a top-secret, ultra hush-hush vessel. Your clearances had to have clearance just to deliver *food.* Yet, this little horsefly was just gonna get to pull on up, huh?

Vinnie heard the automated announcement coming in from the approaching vessel that gave its registration number and name. *The Betty, huh?* He took the numbers the little ship's feminine computer voice had given him and punched them into his console.

"Registration code of approaching vessel," *Father* intoned, "is nonexistent. There has been an error. Please input number again."

The hell there's been an error, Vinnie thought, annoyed. He punched in the code again, much more carefully.

"There is no such registration number listed with United Military Systems," *Father* told him. "If there has been no input error, then the incoming vessel is unregistered."

Not possible, Vinnie thought. He notified the general again, at once, then contacted the incoming vessel, demanding its authorization code before permitting final approach. *Even if it* were. . . . *They wouldn't have the balls to pull into a military station!*

Vinnie expected the *Betty's* authorization to be immediately canceled. That would be pretty interesting in itself. Either the ship would veer off in a righteous hurry, or, if it really needed to dock because of damage or injury to the staff, then it would request aid on a mayday code. If Perez rejected that . . .

If he rejected it, I might have to actually shoot the ship down! Distephano considered that. He had enough firepower under his thumb to scatter the small vessel into atoms. He watched the ship growing larger.

What he got was not what he expected. General

Perez's voice—*the Old Man himself!*—barked into his ear through his headset.

"*I* gave that ship authorization to dock, *Soldier,*" Perez said irritably. "What's the problem?"

The surprise of hearing Perez's own voice, instead of an automated response—which Vinnie usually assumed came from some other officer—thoroughly rattled him. Distephano groped for words.

"Uh, I'm sorry, sir, it's just . . . the registration numbers, uh . . . !" He gulped and pulled himself together. "Sir! No problem, sir! Docking will commence, sir!"

"You see that it does!" Perez snapped.

Vinnie gazed at the incoming ship. *It's a pirate, a fucking real, one-hundred percent, outlaw pirate vessel. No registration numbers. No official anything. And it's coming in on Perez's own invitation. How about that!*

With a smug smile, Vinnie remembered his C.O.'s warning when he'd taken this assignment. *Once you're out there, boy, you just remember—don't ask. Don't tell. Anything. They better not come back to me and say I didn't train you right.* Yeah, this gig was bound to lead to bigger and better things—providing he didn't piss off the Old Man again.

You can bet that won't happen twice. It's C.Y.A. all the way for this boy.

The small ship held steady on her approach. He could see her clearly now. She even *looked* like a pirate, painted in drab camouflage colors that would mask her appearance if she had to fly low over a plant-covered landscape. A versatile little vessel, she was obviously designed for space, but had angled side compartments that could easily reconform to aerodynamic wings for atmospheric flight. She also had tail fins to make her more agile in the air. But she was an old vessel, patched in many places with mismatched parts, dirty and banged up. She was a stark contrast to the hulking, dark *Auriga* that dwarfed her.

Vinnie blinked, peering at some graphic painted on the fuselage. *What the hell . . . ?*

He started to laugh. He was a World War II buff, so he recognized instantly the stylized, antique rendering of what had once been called a "cheesecake pinup." Right under the ship's name, a round-hipped, buxom woman in scanty, form-fitting clothes, suggestively rode an antique rocket across the fuselage of the small ship.

Yeah. The Betty, sure enough. Things are sure getting more and more interesting around here, after all.

Aboard the *Betty,* things were always interesting. At least, interesting enough for her captain, Frank Elgyn, a reedy-thin, angular man in his midforties, whose dark eyes and prominent nose added to his predatory appearance. He shifted in the copilot's seat, and propped a booted foot against the console. He'd just been asked for *an authorization code* from some green-horned, wet-behind-the-ears grunt! He turned to the chair next to him and laughed lightly. His pilot, Sabra Hillard, a tall, strong-bodied woman, grinned back at him and shook her cropped head.

Like there might be *an authorization code* anywhere in existence for *this* ship, making *this* run, with *this* cargo. Sure.

He settled back in the seat. Sabra had her favorite music blaring—the cacophony of its modern beat pulsed through the floor. He made no attempt to lower the sound. Pilot got to pick the tunes. It was as close to a "rule" as anything they had aboard the *Betty.* He addressed the grunt over the comlink.

"My authorization code is 'fuck you,' son."

Beside him, Sabra gave a snort of laughter. Elgyn noticed she was playing some video space battle game at the same time she was piloting the ship in. It was amazing how many things that woman could do at the same time. Made him warm just thinking about it. He caught her gaze and gave her a meaningful look. She returned it.

"Now, open the goddamn bay," he told the soldier, "or General Perez is gonna do a Wichita stomp on your virgin ass."

Apparently, the general had already conveyed that message, because the *Auriga*'s automated computer voice was giving Hillard the coordinates she needed.

"Bring us in on three-oh descent," he told Hillard. "Ride the parallel."

She never took her eyes off her video game. "Darlin', it's done."

Elgyn got out of the chair as the space station grew larger in their foreground. "Don't cut thrust till six hundred meters. Give 'em a little fright." He stroked her cheek with his thumb before leaving, and she gave him a wink.

He glanced around the rest of the cockpit, the assorted makeshift equipment, mixed in with out-of-date games, bits of clothing, all the flotsam and jetsam of their crew strewn here and there. In the middle of all the organized chaos stood Christie. The massive but handsome dark-skinned man made any space he was in look small, Elgyn thought admiringly. A good man to have at your back—assuming he was on your side.

Christie was busy strapping on his armature. The complicated apparatus with its intricate micro-pulleys and gears was the same color as his mahogany skin, and the mechanical system his own design. Strapped to his powerful forearms below the elbows, it all but disappeared, and allowed him to carry weapons where few people ever thought to look.

Elgyn approached the man. "We're coming in. Time to enjoy a little of the general's hospitality."

"Oh, great," the big man sneered. His expressive, dark eyes rolled to convey his contempt. "*Army* food!"

Moving closer, Elgyn helped Christie tighten the last strap on the apparatus. "It'll keep us till we can get the family wagon up to spec. Assuming the natives are friendly."

Christie listened to what Elgyn *hadn't* said. "We expecting any trouble?"

Elgyn hesitated a bit too long. "From Perez? I doubt it, but better to be on guard."

Christie didn't ask any more questions, didn't make another comment. He just nodded once, shaking his lion's mane of dreadlocks into place, and the rest was understood.

The engine room of the *Betty* shared space with the cargo bay. It was there that Annalee Call and John Vriess were busy working, trying to squeeze just a little more life into the antiquated lump of machinery they jokingly called a *stabilizer.* Call knew Vriess was looking forward to this docking. They were really stretched now, some of their equipment just way too old to be refurbished anymore. They'd been doing their best, but Elgyn was hoping the Army would let them have some spares—a little bonus for a job well done. Call and Vriess both hoped Elgyn was right.

Call, a slight woman with delicate features, was standing beside the square block of machinery, her small, thin fingers capably getting into some of the smaller parts of the temperamental unit. Meanwhile, Vreiss, a blocky, middle-aged man with thinning, sandy-blond hair, a strong jaw, and bulbous nose, was stretched out on his dolly on the ground. As the other engineer pushed himself under the equipment to attack the overhaul from the bottom, Call lowered the upper portion of the stabilizer down over its bottom half by means of a magnetic chain hoist. They'd spent hours refitting—*again*—the brain of the machine. Now they had to rejoin it with its mechanical bottom and get the whole thing to agree to work together in harmony.

As Call matched the machinery up and demagnitized the hoist, she found herself becoming more aware of her coworker. Call liked working with Vriess. He was hardworking, inventive, and focused on his job. A lot more than she could say for some of the people on this ship. She released the chains from the upper system and watched the hoist retreat back to the ceiling.

From beneath the machinery, Vriess started whistling a little tune, something they'd picked up in some bar on their last port of call. She smiled, remembering that evening. That was another reason she liked working with Vriess. He was usually cheerful and easygoing.

She picked up the tune herself, whistling along, the two of them making an impromptu little harmony as they worked steadily.

Distantly, Call was aware of another person entering the area. She kept whistling, trying not to tense, trying not to telegraph her feelings. If she wasn't careful, Vriess would pick up her tension. She didn't want to distract him while he was working. She kept whistling, only allowing one part of her to pay any attention to the man strolling on the high catwalk that overlooked the engine room.

It was Johner. Call didn't know his first name, or even if he had one. Not that she would care. She wouldn't care if Johner died. She hated the man. She hated everything he was, everything he did. There were days when her major job aboard the *Betty* was making sure Johner didn't know how much she detested him. Johner would enjoy it too much for her to give him that satisfaction.

The wiry tech made sure Johner's appearance didn't distract her from her work. He'd ridicule her if she dropped a screw or skinned a knuckle because she wasn't paying attention. And she didn't want to alert Vriess that Johner was there. Maybe if they both ignored him, he'd just go away.

Fat chance, Call thought, as the tall, thickset, powerful man stopped walking right above them. He grinned at her, his narrow, ice-blue eyes reminding her of a pig's. He was without a doubt the ugliest man she'd ever seen, and the ragged scar that crossed his face didn't do a thing to improve his appearance. But it was his meanness of spirit that made him truly hideous. Call continued ignoring him. He just grinned more, his scar pulling the smile up into a gross parody of a human expression, and started humming the tune along with them. But Johner's version of the song had a mean twist to it, a rough, ugly edge that matched his outlook.

From the edge of her peripheral vision, Call noticed him remove his pocket knife, flip it open, and use it to clean under his thumbnail. She turned her head, so he could continue his personal grooming without her awareness, and forced herself to keep whistling along with Vriess. She increased her volume, hoping Vriess wouldn't hear Johner's contribution. She didn't see Johner dangle the knife in the air over Vriess's legs, or drop it.

She saw it hit, though.

The small blade embedded itself to the hilt in the meaty part of Vriess's left leg. Call felt a rush of anger she couldn't ignore, and stood outraged, mouth open. She didn't know whether to shout or curse or hurl something at the son of a bitch.

Beneath the stabilizer, Vriess kept whistling, completely unaware.

"What is **wrong** with you?" she hissed through her teeth at the chuckling Johner.

Now that she was no longer whistling, Vriess finally realized something was going on, and pulled himself out from under the machine, rolling the dolly well clear of it. He spied Johner on the catwalk, and glanced at Call, confused by her anger.

"Just a little target practice," Johner said, completely unashamed. He indicated the man on the dolly. "Vriess isn't complaining."

Call looked worriedly at the other mechanic, then glanced at Vriess's thigh, so that he would follow her gaze. When he spotted the knife jutting out of his leg, he yelled, "Goddamnit!" Hitting a lever on the dolly made the back of it snap up. Then the seat rose, and the leg rests folded, and it was once again the versatile, mechanical wheelchair Vriess had built himself. Paralyzed from the waist down, the capable, middle-aged engineer glared at the small penknife embedding in his unfeeling leg.

"Johner, you son of a whore!" Vriess swore angrily, and with all the strength in his powerful arms, flung his wrench at the man.

But Johner ably dodged it, laughing that much harder. "Oh, come on! You didn't feel a thing!" Johner thought that was an absolute riot and laughed even more.

Now, Vriess looked embarrassed, which made Call even angrier. Without making a big deal about it, she took out a clean handkerchief from her back pocket, grasped the knife, yanked it out, and put the folded handkerchief over the seeping wound. Vriess held the cloth in place tightly, waiting for the blood flow to stop. Neither of them talked about it, they just worked together to get the job done.

Call glanced up at the catwalk and the ambulatory bastard she could not call a man. "You are an inbred motherfucker, you know that?"

What did Johner care what she called him? He'd gotten a rise out of both of them, so he'd won. Still chuckling, he held out a hand. "I'll take that knife back now."

Call was just about to fold the blade down and toss it back to him when she reconsidered. She was too angry to be so cooperative.

Vriess was watching her. He touched her elbow. "Call, forget it. He's been sucking down too much home brew."

She knew Vriess wasn't afraid of Johner, in spite of the man's size and advantage. But it would be like him to worry about *her*. Despite her wiry muscles, she was little, slight. And Johner had no qualms about hurting anyone. He thought that was *fun*. But Call didn't care. She was tired of stepping lightly around the abusive bastard.

In one swift move, she jammed the knife blade between two welded metal supports and snapped the blade off clean.

Johner's face went dark with rage. He pointed down at her. "Don't push me, little Annalee. You hang with us a while, you'll learn I'm not the man with whom to fuck."

Call stood her ground defiantly. Size didn't count for everything. She could take care of herself, and if he wanted to find that out for himself, well, fine.

The two of them stared each other down for a moment, and then, to her amazement, Johner blinked first. Still blustering, he left the catwalk.

Call pushed her short, dark hair out of her nearly black eyes and worked her jaw back and forth, still fuming. The pleasant work environment she'd been enjoying with Vriess was shattered.

Until he smacked her lightly on the hip, and quipped, "We really have to start associating with a better class of people."

Sabra Hillard's expert, rough hands hovered the tiny *Betty* under the huge underbelly of the oversized, bloated *Auriga.* "My tax dollars at work," she muttered to herself, then grinned, remembering she never paid taxes.

Above her, the docking port's massive doors slid open. In her headset, the *Auriga*'s computer intoned, "Commence docking."

"Aye, aye, Pops," she muttered moving the vessel into position.

The *Auriga*'s massive electromagnets moved into position as Hillard nestled the small ship in the docking port. With a great clanging of metal, the *Auriga* positioned its magnets against the *Betty*'s hull and secured her in place.

Like a baby in a safety seat, Hillard thought. *Now why does that thought make me so uncomfortable?* A restraint, after all, was still a restraint.

"Docking is completed," the *Auriga*'s *Father* told her. "You may disembark."

Even the computer sounded like it was giving orders. Shrugging off her apprehension, Hillard hit a comm button. "Avast, me hearties! All ashore who's goin' ashore. Remember. The *general* said no weapons aboard the *Auriga.* Meet'cha at the airlock, guys." She signed off.

Why did docking in a station this big always make her feel like she was being swallowed alive?

5

Perez watched his soldiers prepare for the disembarking crew of the *Betty* from an elevated catwalk high above them. His critical eye scanned every soldier, alert for any signs of sloppiness or disorder. The troops looked good. The corridor outside the airlock was as pristine and shipshape as the rest of the vessel. Just the way he wanted it. And well it should be. He'd hand-picked every one of the soldiers aboard the *Auriga* himself. Each one was looking for bigger and better things, higher commissions, more interesting action. Being under Perez's command guaranteed them special consideration when they finished their tour of duty. So far not one of them had let him down. He knew they weren't about to start now. Not with him standing right here watching them.

The air lock cycled and *Father*'s voice intoned, "Cycle complete. Doors opening."

As the pneumatic doors lifted with a groan, the crew from the small pirate ship was slowly revealed to the soldiers. Perez couldn't help but wonder what some of his troops thought. Everything aboard the *Auriga* was spit and polish, the way Perez demanded it be. Each soldier below him was dressed identically, groomed identically. Male or female, big or small, ethnic origin—none of it mattered. They were a unit responding to a single leader.

Not like this ragtag bunch, he thought derisively. The only thing similar about them was their dissimilarity. Their clothes, their hair, the way they stood, the way they walked. . . . *Or rolled,* Perez thought with some amusement as one of the crew members disembarked in a mechanized wheelchair. He shook his head. It was such a bizarre, eclectic group, Perez couldn't imagine how Elgyn ever got any of them to follow even the most basic orders. He wondered how they survived out in space in that ramshackle ship where discipline and order were the only things that could keep you alive.

The *Betty*'s crew shuffled forward into the hold, approaching the troops. As they did, Perez reevaluated his assessment. He watched their wary eyes and tense posture, noted their leathery skin, the mechanics' grease so imbedded in their flesh it was like a tattoo. There *was* something they had in common, he realized. Each was marked by a visible toughness that wasn't just bravado. Just like his soldiers, this crew would kill if they had to. *Even,* he suspected, *that little girl in the middle. Wonder where she came from? Elgyn didn't mention taking on new staff.* Perez tried not to wonder if they had already killed. He shook the thought away. These were pirates in every sense of the word, but Perez saw nothing glamorous about it.

Smugglers, he thought grimly. *Admit it, Martin. They're nothing but thieves and murderers. And you hired them. Why flinch at inviting them in? It wasn't as if you had a choice.*

The eclectic group slowed as it reached the point where the soldiers stood ready to search them. Cooperatively, several of them lifted their arms to be frisked. The huge black man in the forefront raised his arms high, his open shirt revealing his massive, rippled chest. As the soldier before him frisked him efficiently, the black man shook his head, incredulous. The *Betty* crew mumbled comments among themselves.

Suddenly, a sensor light on another soldier's glove began blinking. The woman with the activated signal looked up at a big, ugly scarred man and said firmly, "No firearms allowed on board, sir."

As the scarred man grimaced, Perez thought at him, *Be nice to her, friend. She's a champion hand-to-hand combat specialist. She can probably take out your whole crew if you get on her nerves. And your ugly mug won't phase her for a nanosecond.*

The scarred man opened his jacket cooperatively, showed the soldier what was inside that had triggered the sensor. A big silver thermos.

"Moonshine!" he explained. "My own. *Way* more dangerous."

The *Betty*'s crew all laughed.

The soldier showed not a bit of emotion. "Sorry, sir. You're free to go."

Just then Elgyn finally spied Perez on his platform and walked toward him. "Wha'd'ya think—we're gonna hijack the vessel? All *six* of us?" His crew laughed again.

Perez waited till they quieted down. "No—I think your asshole crew is going to get drunk and put a bullet through the hull. We are in space, Elgyn." He waited for his soldiers to take a turn at laughing, but they were all too professional for that and maintained their demeanor.

The searches were complete, and Perez waived the *Betty*'s crew to go on into the *Auriga*.

The wheelchair crewman was the last of the group to move forward. He finally jockeyed his automated chair to the woman soldier who'd found the thermos. "Wanna check the chair?" he asked the soldier sweetly.

The woman's face never cracked. Perez knew she was experienced enough to know that man was hoping she'd check a lot more than his *chair*. The soldier merely raised her arm, pointing to the group slowly getting ahead of the paralyzed man. With a smirky grin, he rolled on after them.

Perez left, too.

Fifteen minutes later, in his private quarters, the general's door signal chimed. He knew who it was, and told *Father* to open the door. Elgyn stood there, leaning jauntily on the frame. He sauntered in, nodding at the general, and moved over to the table Perez had prepared earlier.

There, stacked on its broad, flat surface, were neat, pre-counted, tabulated, and bound, thousand-dollar bills. There were many stacks. More than Perez wanted to think about. The bills were well worn, nonsequential. They were perfectly square, bright green, and each one of them bore the insipid face of some obscure congressional leader from the last century. Perez couldn't help but think they should be bright, bright red. Blood money.

Elgyn sat slowly into the chair Perez had left there for him, even as Perez sat across from him. The expression on Elgyn's face could only be called *satisfied*. He wore a little smile as he peered over the stacks, thumbing them, quickly counting them.

"This wasn't easy to come by," Perez commented idly.

Elgyn raised his brows. "Neither was our cargo. You're not pleading poverty, are you?"

Realizing he'd been misunderstood, Perez clarified, "I mean the bills. Hardly anyone's got cash these days." *Never mind so much of it.*

Elgyn grinned, following him now. "Just the ones

that don't like their every transaction recorded. The *fringe* element. Like *you*, for example."

The analogy stung. *Tell yourself again, Martin, how you are serving your country.* Perez lifted a small, rectangular packet off the table, and picked up a glass. "Drink?"

Elgyn nodded, the gracious guest.

Perez tore off the protective covering of the little plastic cartridge and popped out its solid brown gel cube into a glass. Passing the glass under a handheld laser, he handed the now liquefied beverage to Elgyn. Then he prepared one for himself. It was good scotch, if not the best.

"I'm guessing whatever it is you've got going out here isn't exactly authorized by Congress," Elgyn said, sipping the drink. He raised it up as if in a toast after sampling it.

I'm so glad you approve of the vintage, Martin thought irritably.

No, this project wasn't approved by Congress, or by any *official* government agency or military panel. But Perez never lacked for funds or resources. Still, whenever he had to deal with the likes of this pirate, he couldn't help but question the entire operation. Not that he could afford questions. He had a job to do, a mission to accomplish, and complete carte blanche to get it done any way possible. He had to believe that the future advantages of this work would outweigh whatever sacrifices had to be made now.

Perez had little patience with Wren's pie-in-the-sky scenarios about advanced medicines and biochemical miracles. He could only think about creatures that, with electronic implants to control behavior, would be transformed into the quintessential ground troops. In fact, Wren and Gedimen had recently reported that the Aliens' intelligence appeared to be much higher than their scanty historical data would indicate. To Perez, that was an added plus——smart animals would be much easier to train.

He had to believe that, in his lifetime, the needless forfeit of valuable, well-trained men would be ended forever. Instead, human soldiers would only be used for mop-up operations after the conflict ended—appropriate work for men who could think, assess, use judgment.

Eventually, different forms of the Aliens would be bred to create beings more advantageous to specific combat conditions, then they would be trained for specialized functions. They would enable the military to reclaim crime-ridden cities, safely prepare new planets for colonization by eliminating dangerous species, begin a new era of peace and productivity—

He stopped his wandering thoughts as he looked across at Elgyn. This pirate would understand none of this. When they had negotiated over the job, Elgyn had not even asked what his specialized cargo would be used for. His only interest had been the pile of money now sitting between them.

Perez and Elgyn were both human, but clearly they were two completely different species.

Perez changed the subject. "Where'd you pick up the new fish?"

Elgyn chuckled. "Call? Out by the handle. She was looking for a maintenance gig."

"Makes an impression," Perez commented dryly.

"She is severely fuckable, isn't she?" Elgyn agreed. "And the *very devil* with a socket wrench. I think Vriess somewhat pines." He picked up the stack of bills closest to him, ruffled them, then held them up to his nose and inhaled. His expression was one of a man smelling the finest bouquet of wine, or the clean sharp tang of a well-ripened cigar. "She is curious about this little transaction. You can hardly blame her. Awfully cloak and dagger. . . ."

Perez resented the fishing expedition. "This is an army operation."

Elgyn saw right through that. "Most army research labs don't have to operate outside regulated space. And they don't have to hire *private contractors* . . . . And they don't call for the kind of cargo we brought."

Perez realized Elgyn was angling for something. A bonus? He'd have to lay it on the table. "Do you want something, Elgyn?"

The reedy man sat back, all relaxed and easygoing. "Just bed and board, couple of days' worth. Vriess'll want to snag a few spare parts. If we're not *imposing.*"

Perez wondered again if he were making a mistake. When he'd first engaged Elgyn in this project, he'd seriously considered killing the crew and destroying the ship after the delivery, then decided it could backfire, raise more problems than it might solve. Maybe he needed to rethink that. It would be good to have the crew right here and the ship docked while he reconsidered. "Of course you're not imposing. Keep out of the restricted areas. Don't start any fights, and *mi casa* is yours, too."

Elgyn raised his glass in gratitude and finished the drink.

"I trust, of course," Perez added, "that you can mind your own business."

The man was all smiles. "I'm famous for it."

Yes, Perez thought. *That's true, you are. That was why I hired you in the first place.*

Back on board the *Betty,* in the cargo hold, Call slipped on her gloves and walked up to Christie.

The big man eyed her neutrally, then asked, "What happened to Johner?"

She shrugged. "You know Johner. He's in party mode already."

Christie shook his head. "Shoulda figured. In that case, thanks for the help."

She nodded, as if to say, *no big deal*.

She heard the clanging sound of air-lock doors opening, and heard the *Betty*'s feminine computer voice intone, "Air locks have cycled. Doors opening. Ramp is lowering."

Call and Christie moved over to the automated hand trucks that held the first containers of "cargo."

As soon as the big doors were completely opened, they touched the controls on the hand trucks and moved the big boxes onto the ramp now running from the *Betty* to the *Auriga*. The metal and plasti-glass boxes they were jockeying were nearly three meters high by one meter wide. The *Betty* had twenty of them to unload. The general's special cargo.

And inside each cryotube slept an adult man or woman.

Call didn't want to think about that. It wasn't her *job* to think about that. This was the cargo. Her job was to deliver it. That was all. She'd get a cut, and salary beside. That was what she'd signed on for, after all.

Still, she asked Christie in a quiet voice, "You, uh, you think Elgyn knows what Perez wants them for?" She nodded at the cargo.

Christie looked at her curiously, as if suddenly remembering that she was new. "I can assure you with complete confidence that Elgyn hasn't spent *one minute* thinking about the general's plans. He only cares about the good general's *cash*."

She nodded once, then started to turn away, but Christie took hold of her arm with surprising gentleness. His tone reflected the same demeanor. "Call— Elgyn doesn't worry about that stuff, and he pays us not to think about it, either. Okay?"

Surprised by his brotherly concern, Call was able to fix a smile on her face. "I'm okay. Let's get it done."

She pushed the hand truck forward, across the ramp, into the *Auriga*.

Just do the delivery. Don't think about it. Don't think about them. Sleeping people . . . .

Walking beside the quiet Christie, she moved into the *Auriga*, pushing the tubes between silent, stationed soldiers, until they ended up before a big door marked, RESTRICTED AREA. There were more soldiers in front of the door. As they saw Call and Christie approach, one of the soldiers knocked on the door.

Immediately, it whooshed open. Call could see a tall, medium-built man standing inside, wearing a lab coat instead of a soldier's uniform. He didn't much look like a soldier either. The name on his lab coat read, "Wren."

The two *Betty* crew members approached the door, but just as they were about to go through it, one of the soldiers stopped them. Other soldiers stepped forward to take the cryo-units. Christie glanced at her and nodded, so she released hers to them even as Christie did the same. The guards wheeled the boxes inside the restricted area, and Call and Christie went back to the *Betty* to get the next ones. The soldiers wouldn't enter the *Betty* any more than she and Christie would be allowed to enter the restricted area.

But as Christie and Call headed back for more cargo, Call couldn't help looking over her shoulder to watch the soldiers move those sleep chambers deep into the restricted area.

Where were they going? Would they wake the sleepers or keep them under? How much space did the restricted area take up?

The doors closed behind the soldiers, before Call could find any answers to her questions. She turned back to the *Betty* and the task before her.

Hand twenty sleeping men and women over to an out-of-the-way military research installation. Yeah. A real simple task.

* * *

At least, Wren thought gratefully, Gediman's not prat-
tling on now.

In fact, as the entire group of researchers gathered
in the viewing area, no one was speaking. Well, after
all, what was there to say? They'd all read the reports,
the history, but until now, there were no living wit-
nesses to what they were about to see. It was a momen-
tous occasion. And it deserved the respect of silence,
in honor of the men and women who were about to
make the supreme sacrifice.

Wren leaned forward as the others shifted quietly
behind him and brought the various computer screens
on line. They would be able to view everything from
every conceivable angle if they wanted. Or, they could
just watch it all through the huge viewing port over-
looking the adjacent chamber. He realized suddenly
that they were all breathing in unison.

He swallowed, and manipulated the controls.

Through the monitors, they could see a sweeping
pan of the entire area. Twenty cryochambers were on
inclined platforms in a circular, pie-shaped pattern, feet
to feet. Wren handled the computer controls, and
slowly, by increments, the chambers were individually
elevated at the head until they were each standing upright. The units were then mechanically secured into
position.

Wren manipulated more controls, changing the
cryomix in the chambers. Slowly. Slowly. He couldn't
allow the subjects to be damaged now. They were far
too valuable.

After a reasonable period of time, when the cryomix
looked right in the readout, Wren had the computer
open the transparent lids of the chambers. It was clear,
in the monitors, that some of the chamber's inhabitants
were already stirring. He could see eyes twitching, lips

moving, other signs of gradual wakefulness. The read-outs were good. The inhabitants were all waking, all fully functional, all in good health. Prime subjects.

Wren glanced sideways at Gediman when the man shifted nervously. He could tell Gediman was uncomfortable. Wren glanced around at the others. Carlyn was rubbing her arms as if cold. Trish had folded her arms and stared unblinking through the viewport as if she would not permit anything happening here to touch her. Kinloch stared openmouthed as if he couldn't believe he was here, watching this. Sprague and Clauss were conferring quietly, while glancing nervously through the window. Clauss kept nervously rubbing his throat. Wren turned away from the group, not wanting to be distracted.

Well, they *should* be moved. It was a powerful moment. One they would remember forever.

It was time. Wren handled the controls, tapped in a sequence, and from the ceiling, a large tubular device descended. Surrounding the big transport arm were individual shallow containers. Sitting in each container was a massive, obscenely organic Alien egg. If such a thing could even be called an egg. It was a living organism itself, pulsing wetly with the life contained within. Sitting firmly on its large end, the narrow end pointed up, with four flaplike folds forming an odd orifice at the cusp. Massive veins cording over the surface of each egg trailed into the containers. He and Gediman had speculated for hours as to their purpose. Clearly, they stabilized the egg, and possibly, in their own environment, they pulled sustenance from the ground itself to maintain the larvae within for years if need be.

Wren pulled his mind away from speculation as the transport arm positioned individual egg-holding containers in front of each hibernation chamber.

The eggs settled as the transport arm stopped moving them. Within moments of being placed in range of another living organism, the eggs, which had been fairly static up to now, suddenly showed signs of life. They could see dim shapes moving within. The flexible walls of the eggs actually quivered.

The remote transmission equipment allowed them to not only see what was happening, but to hear it as well. The eggs made *sounds*. Wet, slurping, sucking sounds. The kind of sounds you heard in surgery, when you were manipulating organs in the cavity of a living body.

Behind him, Wren realized that everyone in the room had finally stopped fidgeting. Unconsciously, he lifted his arm to blot the sweat from his upper lip with his sleeve.

In the cryounits, one of the sleeper's eyes fluttered, then opened completely. The slender, dark-haired man blinked, showing the typical groggy, dry-mouthed aftereffects of the hibernation drugs. The name on his chamber read "Purvis."

The egg standing before his unit trembled, then suddenly opened, four flaps folding back like a large, irregular mouth. Hurriedly, Wren manipulated the controls, making cameras dolly around to view the mysterious interior. Oh, they'd analyzed the contents through every remote sensing device at their disposal. They'd even named some of the contents, even though they were still guessing as to their purposes. But it wasn't the same as *seeing* it with your own eyes.

The egg sitting next to "Purvis's" chamber opened next. Then one across the room. Then another, and another. The sleepers were still only semi-aware, blinking sleepily, looking around, disoriented. They knew they weren't where they had been when they'd gone to sleep, but clearly they couldn't tell where they were now, or why. And they were still too drugged to do anything but blink and wonder.

At last, every single egg sat open.

Wren held his breath, and wondered if every one else in the room with him was doing the same.

Finally, cautiously, six long spindly legs emerged from the egg in front of Purvis.

Slowly, Purvis began to come out of cryosleep. Amazing thing, hibernation. One second you're awake and settling in for a long winter's nap and the next second you're waking back up a jillion light-years and a bunch of months from wherever you'd been. He felt himself warming up, loosening up, as the cryodrugs were flushed from his system.

He was aware enough to speculate about this upcoming job. The Xarem refinery was pretty far off the beaten track, so they had to pay better than some of the other plants. He'd heard, too, that they had better amenities, precisely because they were so far out. The package they'd offered him was good. He just hoped the working conditions lived up to the hype. He'd had enough of "luxurious accommodations" that turned out to be gang dormitories with no privacy.

His feet tingled, and he started to stretch. Two years on Xarem would be better than five years anywhere else. He'd re-up, too, if the bonus looked good. He started to blink, look around.

Hmmmm. Weird recovery area. He wasn't used to having his cryotube actually moved. Usually recovery went on aboard ship. After waking, you got up, took a shower, collected your things . . . .

He glanced around. The arrangement of the tubes was different than they'd been aboard the ship, too. He blinked hard, trying to clear his vision, and finally noticed the huge ovoid *thing* sitting right in front of him.

What the hell is that? He didn't think there was any

weird extraterrestrial life on Xarem, plants or animals. So what the hell was this thing? And even if it belonged on the planet, what would it be doing in the compound?

The oblong monstrosity jiggled suddenly, shifted, as if alive. The surface of it was wet, glistening with some kind of slime. Purvis tried to draw back, repelled, but there was no where for him to go. The top cover of the cryotube was opened, but that only exposed his head and upper chest. His arms and body were still confined in the tube. He swallowed, trying to find his voice, wanting to call for a steward, for someone to check this thing out—and release *him* from the tube.

But before he could, the top of the thing opened up.

Purvis felt a wave of nausea as the folding flaps made ugly, squishy sounds.

What the fuck is going on here? He glanced around at the other chambers, suddenly realizing, as his mind grew clearer and clearer, that one of these grotesque things rested in front of every cryotube. *Why? What for?*

Suddenly, something long and insectile began to emerge from the top of the thing. Slender, fingerlike appendages felt their way tentatively around the surface of the oblong mess. Then, finally, the creature the spidery legs were attached to emerged. It looked like a nightmare combination of a soft-bodied scorpion bred to a horseshoe crab.

What is that, some kind of bug? Purvis hated bugs, small ones, big ones, all kinds. It was one of the reasons he worked in space. You almost never saw bugs in space! And if this was a bug, it was the mother of all of them. It stood poised on its long legs, balancing like a dancer.

He'd seen enough. Panicked, Purvis repeatedly slapped the controls inside the chamber, trying to get it to release him so he could escape and get as far away from this monster bug as he could. But the controls wouldn't respond, no matter what he did. He stared around wild-eyed. Most of the hibernators weren't as aware as he was, didn't realize what was going on.

The creature shifted slightly, bounced lightly on its legs. Purvis's eyes were huge, his mouth agape in shock as he took in a deep lungful of air, to scream for help.

Just as he started his shout, the creature sprang explosively at him, faster than he could follow. Something rubbery, cold, and wet slapped him hard in the face at the same time he felt his entire head grabbed in a giant hand. A long, thin whip wrapped itself around his throat, strangling him. Then he realized what it was. The monster bug, that *thing*, was *on his face*.

Purvis lost it completely, and tried screaming wildly, hysterically, but his voice was cut off before any sound had a chance to emerge. As soon as he opened his mouth, it was filled with something fibrous and fleshy, viscous and slimy. The taste, the feel was disgusting and his empty stomach heaved, even as he struggled to breathe around the thing shoving into him, filling his mouth, ramming down his throat, forcing its way into his windpipe, into his gullet. He kept trying to scream harder and harder, as he whipped his head back and forth wildly, trying to dislodge the thing. His hands and arms were still trapped in the cryotube, so he tried to bang his face against the sides, but couldn't. His arms thrashed, his legs kicked uselessly, but nothing helped, nothing. More terrified than he'd ever been in his entire life, Purvis yielded completely to the suffocating fear and voided helplessly.

He could see nothing, hear nothing, experience nothing but this invading organism raping his face. Then the clammy cold of the creature seemed to invade his very bloodstream, and spangles danced before his eyes. His struggles slowed, grew more feeble, and he wept. He was dying. Oh, God, he was dying! He was being slowly killed by some horrible Alien bug. He sobbed, as the cold overwhelmed him, chilling the blood in his veins, paralyzing his body. If he could only stop feeling . . . .

Finally, his wish was granted, and the chilling cold enveloped his mind as totally as cryosleep. As it did, he was dimly aware of the thing on his face tightening its hold on his head, as the whiplike tail wrapped itself snugly around his throat. Together, the two eased into sleep, one resting more comfortably than the other. And Purvis began to dream horrible dreams, and none of them were about Xarem.

In the observation room, Wren heard Carlyn vomiting noisily in the back of the room. Sprague and Kinloch were with her, holding her up, trying to help her. Wren realized she was crying. At some point Clauss had left the room in a rush.

Beside him, Gediman was quiet, introspective. He was also white as a sheet. On his other side stood Trish Fontaine. Her arms were folded tightly over her chest, and the small woman radiated a quiet rage. Wren blinked up at her, surprised.

"You said they wouldn't be aware of what was happening," she said accusingly. "You said they wouldn't feel it."

Wren took a deep breath, collected his thoughts. He needed these people. He couldn't afford to lose their loyalty now.

"You saw their readings. They were still at forty percent. There was so much cryocool in their systems, they were barely awake. If they felt anything, experienced anything, it was like a dream, that's all. You've read the records. After the implantation they won't remember anything. And we probably only need to keep them semiaware during incubation. We can anesthetize their spines before the eruption of the embryo. It'll be pain-free, like I told you."

She glowered at him, clearly disbelieving, then deliberately turned her back and went to help with Carlyn.

Wren was dismayed and turned to Gediman, but his associate was transfixed by the viewport. Angrily, Wren addressed the whole group.

"Listen, this is *science,* people, raw, untried science right before your very eyes!" They all glanced at him, their revulsion plain. "And yes, it's not neat, and it's not pretty, but it's still *science.* Are you aware that in the twentieth century, during the Manhattan Project, when scientists were struggling to invent the atomic bomb, some of them believed that detonating that first bomb might ignite the hydrogen in the atmosphere? If that had happened, the atmosphere would have *caught fire* and there would have been complete annihilation. Yet, even fearing *that,* they detonated that experimental bomb. You have to take *chances* in science, if you're going to move forward, if you're going to discover *anything.*"

The crew just stared at him solemnly, then turned away again.

Wren glanced irritably at Gediman, wondering where all his glibness was now that he needed it. "I don't know what their problem is. They read the literature. They knew what they'd signed on for."

Gediman couldn't pull his eyes from the massive window. The hibernators had all stopped struggling, and were just lying quietly now, in a state imitating coma. According to the remote sensors, the implantation had already begun. Twenty face huggers embraced twenty human heads, their oxygen bladders generously pumping air into the humans, sustaining their lives.

Finally, Gediman spoke. His voice was reedy, thin. "Reading about it is one thing. Seeing it—Seeing it is something totally different." He swallowed hard and distractedly touched his own throat.

As Wren turned back to the video screens, he had to consciously stop himself from doing the same thing.

6

Call and Christie caught up with the group just as they were about to enter the mess hall/recreation area.

Vriess grinned at the woman from his chair. "You guys all done?"

Call gave a nod as Christie said, "Unloaded and signed for. Every last one of them. I take it our glorious leader is still with *El General?*"

"Who, Elgyn?" Hillard asked casually. "I guess." She spoke to Vriess. "You been 'shopping' yet?"

"On an empty stomach?" the seated man asked. "You gotta be kiddin'. After we finish with this here four-star restaurant, then I'll check out the wares. A man's gotta have priorities."

The group chuckled as they all moved forward through the open doors. The place was cavernous, Call thought, especially compared to the cramped confines of the *Betty*. It was capable of seating every soldier for a meal at once, if need be. Yet the space was arranged so it could also be used for team sports, or other athletics. There was a basketball hoop set up at one end, near an array of boxing equipment and fitness apparatus.

They were late for dinner, and the only other person in the place was a lone woman toying with a basketball over by the hoop. She was tall, slender, with shoulder-length wavy brown hair. Call assumed she was either a soldier or a researcher off duty.

The others were looking over the area, too. Then Johner spied the strange woman and muttered, "Oh, oh."

Involuntarily, Call felt herself tense.

Johner smiled and said, "You're right about that, Vriess. A man's gotta have priorities." He sauntered over to the woman, and several of the others trailed a discreet distance behind. Call wasn't sure if it was group dynamics, or a sense of impending trouble. She doubted if anyone serving aboard the *Auriga* would be an easy target for the grotesque Johner.

Brazenly, Johner came up behind the woman. Placing his hands on her shoulders he asked in what he must've thought was a seductive tone, "How about a little one-on-one?"

Call wondered how far Johner ever got with his charge-ahead notion of romance. She had trouble believing that he'd ever gotten a piece of ass in his life for free.

The woman turned her head just slightly, just enough to let him know she was aware of him. Her expression wasn't welcoming. She turned back around as if dismissing him, and kept dribbling the ball.

"What do you say?" Johner pressed, rubbing his nose into her hair, inhaling her scent.

Call heard her clearly. "Get away from me!" The warning was firm, but there was a note of weary resignation in it.

"Why should I?" Johner asked coyly.

"You'll regret it," she said flatly. There was nothing coy in her voice.

Johner pressed himself against her, rubbing himself

against her ass. Call felt her gorge rise. He nuzzled the woman's long neck, murmuring. "Are you gonna hurt me then? I think I might enjoy that." His small, nearly colorless eyes narrowed and his twisted smile was hideous, but then everything about Johner was hideous.

The woman turned her head. The parody of a smile she gave him was just as unattractive.

Distantly, Call realized that none of the crew had moved toward the mess tables, that they were all standing expectant, waiting for trouble. Apparently, this was not an unanticipated scene with Johner. Unconsciously, Call felt herself leaning forward, wanting to lend support to the strange woman. She knew that wouldn't be viewed well by the crew but . . .

Vriess tugged at the hem of her shirt. She glanced at him, saw him shake his head slightly. *Don't get involved, Call,* she could hear him warning.

She turned back to Johner and the woman, and wondered if calling Johner over to eat with them would distract him enough to—

Without warning, the woman erupted, slamming a vicious elbow jab into Johner's stomach. Immediately she pivoted halfway, firing a fist into his face, suckerpunching him hard. Call was stunned to realize that through all that, she'd casually hung onto the basketball with the other hand. The big man was actually airborne for a second, then hit the slick floor and slid.

The crew of the *Betty* was stunned, not that the woman had struck out at Johner, but at the amazing force she'd used. Call blinked as Johner kept sliding until he was stopped by a pile of pedestal-style punching bags that crashed over onto him in a tumble.

Before Call could absorb what she'd seen, Hillard gave a shout of rage and jumped the strange woman. The woman pivoted again and easily tossed Hillard off. Call gaped in surprise—the pilot was a tough, deadly fighter, but the other woman threw her as if she were a child. Hillard slammed into the deck, her own momentum working against her. As an afterthought, the woman chucked the basketball, and Hillard took it right in the gut without warning. It knocked the wind out of her with a rush that left her gasping.

Christie, his overdeveloped, dark muscles suddenly standing out in sharp relief, grabbed one of the pedestal punching bags and slammed it into the woman's head, base-first, with all the strength the big man had. Call gaped in shock as the stranger took a blow from the flat end of the weighted base right in the face without flinching, like a boxer. Nothing showed in her expression, except for a small trickle of blood oozing from her nose.

Christie was just as dumbfounded, and let her have it again, harder if possible. Once again the woman took the blow, absorbed it, and stood her ground. With a roar, Christie launched the weapon again. This time the woman's hand shot up, grabbing it on the shaft, stopping it in midblow. With little effort, she ripped the object from Christie's grasp—*Christie's!* Call realized numbly—and tossed it away.

Then she was on him like a wild animal. Burying one hand in his hair, she grabbed his jaw with the other while he struggled futilely to toss her off. He started shouting, clawing at her, punching, doing everything to dislodge her, as she tried to break his jaw. It was a terrifying tableau.

Call started to move forward to help Christie, when Vriess clutched her shirt. "Stay out of it!" he ordered. She hesitated, but obeyed.

Suddenly, Johner was back on his feet. He ran to the two struggling figures and slammed a meaty fist into the woman's unprotected kidney.

The woman's head snapped around, and her face contorted—in rage, not pain. She dropped Christie like an afterthought, and he collapsed like a doll. Unexpectedly the woman dropped, too, landing on her knees, her hand snaking out. In one coordinated move she latched onto Johner's crotch with the same crushing strength she'd used on Christie's jaw. Johner screamed, an agonized high-pitched sound. As he fell to his knees, the stranger fired a punch to his gut, folding him completely.

In the midst of this mayhem and the moans and shrieks of the injured crew, a man's voice suddenly rang out clear and firm.

"RIPLEY!"

Call turned at the sound, saw four soldiers, guns drawn, aimed right at them—no, not at *them*, at the woman. Among them stood two lab-coated men, one slightly behind the other. She recognized the first. He'd taken delivery of the cargo. The name "Wren" was stamped across the pocket of his white coat. Slightly behind him stood a man with the name "Gediman" on his coat. Gediman looked twitchy as hell, but Wren was an ice man. It was easy to see who was in charge.

The woman Wren had addressed raised her head slowly, her expression once more collected, dispassionate, as if she hadn't just mopped the floor up with them—a group that prided itself on being the toughest of the tough.

Call turned back to stare at the woman. *Did he say Ripley?* Call blinked, stunned. *Ripley?*

Everything stopped. The *Betty* crew started to back off. Christie struggled to his feet, moved his arms behind his back as if at ease, when Call knew he was anything but. Hillard managed to stand under her own power. But Ripley still clung one-handed to Johner's shirt as if unwilling to release her prey, now that he was down.

"Let's not have a scene," Wren said quietly, as if speaking to a child. As if they hadn't already had a scene, and a horrendous one at that. As if he didn't have four trained soldiers holding guns on one lone woman. As if he had any real control over her.

Amazingly, Ripley released the man, then moved away. She stood apart from everyone, showing no allegiance to anyone but herself. She moved her head in the kneeling Johner's direction and said casually, "He . . . smells."

As if that were a plausible explanation for what had happened, Wren nodded.

Johner finally managed to grab enough air to speak. "What the fuck *are* you?" He was nearly sobbing in pain.

Ripley turned to him, stared at him contemptuously, then turned that half-lidded hollow gaze on all of them. Without saying a word, she wiped away the drop of blood sliding down her upper lip and flicked it away. It was no more important to her than any of them were. The *Betty* crew, the soldiers, their guns, Wren, Gediman. . . . Call watched the drop of blood land on the floor. Dismissed.

As if she'd just gotten too bored with the whole tableau to continue, Ripley scooped up the discarded basketball from the floor, sailed it the ridiculous distance to the hoop, and watched it go right on through. Then she turned and left.

Wren signaled his approval to the soldiers, who lowered their guns. She heard him say to Gediman, "She is something of a predator, isn't she?"

He admires her for it, Call realized.

Gediman was still as nervous as a cat. He tittered foolishly and mumbled, "Well . . . the guy does smell."

The two researchers and the soldiers filed on out of the mess, leaving the *Betty* crew to pick up the pieces of their damaged shipmates. Call helped Christie over to a bench, as Hillard gave Johner a hand up. She knew none of them would feel much like eating now.

As an afterthought, she glanced back toward the

doors Ripley had exited through. When she did, she couldn't help but spot the little drop of blood on the floor where Ripley had flicked it.

A tiny plume of smoke drifted up from the stain. Beneath it, the floor was bubbling.

As late night descended on the *Auriga,* the crew of the two ships found various ways to entertain themselves—safely.

In the privacy of her assigned quarters, Hillard lay stretched out nude on her bunk, her expression blissful. Sighing soft moans of contentment, she indulged in the sensations overwhelming her. Her body ached from the altercation in the mess, but this was making up for it. She deserved it. She intended to enjoy every second of it.

She smiled over her shoulder at the man giving her such intense, intimate pleasure.

Elgyn smiled back at her as he massaged his lover's aching, tired feet.

In the privacy of his quarters, General Perez conscientiously waxed his boots himself, according to regs, by methodically melting the wax with a hand laser, applying it to the leather in a smooth layer, then hand-buffing it to a mirrorlike shine. It was a Zenlike task that kept hands busy and minds relaxed. And it allowed him time to mull over the future of his project.

Down in the ship's stores, Vriess rolled along vast corridors of bins filled to overflowing with neatly categorized and labeled parts. Thousands of parts. Maybe *millions* of parts. He was in mechanic's heaven. And everything was new, new, *new!* Perfect, state-of-the-art, high-end stuff. Only the best for General Perez. Already Vriess's arms were full of cables, printed circuit boards, components. He halted before a bin of diodes, nearly rolled on, then reconsidered. Grabbing a box, he was about to move away when he had second thoughts. Glancing around guiltily, he took a second.

In the living room of a joined suite of rooms, Christie, Call, and Johner sprawled in front of a video screen, passing around Johner's thermos of home brew. After this afternoon's fight, none of them had much to say. Call was surprised that neither of the two men or Hillard seemed to resent her lack of involvement, but she was the new kid after all, and she was small. Vriess had stayed out of it, too, and only a fool would think him helpless.

Johner, Christie, and Hillard, along with Vriess and Elgyn, had been together longest. Vriess didn't talk about it much, but he'd once indicated they'd all been mercenaries way back when—before Vriess was paralyzed.

On the screen, a gleaming black and chrome state-of-the-art revolver turned slowly for the viewing audience, while beside it scrolled all the weapon's specifications. The gun was so sophisticated, Call thought, that it ought to be able to load itself. It could be yours, the announcer promised, for a sum of credits at least equal to that needed to purchase a late model space ship.

Johner passed her the thermos without moving his eyes from the screen. She took it and splashed a little more of the lethal brew into her glass.

* * *

To each, their own relaxation.

In the restricted area, Gediman worked alone. He walked into the moving observation room that would allow him to quietly observe the progress of the first developing Aliens. He did not allow himself to think about the sleepers in the cryotubes and the face huggers attached to them. He did not allow himself to think about their screams as the erupting embryos emerged. That was not his job. He was a scientist on a mission, and his job, right here, right now, was to observe the developing Aliens that had already been born.

It was too bad they didn't have more historical information. Gediman considered it a scientific tragedy that they couldn't go back to planet LV-426, where the Aliens were originally discovered by the *Nostromo* crew. The wealth of information that must have been there! But the derelict ship with its bizarre cargo of thousands of eggs had been destroyed when the nuclear reactor of a damaged atmospheric processor had exploded, leaving nothing behind but radioactive waste and a crater nineteen megahectares in size. LV-426 would never be habitable again.

Ripley had escaped the destruction of LV-426 with a few others, but had ended up on Fiorina 161 when her ship had malfunctioned. A single warrior Alien had emerged there, waiting for the Queen that Ripley had unknowingly harbored. But that warrior had been destroyed, and Ripley had committed suicide to ensure the Queen inside her would never emerge.

That might have been the end of human contact with the Aliens, since all attempts, both by military scientists and private corporations, to discover the Aliens' planet of origin had failed to turn up a single clue, in spite of the hundreds of surveyed worlds that existed. The secret of the nearly perfect organisms had died in the holocaust on LV-426, until the discovery of Ripley's preserved blood and tissue samples from Fiorina 161.

That had been twenty-five years ago. The original samples had yielded little information, and they'd nearly been destroyed twice. Ten years ago, however, Mason Wren, a military scientist, had seen the potential there, and somehow managed to convince some very important people in Weapons Research of the possibilities. It had been his project ever since. But only in the last two years had the rest of the crew been ready to believe in Wren's vision. That's when they'd all been moved to the *Auriga*. That's when they'd suddenly been given *everything* they needed to make the project work. That was when the cloned cells from the samples began to survive and grow.

And now they were *here*. Facing the practical application of all that scientific research. There was still so much to *learn*. Patiently, he watched the monitors, electronic readouts, and the specimens themselves.

Gediman couldn't deny the research crew's amazement at the speed with which some of the embryos burst from their hapless hosts, never mind their incredibly rapid development. Wren couldn't be sure if the growth was accelerated by the work they'd done, or if it was a natural variation. Previous records had been spotty as to the time span elapsed, and the sample size was too small to indicate norms or trends. Of course, they were still waiting for most of the embryos. . . .

He moved the observation room along the track, pausing when he reached a specific cage. Manipulating the controls, he moved the booth right up to the cage's wide, clear port.

Inside, he could see two nearly adult-size Aliens that seemed to be hibernating. They were curled up on the floor, folded as small as possible, totally still. He made notes, checked the time. Suddenly, a third Alien moved up to the window from the shadows.

Gediman jumped involuntarily, having been unaware of the creature until it simply *appeared*. It

loomed before him, dark, massive, malevolent, and totally *Alien.* The bizarre, elongated head, the huge tail,
the six-fingered hands, the external, silicon-sheathed
black skeleton, the monstrous dorsal horns. The beast
grew still.

So, are you observing me? the scientist wondered. It
was an eerie sensation for Gediman to be watched by
such a big predator—a predator with no obvious eyes.

*But you can see just fine, can't you? Special sensors
in that tubular head of yours, for heat, vibration,
sound, scent, movement—Three hundred and sixty de-
grees of awareness, far keener than any eyesight or
hearing known. An amazing creature.*

He saw again the cryotube that held the man named
Purvis. Saw clearly the stark terror on Purvis's very
aware face as the egg opened up before him. Saw the
face-hugger attack and Purvis's desperate struggle. . . .

He blinked, trying to erase the image. Purvis still
had his embryo. Apparently, the man had borderline
low thyroid function, not enough to treat, just enough
to make the development of his embryo slower than
some of the others. . . .

*Forget him. Just because you noticed his name. For-
get it all. You had to go there to get here. And now
you've got them. This is just the beginning.*

The Alien observing him moved stealthily, closer to
the window. As if drawn to it, Gediman, too, moved
nearer on his side of the port. Slowly, the Alien's thin
lips curled up, out of the way of its chrome-colored
teeth. Opening its massive maw, it slid its rigid tongue
forward slowly, as if for Gediman's scientific perusal.
The tongue flexed its own teeth, and the shaft of the
tongue dripped clear mucous.

Gediman forgot all about Purvis, forgot all about
face huggers, and stared enraptured at a sight no one
had ever seen before without dying. He found himself
grinning. "Is that a distended externus lingua . . . or
you just happy to see me?" he muttered.

Distracted, he placed a hand against the port to support himself, then found his nose bumping the specially-designed, steel-strong, clear plastic they still called "glass," his forehead and one cheek plastered against it like a kid as he tried to get an even better look.

Without warning, the Alien's tongue shot out like a whip and struck the glass right by his eye. Gediman leaped back, his heart racing, his hands suddenly clammy. Without tearing his eyes away from the creature, he moved toward the center console.

"Time for the first lesson, puppy," Gediman told it, and slapped his hand down on a big red fail-safe button.

Instantly, jets of liquid nitrogen squirted the Alien, creating clouds of nitrogen steam as soon as they hit the air. The monster screamed frantically, darting back to the middle of the cage, tromping all over its sleeping fellows, rousing them, panicking them. They all joined in the shrieking melee. Gediman released the button.

The warrior who'd been squirted spun his obscene head toward Gediman, his huge, scorpionlike tail lashing wildly. The other two cringed back, clearly unsure of what was happening. The first Alien moved to the port again, but Gediman reached for the red button, pausing just above it.

The monster froze. Gediman did, too.

From a distance, the Alien extended his tongue threateningly, but made no move to advance on the window.

Gediman nodded approvingly. "So, we're a fast learner, huh?" He reached for his notebook, satisfied.

The big warrior quivered in the small, strange place, his rage boundless. That little, soft prey hurt me, burned me! He whipped his tail in fury, as he watched the prey manipulate his devices, perform functions the warrior could only guess at. The warrior stared at the dangerous red pad in reach of the small being. He read the words "Fail-safe," written beside it, and "Warning! Nitrogen jets!" He watched the small creature—the name "Gediman" printed on it—as it made words appear on a device it held. The prey radiated satisfaction, pride, accomplishment, as if it had fully realized its true function.

Not that it mattered to the warrior. To him, the prey had only one true function, the same as any other species. He lashed his tail, extended his tongue in warning. Atmosphere whistled through his dorsal pipes. He hated this Alien environment, longing for the steaming warmth of the crèche, the strength and safety of his own kind. Even with the two others nearby, he suffered the aloneness of his own individuality. It was time to build the crèche. Time to join with other warriors and serve the Queen. It was why he lived.

He watched the prey, learning almost everything about it that the warrior would ever need to know.

He could not smell it yet, but he could smell others of its kind, their scent carried through the thin air. They were warm-blooded oxygen breathers. He could see the color of its exhalations even through the clear barrier. He could see the color of its red blood through its pale veins, analyze its chemistry. He could gauge its weight, its muscle mass, its ability to resist. He knew how strong it was, how weak. He could see the color of its emotions, whether it was hot or cold, and whether it felt pain or fear. He could see it felt fear of the warrior—but not enough. Especially not now that it proved it could hurt the warrior. The "Gediman" radiated the color of pride, of accomplishment.

I will remember that color when I come for you.

And I will come for you.

The Gediman's body would be building materials

for the crèche. Once it was secured there, the warrior would decide if it would serve as food for the Queen, or if it was suitable to bear her young, or even if it would serve as food for the young. He could decide, even, if Gediman should bear young **and** also be its first meal.

And since you have hurt me and taken pleasure in it, I will decide to do with you whatever will keep you alive the longest.

The warrior would watch until the Gediman's pride melted away, and with it every emotion it ever had, until there was nothing left but fear, an all-encompassing fear like the Gediman had never known. Fear made the host, was critical for it. It made the organism receptive, opened the pathways for the young, allowed them to take solid root, to grow, to change the host to fill its needs. Fear was critical for that. And when the young had left their Alien womb, then the last burst of fear and pain tenderized the host's meat, to feed the small young.

The big warrior lashed his tail, transmitting everything he thought and planned and felt to his brothers and his Queen. His Queen, his Mother, sent her love and approval. It would happen soon. The warrior would see to it. And this small human, this Gediman, would be the first. The first womb. The first food. And he would live to know it all. The warrior would see to that as well.

The Queen approved.

Back in the suite, Call glanced at the specs on a bizarrely designed dagger now being displayed on the screen as she decided she had had just about enough of videos and alcohol. Hell, nights on the *Betty* were usually more interesting than *this*. She attempted to get up, but fell back as if unbalanced.

The two men chuckled amiably.

"Jesus, Johner," she complained, scratching her head, "what do you put in that shit anyway? Battery acid?" She stared at her empty glass as if trying to figure out how it got that way.

"Just to add a little color," Johner told her defensively, then he and Christie cracked up, slapping palms.

"That's it for me," she decided, and hauled herself out of the chair and staggered off. She tried whistling that little tune she and Vriess had been harmonizing on before, but now it sounded a little rough around the edges.

Outside the suite, Call rounded a corner. Once out of anyone else's range of vision, she straightened up, perfectly sober. Glancing around, she made sure she was alone, then walked purposefully down the hallway. Following the route she'd preselected, she moved on until she reached the area clearly marked RESTRICTED.

From here on in, she knew, every door would be a barrier. Rummaging in her pocket, she removed a locksmith's master key ring. On it were a dozen microspray capsules, most of them her own invention.

Watching over her shoulder, straining to hear, using every sense she had, Call made sure she was still alone, still unobserved as she proceeded to violate lock after lock. Some of them required rapid code input, plus the right combination of spray chemicals into breath analyzers. Some of them only needed one squirt from the right capsule. But none of them were able to resist her.

Finally the last door opened silently before her, just enough to allow her slender frame to slip inside. Hesitating briefly, she entered the cell and closed the door behind her. Still no alarms. Clearly they were no longer watching the occupant of this cell as closely as they had at first.

The cubicle was tiny, dark, and for a moment Call

thought she'd picked the wrong one, that this one was uninhabited. There was nothing in here—no sink, no drinking water dispenser, no toilet, nothing. All she could see was sharply defined shadows and contrasting bright areas that divided the small space of the cell into seperate areas. Then her eyes adjusted to the stark lighting and she could make out the sole of a sneaker facing her from the edge of the darkest shadow. She looked again. The sneaker was attached to a leg that nearly disappeared into one of the shadowed areas. The lone occupant of the cell was curled up within that shadow, cleverly rendered invisible to anyone who might be observing her from above.

Clinging to the darkness, Call moved silently toward the figure, then crouched low, edging toward the same dark area that obscured the sleeping figure. She could barely make out the shadowy form curled up, fetallike, in spite of her close proximity. Moving silently, Call crawled into the limited space, for once grateful for her small, compact body. The darkness enveloped her completely. Now they were both hidden. No sooner had she concealed herself than a shadow passed overhead.

It was a guard making his rounds above the cell, his booted feet passing over the grill in the ceiling. Call stopped breathing.

Finally, he was gone. Call turned back to the sleeping woman, waiting for her to register some awareness of the invader's presence, but the figure slept on, brown hair obscuring her face, the rise and fall of her breath steady, regular. Human. The woman's arms were curled around her stomach as if guarding something there, or perhaps she was in pain. Even in sleep, her strong, attractive features were troubled, as though she were having bad dreams. . . .

You came here to do a job, Call thought, repressing a stab of pity. *So, do it. Just because she looks like—*

With the silence of an assassin, Call extended her right hand, and her concealed stiletto slid into it. At the touch of a button the blade emerged soundlessly. The silvery weapon was almost a foot long, with a deadly point. Call always felt projectile weapons were for cowards. She liked to work close and quiet.

She crouched, drew her hand back unwaveringly. *Stop staring at her. Do what you came here to do.*

She swallowed. One quick move, and she'd puncture the heart. Clean. Neat. Ripley would never know. It was the kindest thing she could do for her.

Suddenly, the still figure stirred in her sleep. Call froze. The woman's head tipped back, her long throat exposed. Part of the lacing on her brown, form-fitting jerkin separated over the breasts and belly. Her pale skin could be seen even in the shadow.

Call moved the tip of the stiletto and parted the drab, laced bodice a little more. She blinked, staring at the scar. A scar? A **scar!**

No!

Softly, the woman's voice asked casually, "Well?"

Call jumped, sliding back a bit. She was so startled, she nearly dropped her knife.

"You gonna kill me, or what?" Ripley asked, in her usual flat monotone.

Call's jaw tightened. "There's no point, is there?" With a rapid flick of her wrist, the stiletto whipped back in place up her sleeve, just as quietly as it had emerged. "They've already taken it out. Christ . . . is it *here*? On board?" She felt icy inside, still trying to absorb the fact that she was too late.

Too late!

Ripley was smiling grimly. "You mean my *baby*?"

Call was shaking her head, barely aware of the bizarre reality of herself having *this* conversation with *this* woman. "I don't understand. If they've got *it*, why are they keeping you alive?"

A small shrug. "They're curious. I'm the latest thing."

Call battled a flood of impotent rage. She hadn't counted on being *late*. Then she forced herself to snap out of it. She looked meaningfully at the woman near her in the confined space of the sharply outlined shadow. Soundlessly, she flicked the knife back into her hand, released the blade, showed it to Ripley.

Her voice gentle, Call offered a gift. "I can make it all stop if you want. The pain . . . this nightmare. It's all I can offer you." *You deserve so much better.*

Ripley's expression grew more open, and Call watched it fill with an unspeakable sadness that tore at her. Without answering, she opened her hand, then pressed the palm calmly against the point of the blade.

"What makes you think I would let you do that?" she murmured.

Then Ripley pushed her hand firmly onto the tip of the knife until the blade went completely through, emerging out the back by at least four inches before she stopped.

Call's eyes went wide, her mouth opened. It was the same expression she'd worn in the mess hall. "Who *are* you?" she whispered, staring at the impaled hand, the thin trickle of blood dripping from it, the lack of reaction from the woman.

Her voice flat, she stated simply, "Ripley, Ellen. Lieutenant, First Class. Number five-one-five-six-one-seven-zero."

Call could only shake her head. "Ellen Ripley died over *two hundred years ago.*"

That bit of knowledge seemed to move the woman; surprise showed mutely on her face. She pulled her hand off the knife, grimacing slightly at the pain, as if it were a minor thing. "What do you know about it?" She tried to make the sentence sound distant, but an undercurrent of interest was there.

"I've read Morse," Call said, tightly. "I've read all the banned histories. Ellen Ripley gave her life to protect us from the beast. You're not *her*."

The woman called Ripley looked away, at some distant point only she could see. "I'm not her? What am I, then?"

Good question. Call watched in awe as her knife blade sizzled and smoked, melting right in front of her, leaving only a sharp-edged stub. There was Ripley's answer. She showed her the steel. "You're a *thing*. A test construct. A clone. They grew you in a fucking lab."

That grim humor flashed again. "But only God can make a tree."

Call felt a sudden need to connect with . . . with this simulacrum, this *shadow* of Ripley. "And now they've brought the beast out of you."

The sadness again. Soul-deep sorrow. A depth of pain Call could only guess at. "Not all the way out."

Call didn't understand. "What?"

Ripley looked at her, allowed eye contact. Her gaze burned Call, seared right through her the way Ripley's acid blood had dissolved her knife. The woman whispered, "It's in my head. Behind my eyes." For the first time, she appeared human, vulnerable.

"Then *help* me! If there's anything *human* in you at all, help me stop them before this thing gets loose."

The woman's desolation was bottomless. "It's too late."

For a second Call misunderstood. *Too late for me?* She suddenly became painfully aware that she was crouched in the dark, inches from this . . . this . . . Call didn't know what to call her. This predator who could probably kill her one-handed faster than she could ever react in defense. Her knife would be useless—

When Ripley raised her hand toward Call's face, the younger woman flinched. Ripley froze for a moment, then her hand moved again. Ripley stroked Call's forehead, moving a strand of hair back. It was a gentle, nearly sensuous gesture. The way a mother would touch her child, a bit of grooming, a bit of comfort. . . .

"I've come to terms with the idea," Ripley muttered, and Call realized she was referring to the monster she'd birthed. That the creature lived. That she would bring forth a new plague. "It's inevitable."

Call pulled herself together, her face stern. "Not as long as I'm around." She tried not to think about how ineffectual that must sound. She hated her small frame, her soft, lilting voice. Not for the first time she wished she was built like Christie.

"You'll never get out of here alive," Ripley said sadly, as if she were instructing a foolish child.

Hearing the waver in her own voice, Call insisted, "I don't give a damn!"

Ripley raised an eyebrow, amused. "Really?"

Lightning swift, Ripley's hand lashed out, grabbing Call by the throat, and suddenly there was no air. Instantly, Call swung the stub of the melted blade, trapped by the confines of the small space and hampered by her own rising terror.

Ripley slammed her arm to the floor, loomed over her. Call had to fight panic, try to keep her mind clear. The predator's eyes sparkled over her face. With infinite sadness, Ripley offered, "I can make it stop."

Call heard herself actually whimper, and knew her stark terror was plain on her face. Her eyes pleaded for mercy.

As quickly as she'd been grabbed, Call was suddenly released. Ripley slid away from her. Once more, the woman curled back up in a fetal ball, back against the wall, hiding as far within the shadows as she could.

What are you doing? Why do you even need to hide? What do you think they want from you now? No wonder there were no furnishings in the cell. If they'd given her a cot, no doubt she'd be curled up under it, completely out of sight. *Is there some measure of safety and comfort you find by curling into this little dark place? Is it some long-forgotten childhood memory hundreds of years old?*

"Go," Ripley ordered her, dead-voiced again. "Get out of here. They're looking for you."

Unnerved, Call shoved away from her, fearing she'd change her mind, understanding that whether she emerged from this room dead or alive was entirely up to the whim of this woman. She scrambled away from the shadow, suddenly heedless of being discovered by the guard and, sucking air desperately, she scuttled like a crab for the door.

Her purpose here, her entire mission, was forgotten in a fog of self-preservation. Call couldn't believe how strong that instinct was, how it drove her to escape. She fumbled at the door, found the mechanism, forced it to open.

She darted from the room, all caution forgotten in her panicked flight. Two steps outside the cell something cold and metallic touched her neck, but before she could turn and defend herself the charge struck her hard, burning her skin, igniting her nerves, coursing a blast of electricity down her spine, through every nerve—

She shouted once, then everything went dark as she collapsed.

Wren watched the petite, dark-haired woman crumple to the ground with smug satisfaction. As two soldiers grabbed her under the arms and hauled her up, he thought, *Just who do you think you are to try to interfere with a top-secret research mission? Did you really think you'd succeed?*

He was so enraged, he was grateful that the presence

of the soldiers would force him to maintain his profes-
sionalism. As Call shook her head dazedly and started
to regain consciousness, Wren growled at her, "I think
you're going to find that this was ill-advised."

He asked the nearest soldier, "Where are her
friends?"

"As far as we know, sir, they're all in separate
quarters. . . ."

"Sound the alarm," Wren ordered. "I want them
rounded up—now!"

Ripley curled up tight within her shadow and stared
into the darkness, trying not to let the young woman's
words touch her. She was tired, so very tired—But she
didn't dare sleep.

I don't wanna sleep, a small, thin voice said in her
head. *I have scary dreams.*

Who had said that? Ripley couldn't remember, but
the memory stabbed like a knife.

She couldn't sleep . . . she felt as if they could touch
her in her sleep. Her mind was unguarded then, and
brought them to the surface. All the monsters, the *real*
monsters. Moving, breathing, seething—dreaming,
planning, waiting. . . .

She shuddered.

They were a perfect organism, with only one true
function. And that woman, that small, young woman,
she couldn't understand. . . .

Its structural perfection is matched only by its hostility.

Ripley could not recall who had said that to her or
when, but she remembered it, nonetheless. It filled her
with a crushing sadness. The thought of that idealistic
young woman's zeal, her determination, depressed her
even more. For Ripley could see the barest shadow of
what she had been in that woman's eyes. What fate and
the universe's worst luck had made her.

And what has fate made me now? she wondered hollowly. She didn't know. Had it made her Ellen Ripley, as her chaotic mind insisted, or had it made her a quisling, a changeling as grotesque as . . . as . . .

I prefer to be called an artificial person.

She blinked, looking at the rapidly healing mark on her palm, all that was left from the woman's knife.

In the stillness of that moment, her eyes drooped, her body sagged, and she slipped into sleep unawares. And then it was there, waiting for her . . . behind her eyes. . . .

Her longing for the steaming warmth of the crèche, the strength and safety of her own kind. Alone, she suffered the isolation of her own individuality. Only in sleep could she join them, rejoice with them. It was time to build the crèche. Time to join with other warriors and serve the Queen. It was why she lived.

The warrior lashed her tail, transmitting everything she thought and planned and felt to her Queen. And her Queen sent her love and approval back to her warrior. It would happen soon. The Queen would see to it and the warrior would make it happen. And this shell that was human, this Ripley, would be the mother of them all. The first womb. The first warrior. And she would live to know it all, to share the glory with them. The Queen would see to it, for Ripley was the keystone of the hive. The nurturer of the crèche. The foundation of the Newborn.

Ripley twitched helplessly in her sleep, making soft sounds of protest and pain. The Queen shared her dreams, and approved.

7

Christie was just about to tell Johner that he'd had enough of both his terrible home brew and his company, and get his own self on to bed when the doors to their suite suddenly slammed open. He and Johner were instantly on their feet as four soldiers charged into the room. Before either man could do anything, they were staring down the barrels of the soldiers' fully charged guns, held ready to fire. The two men from the *Betty* exchanged a quick look. Instinctively, Johner gripped his thermos tight.

"What's the problem?" Christie asked, making no sudden moves. He held his hands at his sides, away from his body. He didn't want anybody here making any mistakes.

"Sir," one of the soldiers said, incongruously polite, "you will come with us. Now."

I guess we will, Christie thought, giving Johner a quick nod.

"Sir," the soldier repeated. "Now!"

Christie glanced at the man. The name *Distephano* was stamped on his helmet. "Sure thing, man. We're coming. No resistance here, is there, Johner?" Carefully, ostentatiously, Christie moved his hands behind his back, clasped them.

"You got that right," Johner mumbled low.

They were marched into the mess hall. Every light was on. In minutes, Elgyn and Hillard were pushed into the room by other soldiers. Elgyn was still adjusting his clothes, having obviously dressed in a hurry. He glanced at Christie, made eye contact. Hillard did the same. No one spoke.

Suddenly, from the doorway, Call was shoved into the room. She stumbled, obviously dazed, rubbing her neck. That doctor, Wren, was with the soldiers manhandling Call, and he was glaring at the little tech. He looked furious.

They've stunned her, Christie realized, tensing. *What the hell could that little girl be up to now? And where the devil is Vriess?*

Elgyn finished with his clothes. He looked straight at Wren. "What the fuck is going on here?"

"Looks like a double-cross, boss," Christie said clearly. He wanted Elgyn to hear the clarity in his voice. He and Johner had been drinking for hours, but they were used to functioning well under a level of alcohol that would kill most men. He knew Elgyn would be concerned about their ability to respond to the situation. Christie tried not to be distracted by Vriess's absence. Were they holding him somewhere as insurance?

Wren scanned the room then asked Elgyn point-blank, "Where is the other one? With the chair?"

Well, if he don't know, then Vriess must still be loose, Christie decided, feeling relieved.

Beside him, Johner growled at Distephano, "Get your fucking hands off me!" His voice sounded sloppy, slurred. Christie wondered if Johner *was* too wasted to function.

"Doctor," Elgyn said reasonably, "talk to me. What's going on?"

What Wren said made no sense. "You're gonna tell me who you're working for right now, or you'll be screaming it, come sunrise."

Huh? Christie thought. *When we got here, we were working for you, ya stupid fuck. Other than that, we work for ourselves—no one else.* The black man exchanged a meaningful glance with Elgyn.

Suddenly, Call stepped forward, her expression grim. "Wren, they got nothing to do with this."

This is about Call? What the hell could one tiny little girl like her do to this bad-ass military station?

Hillard glared at Call. "To do with what?"

Elgyn raised his hands placatingly. "Everybody just calm down. We can work this out. There's no need to get emotional. . . ."

Christie tensed as Elgyn said the code words. Still grasping his hands behind his back, he flexed his forearms. Two guns silently slipped out of his sleeves into his hands. Carefully, he wrapped his big palms around the familiar, friendly gun butts.

Wren was ranting on. "Do you know what the penalties are for terrorist activity?"

Johner mumbled to Christie, "Terrorist?"

Shit, Christie worried, *maybe Johner did have too much booze. If he's out of it . . . too slow to react . . . we're in it deep.*

Finally, Elgyn started to show some temperament. "There's no goddamn terrorists on my crew." He turned his anger on the only one who seemed to have some idea what was going on. "Call, what's this about?"

Before she could answer, Wren interrupted. "I don't give a shit if you're in on this or not. You brought a subversive onto a military vessel and as far as I'm concerned, you fry with her. You hear me?"

Elgyn drew up straight, looking Wren right in the eye. "I do." His eyes moved past Wren. "Christie?"

The crewman never moved, standing stock-still, like a statue. But he'd heard.

Before anyone else could move or react, Christie whipped his weapons from behind his back. Pivoting like a gun turret in a battleship, he fired. The rapidity of his movements belied the accuracy of his shots, as one by one, he hit four of the soldiers square in the heart. Not a single bullet even grazed anyone from the *Betty* crew, in spite of their close proximity to the stricken soldiers.

The powerful bullets, hitting the soldiers at such close range, blew them back, six feet away from the crew. Their chests exploded, blood and tissue and bits of bone spraying the walls, the floor, tables, chairs, other soldiers. The bodies finally crumpled to the floor, but before that happened, the other soldiers began to respond. The one standing next to Christie pivoted, pointing his gun right at the big man.

Christie never turned in his direction, just whipped his gun to the side, and using only his peripheral vision, fired off a burst. The soldier was propelled backward, dead before his finger ever tightened on the trigger.

Another soldier nearer the exit doors roared a challenge and charged forward, firing wildly.

Christie moved out of the line of fire, but the charges ricocheted dangerously close to the slower responding Johner. Johner was almost comical as he danced in place, miraculously managing to dodge the soldier's random fire, while struggling with the cap of his metal thermos. Then Johner was suddenly struck where it would hurt him the most—square in his home brew! The bullet pinged loud, puncturing the top of the metal canister.

Johner looked positively amazed when the bullet accomplished what he couldn't, ejecting the top of the thermos and causing the revolver hidden inside to drop right into Johner's hand. He barely had time to aim the gun—with the thermos cover dangling over the muzzle—at the soldier shooting at him. Johner fired, and the metal cover exploded wildly.

So did the soldier, who screamed as he was hit and fell hard on his back, sliding along the floor, just like Johner had earlier. Only Johner had lived through his experience.

The dead soldier's progress was halted when Elgyn's foot blocked his helmet, as casually as if he were halting a soccer ball.

But then Christie heard an ominous click and realized someone had gotten behind him.

"STOP!" shouted a male voice close to his head.

Christie glanced back. He could just make out the smooth bore of an impressive military weapon trained on his skull.

"Drop your weapons," the soldier ordered him and Johner, "or I blow his head off."

Everyone froze. Christie could see Johner snarling, uglier than ever. The shattered remnants of the thermos were smoking. They had to be burning Johner's hand.

Dropping my weapons is a tad hard for me to do, boy, Christie thought as he ever so slowly raised his hands in the air. He spread his palms, made sure they all could clearly see the apparatus holding the guns in place near his fingers. He'd never come up with a way to release the guns easily for this kind of situation. Maybe because he never thought he'd be in this situation.

The fact that his powerful weapons were suspended close to Christie's hands was something the soldier holding him at bay couldn't have anticipated. Christie spied a bead of sweat running down the man's face. He was quivering with nervousness. He'd have to be careful now. They'd all have to be careful. One wrong move could get him killed.

Coolly, Christie turned his gaze heavenward, scanning the ceiling. Surreptitiously, he aimed the barrel of one of his revolvers at a reinforced corner of the ceiling. He moved the weapon ever so subtly, aiming . . . aiming. . . .

He fired, hearing the high-pitched whine, as the bullet ricocheted and slammed into his soldier's helmet in less than a second. The soldier fell like a tree, the neat hole in the top of his helmet still smoking.

That left one soldier, and one doctor. Wren and Distephano. Christie smiled, lowered his arms, and aimed his weapons at them.

In the Alien observation room, alarms blared and warning lights flashed when the first gun was fired. Gediman and his assistant, Carlyn Williamson, spun to check the video screens. On one of the monitors the mess hall was pictured. As they watched in shocked fascination, *Father*'s perfectly modulated voice warned, "Emergency. Emergency. There has been an armed attack on *Auriga*'s personnel in the mess hall." The computer continued to repeat the message over and over, as they watched the motley crew of the *Betty* defeat more than half a dozen trained, armed soldiers in scant seconds.

It was over before Gediman could collect his wits. Stunned, he watched a huge black man press a revolver against Dr. Wren's temple.

"*Shit!*" Gediman hissed, feeling completely impotent.

Carlyn gasped Wren's name, clutching Gediman's sleeve in reaction. But both of them knew there was nothing, absolutely nothing they could do. They could only stare, horrified, at the unfolding scene.

* * *

Now what the fuck do we do? Elgyn wondered, as everything slowed to a crawl. Christie pinned the doc against him, gun to his head to ensure maximum cooperation. *How the hell do we get off this barge in one piece? By taking Wren hostage? The place will be swarming with grunts any second now.*

Johner, finally getting his act together, disarmed the single surviving soldier. Elgyn watched as Johner noted the soldier's name, used it to get his attention.

"Okay, Distephano, now nice and easy. . . ." Johner lifted the gun right out of the man's grasp.

As soon as the single living soldier was disarmed, Call started moving. "I'm gonna finish this," she growled.

Finish what? Elgyn wondered, still having no idea what had brought all this on. Call knew, though. The captain reached out, snagged a tight handful of her dark, short-cropped hair, yanked her back hard. Her small body nearly whipsawed in his grip.

"You're not goin' nowhere, Call!" he told her angrily.

The warrior watched the changing emotions of the two humans who stood with their backs to him and his brothers. Another warrior stood at his side, while alone in the back of the cage sat the third—the smallest of the three. The second warrior paced nervously, but the first stood his ground, watching, waiting. He eyed the red button, now unnoticed by the humans.

The humans were upset, worried, nervous. Their colors were flaring, whatever was causing their concern still ongoing. There were strange sounds out there, voices, loud meaningless noise, flashing lights.

It was interesting, but it wasn't about to distract the warrior from his primary objective.

There had to be a way to turn the humans' unexpected problem to their advantage.

A memory came to him. From the Mother.

I don't know which species is worse. . . . You don't see them fucking each other over. . . .

It was not his memory, and he was not sure what all of it meant. But there was meaning there, something for him to learn. He considered. . . .

The first warrior turned to his closer brother, transmitted information to him. The second warrior absorbed the information. He stopped pacing. Together, the two looked back at the third. The smaller one understood their objective, their reasons, the whole new concept. He even agreed with it. However, he was also burdened with his own individuality, and edged back against the wall of the cave nervously.

The two larger warriors turned back to the humans, watching them, eyeing the fail-safe. The humans had completely forgotten them in their panic. The sounds, the voices, the images on their machine, were all working to distract them from the warriors. They were a high-strung species, yet adaptable. It was one of the things that made them such good hosts.

They would have to move quickly.

The two warriors turned on the third, who, in spite of his understanding of their need, lost himself momentarily in his individuality. In fear, he bared his teeth at his brothers.

It did not matter.

The two struck as one. The smaller warrior screamed and shrieked, as the two large ones grappled with him, using all their strength, their magnificent tails lashing wildly for balance, slamming into walls, into the clear port in the small space. The dying one shrieked louder, grappling with them as a warrior's

*teeth smashed into his skull, as powerful hands ripped
at his limbs, his tail, his head.*

*The wounded warrior's blood erupted from his skull
as the second warrior's teeth finally punched through
the thick exoskeleton. The first warrior wrenched one
of his brother's arms off and blood spurted everywhere, splashing the clear port, the walls, the floor.
The first warrior could smell the sturdy cage material
begin to melt, hear the sizzling, bubbling destruction.
The dying one shrieked on, offering his life for his
Queen, for his hive, if reluctantly. Finally, there came
a last, triumphant scream, followed by the death rattle.*

*The two surviving warriors ripped apart his chest,
tore the dorsal horns from his back, broke his legs
apart. They were coated in their brother's blood, but
they were immune to its damage. The floor of the cage,
however, bubbled, seethed, melted and grew soft. They
kept tearing at the third warrior, finally pounding him
to pulp.*

*The first warrior felt the Queen accept her son's
sacrifice with sorrow and pride.*

Over the klaxon call of the alarms, over the flashing red
alert lights, *Father*'s calm voice changed its message
from the emergency alert it had been sounded to a new
one. It took three repetitions before the message got
through to either Gediman or his assistant.

"There is serious structural damage to animal holding facility number zero, zero, one. There is serious
structural damage to animal holding facility number
zero, zero, one. The damage is sufficient to breach the
security of animal holding facility number zero, zero,
one. There is serious structural damage to animal holding facility number—"

Damage to the cage . . . ? Gediman forgot all about
the mess hall riot and whipped around to the view port.

He suddenly heard the terrible screams from inside it, though he could barely make out the frantic movement of shadows. A huge tail slammed into the view port, making it quiver. Then there was a sudden splash of liquid on the glass . . .

. . . And then the port on the cage began to melt.

Two of those things are ripping the third one to pieces! What the hell . . . ?

"Dr. Gediman!" Carlyn shouted, pointing at the port. "Doctor!"

Without answering her, he ran to the port. There was a flurry of action within the cage, then everything seemed to stop. He could see scattered pieces of something that had once been alive. There was a heaving, melting mass on the floor. The two remaining living Aliens suddenly turned to look at him. It looked like they were *grinning*!

The mess on the floor began to sink into an oozelike puddle.

Gediman's eyes couldn't open any wider. Horrified, he lurched for the fail-safe button, slammed it down, held it. Looking up at the port, he could see the nitrogen spreading through the cage, but there were no screams from the two warriors. In fact, there were no screams at all. And now the nitrogen gas filled the cage, preventing him from seeing anything. He released the button, waited for the fog to lift, so he could see. . . .

"Oh, god, Doctor!" Carlyn shouted, pointing.

As the gas cleared, the only thing left for Gediman to see was one long tail disappearing into a bottomless hole.

*S*he jerked out of the nightmare with a cry.

Wake up. Be quiet. We're in trouble.

No, that was just a memory.

*She paused, listening, watching in the dark. **Sensing.***
No, not just a memory, not just a bad dream. Some-
thing was happening. Something real.

Gediman stared as the doors to the cage opened. It was
impossible. It couldn't have happened. *They're gone.*
Gone! His only coherent thought was, *Wren's going to*
kill me. My fellowship, my studies, all gone.

He edged into the forbidden territory, the cage, still
trying to absorb the reality of the emptiness before
him. He walked carefully, stepping cautiously around
spots on the floor that were still melting, still bubbling
merrily away. The stench of burning plastic nearly
choked him.

In the center of the room the entire floor was gone,
dissolved, turned to pudding. It wasn't possible. Where
could they possibly go? What could they possibly do?

He leaned over the hole, careful not to step in any
of the melting mess. It was too dark. He couldn't see
anything. Maybe they were down there, trapped in the
ship's grid work, and they could contain them. . . . If
he could only see—

He knelt, peering into the gloom.

Behind him, Carlyn gasped, "Oh, God, Doctor Gediman, *be careful!*"

It was worse than he thought. He could see light
now. The blood had already eaten through *two* levels.

"Christ, Carlyn," he said, "they could be anywhere."

Suddenly, something black and spidery appeared
from under the lip of the melting floor. Gediman, peering past it into the second damaged floor, didn't notice
it for half a second. Half a second too late.

All at once, his brain registered, *six fingers, long*
nails, inhuman hand—

His head jerked back, but not nearly fast enough.

The massive hand enveloped his face, grabbed it, held tight. He screamed, but it was smothered against the silicon-skinned palm of the Alien. His terror bloomed hugely, overwhelming him, embracing him, becoming his all. He didn't care if he couldn't be heard. He had to scream. And he did. Again. And again.

With a strength he had never imagined, the massive Alien warrior dragged him into the darkness of the sub-flooring grid in a move that was almost graceful. The Alien embraced him there under the floor, his arms and tail surrounding Gediman like a lover, holding him close, holding him secure, so that he would not fall. Gently, then, the beast freed his mouth, observing Gediman curiously, as Gediman's lungs powered his frantic screams of total, utter terror.

The creature seemed to smile there in the dark, but like the Cheshire cat, all Gediman could see were those terrible silver teeth, grinning. Grinning at him. Gediman screamed some more.

Carlyn stared wildly as Dr. Gediman suddenly, inexplicably disappeared into the hole in the floor. No, not inexplicably. She knew exactly what had happened. Dear God, she *knew*.

Eyes wide, mouth open, chin quivering in horror, Carlyn edged out of the cage, and slammed her hand on the controls that would shut the door.

*They were out. They were **out**!*

Father was babbling at her about structural damage and breach of security. Terrorists had taken over the mess hall, and now . . .

She ran, panicked, to find someone, to get some help. But here, on the outskirts of Pluto, she knew there was no help. They were all locked in a terrible bottle with the angriest genies of all.

* * *

Call had never known such frustration. She stared at Elgyn. She *had* to get through to him, she *had* to. She could see Elgyn wavering, half believing her, half ready to cut his losses and run for it.

"He's conducting illegal experiments," she nearly shouted at the *Betty*'s captain. "He's breeding—"

Johner, still half drunk, cut her off. "She's a goddamn mole! Ice the bitch—"

She shouted over him, pointing to Wren. "Listen to me! He's breeding an Alien species here. More than dangerous. If they get loose, it'll make the Lacerta Worm Plague look like a fucking square dance!"

Elgyn was clearly considering what she was saying, his eyes darting between Call and Wren.

Suddenly, Christie murmured, "Listen!" and the soft command brought them all to attention, even Wren and Distephano.

It was distant, but they could hear it. Screaming. Terrible screaming. They all froze as they realized. Many voices. Gunfire. The squeal of something high-pitched, horrible. . . .

Wren turned slowly in the direction of the noise.

Suddenly, the male voice of the computer broke in: "Emergency. Animal holding facilities numbers zero, zero, one through zero, one, zero have sustained extensive structural damage that has destroyed their structural integrity. The specimens housed in those facilities are no longer contained. All personnel are to evacuate the *Auriga* immediately. Repeat. All personnel are to evacuate immediately."

Wren screamed, "NO!"

In his quarters, Martin Perez jerked awaked, the klaxon call of the alarm an unexpected jolt. Over the alarm,

Father's calm voice outlined emergency procedures, ordering immediate evacuation.

Evacuation? Perez thought groggily. *That's impossible. The only possible reason to evacuate the Auriga would be if—*

Father's repetitive, if brief, explanation of the crisis made everything clear. ". . . Animal holding facilities have sustained extensive structural damage. The specimens are no longer contained. . . ."

With a frustrated roar, Perez grabbed his military cap, jamming it onto his head as he reached for his slacks. If that clone was responsible for this, he'd personally ensure her complete destruction, right down to every last individual cell.

The research staff scrambled to help the minute they heard *Father*'s announcement. None of them could believe the Aliens were really *out*. That wasn't possible, was it? *How?*

Dr. Brian Clauss had been closest to the animal holding facilities when all the screaming and gunfire started. He raced to the area without thinking, working on sheer adrenaline. Along the way, he'd shed his lab coat. Underneath, he wore the same military fatigues the other soldiers wore.

Entering the compound, he moved cautiously along the track that carried the observation room along its path. He froze, staring in shock at the five dead soldiers that lay before him. Or *were* they dead? Carefully he crouched, staying alert, aware of everything around him. He was closest to a young female sergeant and bent at the knees to touch her neck. Beneath the still warm skin he could feel the pulsing blood, the heartbeat strong, sure. Were they paralyzed? Didn't matter. She couldn't help him, couldn't tell him what had happened here.

Brian rose, moved along carefully, watching everything. On impulse, he reached down, took the sergeant's gun, checked the rounds. Better to be safe. . . .

Wren's orders would be against shooting to kill—he'd want to try to take the creatures, to stun them and recapture them. He'd worked with the head researcher long enough to know that. But, as Clauss looked over the overcome soldiers, and the damaged, empty animal facilities, he found comfort in the weapon he clutched tight against him.

Fuck Wren, Brian decided. The purpose of research was to learn from past failures. He checked each collapsed soldier, and thought, *Uh-uh, not me. I'm not gonna end up like them. One of those bastards surprises me and we'll see who ends up flat out on the floor.* He snapped off the safety, and was ready to party, suddenly very grateful for the weapons training he'd endured for this assignment.

Let's see how those ugly fuckers like eating these huge bore bullets I've got waiting for them. He moved along the row of destroyed cages carefully, silently, respectfully stepping over the fallen soldiers.

Every cage was smashed, every one totally destroyed, even the ones that had been empty! And with a violence that was hard to imagine. As if those animals hated the very concept of their captivity. But that was crazy. They were just *animals* . . . weren't they?

He was standing before the first cage. This must've been where it began. He peered inside, saw a huge melted hole in the floor. How had *that* happened? The light was dim, but he thought he saw something move in the cavernous hole. Was one of them still hiding here?

Clauss aimed his gun, but couldn't see well enough. He listened. Nothing. Cautiously, carefully, he stepped through the shattered port into the cage itself. His entire body was poised, tense, ready to fire. He squinted, now inside the cage, but stayed close to the front, close to the port, as he peered at the hole.

There. Was that it? Something moving? Like a tail?

Brian stared harder, taking aim. He didn't feel like a researcher now. He felt like a soldier. He'd love to kill one of those bastards, after what they did to the soldiers outside, after what Carlyn said they'd done to Dr. Gediman.

The warrior hiding in the observation room waited until the human was completely inside the warrior's old cage, waited until the prey stood poised, watching as one of his brothers lured him with a tail tip. They were so gullible, these humans. He watched as the researcher lifted its weapon to its face.

The warrior waited. . . .

The warrior lashed out with his stiff tongue, slamming it onto the hated red button, holding it down.

The nitrogen gas jets sprayed the human, soaking its clothes, splashing its face, overwhelming it, burning it with terrible cold. The human jerked under the nitrogen shower, grabbing at its freezing, burning face, which only caused its hand to stick there to the freezing flesh. The prey screamed until its lungs froze and stopped moving air. It slammed around the cage in agony, the arm holding its weapon hitting the wall, and breaking off like an icicle at the elbow. It spun again, slamming its other side into a wall, shattering the forearm, but leaving the hand still stuck to its face. Then finally it collapsed, its legs and spine cracking with the force of his fall, its skin seared, its body so brittle it shattered into shards.

The warrior watched it all, able to see what was happening even through the fog of nitrogen gas. He released the button when the human lay still, unmoving, broken and scattered all over the cage. The human would still be useful for food. He'd come back for it later—when the body wasn't quite so cold.

The noise finally filtered down to Ripley's cell. In the darkness, her eyes opened. She tensed, as she always did on waking, and listened with all her senses.

Slowly she emerged from the shadow, and moved into the center of the room. She could hear them, the humans, screaming, firing weapons. She could hear the chaos. So familiar.

And she could hear the warriors, being freed, screaming their victory over the prey who'd tried to keep them captive, the humans who would now become the hosts. Distantly she could hear the Queen as well, sense her joy, her love for her subjects, her approval of their courage.

She listened to the humans and the Aliens with all her senses. She'd heard it all before. . . .

Ellen Ripley couldn't help it. Sitting crouched on the floor of her cell, she started to laugh. It was a joyless laugh, touched with hysteria.

Suddenly, something huge slammed against her cell door. She jumped, no longer amused. It hit again. Again. Again. The door buckled slightly. It hit again, loud, powerful.

Her terrible children. Coming for her.

8

There might come a time when Perez would demand an accounting for what had happened aboard his ship, exactly *who* had fucked up, but he was a good enough commander to know that *now* was not the time. If *Father* determined that the danger to personnel was sufficient to abandon ship, then that was what they would do. All was not completely lost. They could control the *Auriga* from the lifeboats in space, and bring the space station to dock elsewhere while the creatures were trapped within. Trapped without prey. Then they'd have the time to find a way to force them into new confinement units. . . .

But those were plans that would have to wait. Right now he was obliged to get his troops to safety.

His well-trained, handpicked soldiers were responding perfectly, just as they'd been drilled. The nearest lifeboat was powered up, and was already filling with soldiers. Perez directed them efficiently, quickly, wasting no time, no effort. One by one, soldiers slid down the pole into the belly of the lifeboat where they would strap themselves in. *Father* kept track of the personnel, counting each soldier as he or she strapped themselves in place. There should be one more. . . .

Olsen straggled along, late as usual. If he hadn't been such a competent tech—

"Get your ass in gear, boy, and get in that boat!" Perez barked at the jogging soldier.

Olsen hit the pole running, as the lifeboat hatch started to lower right behind him.

Something moving on the edge of his vision made Perez look up.

Suddenly a shadow, black, spidery, *huge,* scrabbled down the side of the dock incredibly fast, then onto the pole, finally sliding under the closing hatch as slippery as oil.

"Sir!" the soldier behind him, operating the docking bay's controls screamed, pointing.

My god! The general stood frozen to the deck, staring in horror as the massive Alien warrior entered the lifeboat. "Open the hatch! Let them out!"

The soldier complied, slamming his hands against the controls.

As the hatch reopened, they could hear shouts, shrieks, human and inhuman, coming from inside the lifeboat.

Those men are strapped in place. Weaponless!

Perez could see blood—human blood—splashing against the clear ports of the lifeboat. The screams intensified.

Perez turned, pulled a grenade off the armed soldier behind him who was standing in mute horror, and yanked the pin.

Just then Olsen bolted out of the hatch as if propelled, his face contorted in frantic terror. He grabbed the rails, the pole, fighting to get out. Huge, dark hands grabbed him around the legs, hauling him down, back into hell.

"Close the hatch!" Perez ordered.

"But, sir . . . !" the soldier protested.

"Close it now!" the general demanded.

The soldier hesitated a scant second, then complied. As the lifeboat lid began closing, the general flung the round grenade, rolling it along the floor.

"Cycle the lock," Perez said.

There was no argument this time. The grenade barely made it through the rapidly closing airlock doors. Just before they sealed, Perez saw the grenade bounce into the lifeboat, just below the closing hatch. Once the hatch and airlock were closed, there was blessed silence—but Perez could still hear those men screaming in the lifeboat. In his mind, he would hear them screaming forever.

Pushing the soldier out of his way, he grabbed the mechanism and launched the lifeboat. He could feel the rumble of the ship as it was ejected through the dock into space. He turned to the nearest view screen, watching its descent.

Then it was out of the dock, free of the *Auriga*. Its clear ports were completely curtained in red now, but he could still see shadows struggling within, behind the screen of blood.

Grim-faced, Perez triggered the remote control for the grenade he still held in his hand. He and the soldier with him watched the vessel explode in the silence of space.

He closed his eyes to give a moment's tribute to his fallen soldiers, then solemnly saluted the rapidly dispersing debris that represented an entire troop. He turned to the remaining soldier beside him.

The young face was wide-eyed and aghast. The sharpness of Perez's voice forced the man to refocus on his general. "Join the next troop in lifeboat two and warn them. Stay sharp! Now, move out!"

The soldier snapped to attention, and saluted. "Yes, sir!" He obeyed immediately, jogging away, leaving

Perez alone to regard the void where a lifeboat full of soldiers had just been.

Alone with his thoughts and burgeoning regrets, Perez lightly touched the view port with his fingertips.

Suddenly, a cold chill shuddered down his spine and he stiffened. He sensed the minute it appeared, somehow *knowing* the exact moment when he was no longer alone. Part of him wanted to dismiss the sensation as imaginary, but the part of him that had kept him alive and thriving all these years in the military knew better. He stared at the viewscreen, unmoving, and finally, dimly, saw its horrible reflection as it stood up slowly behind him.

One of *them*. Rising up, up, up, taller than the tallest man, as swift as a missile, as silent as Death.

Perez stood stock-still, refusing to show fear, refusing to admit defeat. He owed the memory of his dead troop no less. He stared at the hideous reflection as the warrior Alien drew back its thin lips in a chilling snarl, exposing the primary set of silver teeth. Ropy saliva dripped from its maw as it raised its spidery hands to pounce.

Perez's own hand moved cautiously to his sidearm. If he could just be quick enough—He grasped the gun butt firmly and—

He watched the rigid, fanged tongue as it exploded from the monster's mouth and realized, rather than felt, it slam into the back of his skull. The strike was so sharp, so sudden, so precise, that he didn't have a chance to feel the pain, feel the killing blow. He didn't even have time to react.

The hand resting on his gun butt went slack, useless, and there was no longer any sensation on that side. Dazed by a turn of events too extreme and sudden for him to comprehend, Perez touched the back of his head with his other hand, the one he could still use. He came away with a palm full of blood and tissue and dimly recognized it as his own brain matter.

Then his body finally reacted, shutting down all at once like a machine whose power source had been all too abruptly terminated.

As Perez collapsed bonelessly to the floor, his murderer followed him to the ground, mantling its prey for its own purposes. There was no one left to salute the general or even acknowledge that he'd just made the supreme sacrifice for his country and the deadly project he'd so firmly believed in.

"Lifeboat one has been destroyed," *Father* said, its voice sounding incongruously calm. "Lifeboat two has been disabled by unknown forces. There is a shipwide emergency. All personnel are to evacuate immediately. Repeat. All personnel are to evacuate immediately."

"No!" Wren shouted, outraged. They could hear and feel the destruction of the first lifeboat even here in the mess. They could hear shots being fired, things blowing up, people—and other creatures—screaming.

And it kept getting worse! How was this possible? The more *Father* told him about the nightmare taking place aboard the station, the more Wren's rage bloomed.

He spun on Call, the woman who'd started it all. "What have you done?"

"Me?" she shot back.

"All right," Elgyn said, sounding amazingly collected. "Enough of this. Time to bail out. We make for the *Betty.*"

The other woman, Hillard, looked at him worriedly. "The *Betty*'s all the way across the ship! Who knows what's in between?"

Distephano, the soldier, stepped forward to address Wren. He, too, was surprisingly calm. "Sir, we have to go."

Go? Wren thought, incredulous. *All my work is here! I'm not going anywhere!*

But before he could say anything, Distephano said to Elgyn, "Let him go. No quarrel."

Was he bargaining with these terrorist? I'll have his commission!

Elgyn shook his head firmly. "You can have him when we're off. Not before."

The huge black man shoved Wren forward, nearly making him fall. He realized the *Betty* crew still had their guns trained on himself and the soldier. This was ridiculous! Outrageous! He had to get to the lab. . . .

Elgyn leaned over a dead soldier's body and took the man's weapon.

Hillard said worriedly, "What about Vriess?"

The ugly man they called Johner growled, "Fuck Vriess!"

Then, suddenly, Wren understood what was happening to him. He understood these were not people who could ever care about him, his work, or what it represented. How could they, when they couldn't even care about one of their own? And he understood that his life was in their hands.

He glanced at Distephano, realizing that the soldier was his only potential ally, and determined to cooperate until he regained control of the situation. Perhaps, at the right moment—

The others moved them out of the mess and into the corridor to begin their journey.

John Vriess had just finished packing all the spare parts he wanted into the various cubbyholes and stashes that were part of his chair when things started to go wonky.

He heard strange sounds, like muffled explosions. Screams followed. Then the computer urged evacuation, while Vriess tried to figure out what the fuck was going on. Quietly, cautiously, he started out for the *Betty*. He didn't think Elgyn would leave without him, but he knew Johner wouldn't be willing to wait. Even if he did have all the spare parts.

He rolled steadily down the eerily empty corridor, keeping his eyes open. What the hell could've happened aboard this massive vessel that could cause so much damage so quickly that the computer would tell them to evacuate? Core breech?

He was halfway toward the end of the corridor when he heard something. Something above him. Vriess looked up toward the ceiling grid. Through the grates overhead, he thought he saw something moving up there, a bowing of the grid, as if from weight. And he could hear slithering. *Rats? Aboard a barge like this, a military ship? Impossible.* Of course, he'd had to slap at a stray mosquito in the storage hold, which kind of surprised him, but . . .

He heard it again. Whatever it was, it was moving. Toward him. Vriess had the feeling that whatever it was, was *big*. It moved closer, scuttling quickly. Just about overhead. . . .

Vriess reached down over the side of his chair, moving slowly but smoothly, with no wasted effort. Under the armrest he pulled off what seemed to be a decorative pipe, but was actually part of a weapon. He reached over the other side and found its mate. Behind him was the trigger mechanism. All of it cleverly camouflaged into the design of the chair. In three quick moves he had the gun assembled and armed. Still moving with slow, easy motions, he aimed the gun at the ceiling. . . .

And fired!

The blast sounded enormous in the closed place. Something in the ceiling screamed, an incredibly high-pitched, inhuman sound. Vriess could hear it scrambling away from him, letting him know he'd only winged it. Whatever it was. Vriess's eyes tried to track the progress of the creature as it scuttled over the ceiling.

His attention drawn, he didn't see the drop of Alien blood suspended from the ceiling right over his leg. The drop hit at almost the exact same spot as Johner's knife had just yesterday. Then a second struck. And a third.

Vriess didn't become aware of it until he smelled his smoking flesh and clothing, and glanced down to see parts of his leg melting away. Confused, horrified, he slapped at his leg. Some of the stuff eating away at his leg got on his fingers and started burning like hell. He swung his hand, then nearly put it in his mouth before realizing what would happen. The whole while he struggled with the pain, he had to force himself to remain quiet. He didn't want the sound of his pain to attract whatever was hanging out in the ceiling!

Suddenly, a searing drop of burning acid hit his ear, and the pain was so excruciating he had to bite his lip to keep from screaming.

Then, it was back, he could hear it—or could it be a different one? This one was more aggressive, not just scrabbling around the ceiling, but trying to get through it. Suddenly, it broke a corner of the tiling free and shoved its head through. And it was all head, a huge, elongated, nightmare head with no eyes, no ears, no hair, just skull and—

TEETH!

Gigantic, steel fangs, millions of them in a huge maw hissing right at him! Then its mouth opened wide, and something came out and—and—

THERE WERE MORE TEETH!

Vriess cracked finally and screamed hysterically. His finger squeezed the trigger. He fired, and fired, and fired.

The thing with teeth screamed back at him and exploded into a million fragments, all of them raining down on the berserk Vriess.

* * *

The door to her cell buckled as the creatures battered and bashed at it. It could not hold much longer.

Ripley looked around the cell, trying to find something, anything, that might help her. She glanced above, realizing that she had not seen the guard for a long time. Dimly, she could hear the computer voice urging evacuation. It seemed a good idea, but how—?

She remembered something—

Try to break the glass! Hurry!

There was no glass to break.

They cut the power. How could they cut the power? They're animals!

Her eyes searched the cell, found the cables encased in metal, followed them to a metal housing sealed into the wall.

Cut the power!

She punched the housing with her fist as hard as she could, bashing at it the same way the Aliens were bashing in her door, trying to get to her. She hit it again, again, again. It bent, buckled, started to twist. She worked harder, hit harder, all the while feverishly glancing at her failing door.

Finally, she could get her fingertips under a small tear in the metal. She pulled at it, twisting, tugging, until the metal yielded and she yanked it away from the electrical circuits inside.

They were almost through—

Jabbing the side of her hand against the sharp edges of the torn metal, she cut herself badly. Holding her injured hand, she forced more blood out, dripping it on the circuits and cables she'd revealed. Almost instantly, they started to melt. There was a sudden burst of sparks, making her jump back. The cell was plunged into darkness as the lights went out, but Ripley could still see.

Then there was a whoosh and an emergency exit opened in the wall of her cell. With a final glance back at the damaged door, Ripley left the cell.

* * *

Christie was on point, and Elgyn was bringing up the rear. *Like old times,* the *Betty*'s captain thought, but the memories were not fond ones. They were in a single line, with the soldier and the doctor somewhere in the middle, and they were making pretty good time down the corridors of the *Auriga*. The desolation of the big vessel rattled Elgyn. Where the hell were all the soldiers, all the officers, all the researchers? This place was like a goddamned hive, so where were all the bees?

The computer voice urging evacuation was a constant distraction, and if he'd known where they were, Elgyn would've shot every speaker to bits. And that made him think, again, that they'd made an error in the mess hall by not taking more weapons and ammo off the dead soldiers. You can never be too armed or have too many bullets, right?

The crew ahead of him jogged on, passing another semidarkened adjoining hallway. As Frank drew up to it, something caught his eye. He looked again.

A military weapon, some heavy-duty baby, just laying there on the floor. What the hell—?

What could have made a soldier just abandon his piece like that? Elgyn really didn't care, this was his chance to correct the mistake from the mess hall.

Finder's keepers.

Glancing cautiously around, he snatched the weapon up, only to discover yet another one, lying three yards farther up the hall. This was too weird. Shouldering the first weapon, he approached cautiously, and picked it up as well.

This one was nearly glued to the floor with some horrible gummy stuff. As Elgyn lifted the rifle, gelatinous filaments trailed off it like snail slime. Gross.

But it shouldn't affect its performance. What the hell happened to the lights down here?

Behind him he could hear Hillard's voice.

"Elgyn?"

"I'm coming!" he shouted back, and started to turn—

When he spied a third gun on the floor a couple meters ahead of him, just beyond a hole in the floor, where it looked like the decking was simply melted away. Could a grenade do that? Stepping cautiously near the hole, he reached for the third gun.

Something, some sixth sense made him freeze. He had a sudden memory of a boyhood day with his grandfather, when they'd laid a box trap for some squirrels by making a path of peanut butter on crackers that led into the box.

"Elgyn!" Hillard called again.

Leave it. You got two. Let it go, and get the hell out—

Two huge, dark hands shot through the solid floor with inhuman speed, wrapping themselves around his ankles, and giving a sudden, sharp *yank*. The deck plating collapsed around him as Elgyn was pulled down. Flinging his arms wide to stop his fall, his palms slapped the deck as his arms suddenly blocked his descent. He clawed at the decking for purchase, trying to pull himself out of the hole, but those hands were still gripping his legs. His scavenged rifles clattered away from him, too far to reach, one of them falling right into the hole in the floor that was a half meter in front of him.

Elgyn started kicking wildly, trying to rid himself of the taloned hands still gripping him, clawing him, dragging him down. He could feel them on his calves, on his knees, on his thighs, and *whatever it was that had grabbed him* started climbing up his body. He yelled, kicking, pushing against the floor, fighting to get free, fighting for his life.

His entire lower body was embraced, as massive,

unbelievably powerful arms gripped him around the waist, holding him securely.

What is it? What the hell is it?

Something incredibly powerful and razor sharp like a huge spear punctured Elgyn's chest with breath-stealing suddenness. The pirate captain felt every centimeter of its passage as it punched its way through ribs, lungs, heart, until it passed through his back, leaving a gaping hole. Unable to breathe, his heart crushed, Elgyn felt consciousness slipping away, as he continued to struggle in the grip of his murderer.

What is it? What the hell is it that's killing me? And why?

Elgyn's last conscious sight was of something huge and black and hideous coming up from the hole in the floor, gripping his red heart in silver teeth.

9

Christie was halfway down the hall when he finally realized the others weren't with him. He ran back to find them all gathered at the mouth of the last corridor they'd passed. "What the hell's goin' on? We gotta make time!"

No one answered him. They all just stared at the darkened hallway.

Hillard was yelling, "Elgyn! Elgyn!"

Christie pushed his way up front, just in time to see the shadowy figure of his captain being yanked through the floor. "Holy shit!"

He dashed down the hallway, aware of the others running beside him.

The only part of Elgyn that was visible was from the shoulders up. His features were set in a mask of pain and horror.

"Get him out!" Hillard was shouting. "Get him out, dammit!"

Johner and Distephano moved quickly to comply, grabbing Elgyn by the arms, hauling him up out of the floor. Christie stared, transfixed by a huge gaping hole that ran right through the center of Elgyn's chest. He was *dead. Elgyn was dead?* Christie could see clear through the hole and out the other side. Elgyn was dead.

Everyone stared, horrified. Even Wren had paled, his skin suddenly clammy with sweat. Hillard didn't move, but simply regarded her dead lover lying limp in their arms.

A loud crashing sound made them all turn to stare back up the hall. The floor between them and the main corridor exploded upward in a shower of decking and debris, and suddenly the mouth of the hallway was blocked by a vision from hell. Some kind of towering, massive *monster.* Christie dimly remembered Call talking about Wren's science project, about breeding creatures, about . . .

"If they get loose, it'll make the Lacerta Worm Plague look like a fucking square dance."

Oh, yeah, Christie thought, *you got that right, babe!*

The creature opened its jaws, revealing an incredible row of gleaming, stainless steel teeth, then it stuck out its tongue and *hissed*—

The entire group panicked, dropping the body of their dead captain unceremoniously across the gaping hole in the floor and running hell-for-leather in the opposite direction of that—that—*thing!*

They rounded a corner and found themselves facing a dead end.

It planned this! Christie thought frantically. *That thing found a way to lure Elgyn, then used Elgyn to trap us. Now it's got us all. Shit!* He took a deep breath. He had to think, had to think—If they weren't half as smart as that thing, they were dead for sure. Christie pressed himself against a wall and started inching his way to the corner. He needed to know where the hell it was now.

Grabbing hold of Johner's shirtsleeve, Christie

towed him into position beside him. Johner had gone gray, especially around his jagged scar. But at least he was sober. Of that, Christie was sure. Johner was shaking. He'd never seen Johner tremble from fear before. He never even thought he was capable.

"You okay?" Christie hissed at him.

Johner blinked, took a breath. "Yeah. Yeah. I'm with you."

That's what I needed to hear, the big man thought.

Moving his head quickly around the corner, Christie glanced at the Alien. At the other end of the wall, the creature rocketed up out of the floor and started moving toward the dead Elgyn, who was sprawled across the gaping, melted hole. Christie blinked the sweat out of his eyes.

"Is it coming?" Johner hissed at him. "Is it?"

"Dunno. Might be after the body."

In the corner with the others, Hillard let out a soft moan.

Johner was together now, Christie could feel it. He leaned around Christie, taking a look for himself.

"Is he coming?" Christie asked.

"Yep!" Johner said almost matter-of-factly.

Hillard exhaled in a rush. "Oh, great!"

"That's what I say!" Johner said, pulling his gun up. "Let's get it over with."

Christie looked at the scarred man, and the two of them grinned at each other. Then Christie sobered himself, realizing they were a hair away from hysteria.

Christie leaned around the corner to take another look. It was coming for them all right. Eight or ten feet tall, yet as graceful as a spider, it stepped over Elgyn's body and kept on coming.

Until Elgyn's body moved.

Christie stared, disbelieving, but he could clearly see Elgyn's sprawled body through the monster's spindly legs. He motioned Johner to take a look. Cautiously, Hillard joined them.

Elgyn is dead! How the hell—?

The impossible movement must've confused the creature as well, because it turned back, leaned over the corpse. It almost seemed to be sniffing at it. The corpse moved again, heaving slightly. Christie was all too aware of the various, strange things a body could do after death, but this sure wasn't on the list.

Now the monster was sniffing the huge hole in Elgyn's chest. The body rocked slightly as it did, then suddenly, the barrel of a rifle eased out of the hole! Christie blinked, then looked at Johner who was staring just as wide-eyed as he was.

The Alien didn't know what to make of it either. It sniffed the muzzle, then pulled back its lips in a snarl. The barrel suddenly tapped the monster brazenly on its massive head.

Then it fired.

The blast blew its head all to hell and back, and the *Betty* crew dodged back around the corner to avoid being spattered. Christie was the first one back to look. The monster had crumpled to the floor and everything its blood had touched was now melting. Christie edged warily around the corner, his gun ready. Johner was right beside him. Then the others came to see.

The rifle barrel jutting from Elgyn's body disappeared back through the hole, then the body itself heaved upward and fell over on its side.

Two slender hands appeared on the lip of the hole and deposited the rifle there, then the gunner levered up out of the floor. Christie was shocked to see that the shooter was the woman who'd beaten the shit out of them earlier—the woman they'd called "Ripley." She hauled herself up in one smooth move, brushed herself off in a casual way, and shouldered the strap of her gun as if she'd always worn one.

Christie glanced at Johner. He didn't look like he was the least bit interested in putting the make on her now.

No one moved for a long moment until the woman suddenly knelt over Elgyn's body, and started searching him.

Hillard suddenly went tearing up the hall, heedless of any danger. She was furious, as if this woman were the cause of all their problems. "Leave him alone!" she shouted.

Christie flinched, wondering how many of those *things* might be out there, how many might be drawn by their voices.

Ripley barely spared Hillard a glance. Impassive as always, she discovered a handful of ammo in Elgyn's pockets and appropriated it, putting it in her own. Then she straightened up and loaded her rifle, checking it professionally. The rest of them might as well have been invisible.

Call suddenly found her voice. Christie could hear her mutter, "Okay . . . real slow now. What. The. Fuck . . . ?"

Ripley looked at them all then, for a long, uncomfortable moment. Then, without a word, she approached the monster's corpse. Bending over its head she actually *reached into its mouth*. Its maw was open, oozing a clear, sticky liquid, and the beast was still twitching in its death throes.

Christie heard a soft sound beside him and realized to his shock that it came from Johner. The scarred man's eyes were wide with revulsion. *That's right. Man, Johner hates bugs, and that thing looks like the mutha of all bugs!*

Without warning, Ripley grabbed hold of the Alien's tongue. Bellowing a fierce battle cry, she yanked with inhuman force and ripped the rigid, fanged tongue right out of the monster's head!

While the rest of them just stood and stared, Ripley walked over to Call and dumped the hideous, dripping thing in the smaller woman's hands.

"Here," Ripley said casually. "It'll make a great necklace." Then she sauntered a few yards away.

Call stared in horror at her "gift" and let it fall to the floor. Every last one of them shuddered.

Wren, Christie suddenly realized, was trying to keep the entire group between himself and Ripley, but she seemed to be paying him no mind.

In a shaky voice, Johner asked Christie, "What do we do?"

The black man shrugged. "Same thing we were doing. We get the fuck outta here."

"What if there's more?" Johner asked, his eyes wide and feverishly bright. "Let's . . . let's stay here and let the army guys deal with it. Someone will come. . . . I mean . . . where are the army guys?"

Christie didn't like seeing Johner this rattled. He was going to need him if they were ever to get out of this.

"They're dead," Call said. She sounded sure of herself, and Christie wasn't in any position to argue with her. After all, they sure hadn't seen any soldiers since they'd left the mess hall.

Johner suddenly focused on Wren, and his expression grew grim. He approached the scientist, gun drawn. The soldier, Distephano, stepped in his way, in spite of the fact that he was unarmed. Johner ignored him, his eyes, his anger, his fear, all directed at Wren. Call had said that he was the one responsible for creating the Aliens, and Johner must've just remembered that.

"We don't need this asshole anymore," Johner growled. "Let's waste him."

"Step back!" Distephano ordered futilely.

Johner brought his weapon up, aimed at the soldier's face. Distephano never flinched, but Wren cringed.

"Stop it!" Call ordered, pushing her way over.

Johner spun on her, furious, a hair trigger away from exploding. "You got no authority here!"

The short, slight woman didn't back down. Getting right up in Johner's face, she demanded, "We're not killing anybody, except in self-defense!"

Reluctantly, Christie realized it was time to get involved. He spoke to Wren. "Doctor. That thing. That's your pet science project?"

In a small voice, Wren admitted, "Yes."

"And there's others?" Christie guessed. Wren nodded. "How many?"

The doctor glanced around nervously, and Christie realized he was still worried about Ripley, who was now crouched on the floor several meters away. In a barely audible voice, he murmured, "Twenty."

Johner nearly lost it. "Twenty! We're fucked in our pink bottoms if there's twenty of *those* things!"

Every one started talking all at once, nearly panicked, until Ripley's calm voice cut through. "There'll be more. Lots more."

They all looked at her.

"They'll breed," she told them. "In a few hours there'll be twice that number. Probably more."

She rose gracefully from her crouch and approached them. Without showing any more emotion than she had over anything else, she said, "So, who do I have to fuck to get off this boat?"

None of them answered. She made them edgy, nervous. In spite of the fact that she'd saved them from the beast, none of them felt the least bit comfortable having her around.

Suddenly Call stepped forward, pointing at Ripley. "Wait a second here. *She* was the host for these monsters. Wren cloned her 'cause she had one of those inside her."

"That explains a lot," Christie muttered to Johner.

"She's too much of a risk," Call insisted. "Leave her here."

Johner was nodding. "I gotta go with Call on this one."

Bad idea, Christie decided. *We need her.* He didn't know why, he just *knew,* and he was used to following his gut-level instincts, especially when things got tight. Without Elgyn, they had no leadership. Someone had to make a command decision. They were all looking at him. Man, he didn't want this job!

Glaring at the whole group, Christie ordered, "She comes."

Call spun on him, shocked. "She's not *human*! She's part of Wren's experiment! She could turn on us in a second."

Christie watched Ripley through it all. Still that same dispassionate cool. And her eyes—those predator eyes. . . . They were losing valuable time with all this arguing. *Twenty* of those things?

He turned on the entire group. "I don't give a good goddamn whether you people can get along or not. If we're gonna survive this mess, we all work together. We *all* get off this boat. After that, it's every man for his lonesome self." Impulsively, he reached down, picked up Elgyn's rifle, and handed it to Distephano. Johner stared at him in outrage, but Christie ignored him. The soldier nodded at him in gratitude and checked the rounds.

Call was looking at Ripley. "You can't trust her," she warned Christie one last time.

Christie looked at Ripley, then at Distephano, then at Call. "I don't trust anyone."

Hillard, who had been quiet through the whole thing, her attention focused on her dead lover, covered Elgyn's face with her coat.

Johner suddenly realized they were leaving their old comrade on foreign ground without burial, and his face twisted in an expression that might have been regret. "*Vaya con Dios*, man."

Hillard touched Elgyn's hand one last time, then stood up. Call touched her shoulder lightly, trying to comfort her, but Hillard moved away from the gesture, a distrustful look on her face.

Ripley, Christie noticed, was willing to bring up the rear, Elgyn's last position. She was watching them all with an expression of fascinated detachment. He noted Call glancing back at her, and Ripley giving her a cold smile. The woman's expression made him shiver.

"Okay, everybody, let's move out," Christie ordered, taking point once more. Leaving their captain and friend behind, they proceeded on to the *Betty*.

This is the cell block, Christie thought, as they moved into it. *Lotsa doors. Plenty of places for those damn things to hide.* Since they'd left the hallway where Elgyn died, they hadn't see a single Alien. Every place they'd checked had been empty, deserted, but the looming sense of *something* seemed to be following them. Maybe it was just Ripley, bringing up the rear. Christie didn't know, but by now they were all wired for light and sound, waiting for anything.

At least they were acting more like a unit instead of a ragtag bunch of stragglers. Behind him, he knew Johner, Hillard, Distephano, and even Call—in spite of the fact that she was weaponless—were checking every door, every space behind every piece of furniture.

As Christie passed by a closed elevator, he began thinking that maybe, just maybe they would make it. Then, five meters past the elevator, a chime went off.

The elevator! Christie thought, freezing in place, as did everyone else.

Slowly, he readied his weapon, hearing the clicks and whirs as everyone else followed suit.

As the elevator doors slowly opened, Christie turned to face them. The others were already in position, guns pointing toward the opening elevator doors. No one moved. No one breathed.

The interior of the elevator was dark, too dark to see.

Sparks suddenly shot out of the elevator ceiling, making everyone jump, and a light began flickering. In the uneven illumination, Christie saw something folded up, hunkering in the back. At the exact same moment, every person who was armed lifted his weapon.

With a blast of light, the overhead neon bulbs suddenly ignited, throwing bright white light everywhere.

Sitting in the elevator was Vriess, a shotgun in his arms, sighted, ready. His eyes were wide in terror, and he was trembling wildly, sweat pouring off him.

Vriess and the crew all stood there aiming at one another for a long second, each of them not recognizing the other as being human. Then at the same time, the realization hit, and everyone exhaled in relief and lowered their arms.

Johner gasped, "Oh, man!"

"Vriess!" Call called out happily, and ran over to him.

Vriess grinned weakly and said shakily, "Hey, wha'chu guys doin'? Hey, Call."

Christie wiped sweat off his forehead. "Thought you were toast for certain."

Vriess's voice told them everything about his experience they'd ever want to know. "You . . . you've seen that fucking thing?"

"We've seen 'em," Christie replied grimly.

"Shit," Vriess said. "I thought maybe I got 'em all."

Christie shook his head, noticing the burn marks on Vriess's leg and ear. Yeah, his friend had obviously had a real close encounter.

Johner turned to Wren and demanded, "Can we track those things?"

Wren shook his head. "No."

You tellin' the truth there, Doc, or not? Christie wondered.

Johner looked at Christie, really worried now. "We could get to the *Betty*, and they could be all over it! Maybe *inside* it!"

Wren decided to be helpful. "All of the activity seems to have been in the aft sector, by the barracks. There's no reason to suppose they'd move."

Christie watched the doctor doubtfully.

Then Ripley spoke up. "They won't move."

There was a certainty in her voice that Christie found himself believing. The crew was looking at her, still nervous about who and what she was.

"They're breeding," Ripley told them, in that flat, dead voice of hers. "They've got new host bodies to use. They'll stay close. If they send anybody out, it'll be here. Where the . . . meat is."

If they send anybody out. Christie mulled that over. *Like they're people who can think, plan—but maybe they can.*

"The 'meat,' " Call said in disgust. "Jesus."

Christie wanted to know more. He didn't care about the terms. "They're breeding. How long does that take?" He didn't bother asking Wren. He knew a reliable source when he saw one.

"Hours," Ripley said.

"Or less," Wren added. They all looked at him. "The process has accelerated. Something to do with. . . ." He glanced guiltily at Ripley. ". . . With the cloned cells."

Her expression closed down even more.

Okay. Now we know. "Faster we get from here to there, the better," Christie decided.

Johner spoke directly to him. "Well, if we want to make decent time, I say we ditch the cripple." He cocked a thumb in Vriess's direction, then glanced at the man and grinned shamelessly. "No offense."

Vriess grinned back bitterly and flipped his middle finger. "None taken."

Before Christie could tell Johner to go fuck himself, Hillard moved forward. She'd been morose, mourning Elgyn, and seemed to be blaming both Call and Ripley. Christie had worried that, in a pinch, her depression would be a liability. She was holding her head up now, and some of her spirit seemed to rally.

"Nobody's left behind," she ordered firmly, "not even *you,* Johner." Her voice was steady, if quiet and sad. Nobody dared defy her.

Christie turned to Distephano. "What's the best route?"

He thought for a second. "The elevators. They run straight from the top of the ship down to engineering. No stops. But if we get in the shaft, there's a maintenance access tunnel that runs above level one deck. It'll take us right to the dock."

Christie nodded. "Sounds reasonable. How do we reach them?"

Distephano pointed. "Down this corridor, then we angle over and cut through the labs. We can shortcut through them to the elevators.

"Right," said Christie. "Let's do it."

Vriess suddenly started moving in his chair, unhooking and unsnapping parts of it. His weapons. He assembled them quickly, efficiently. Snap, snap, snap. A veritable arsenal was stashed away on the chair, right in plain sight. Christie had to smile.

Vriess caught his friend's amused look. "They *never* check the chair."

Distephano stared, chagrined.

"Call," Vriess said sharply. She looked up, and he tossed her a small but deadly weapon perfectly suited to her size.

"How come she gets a piece?" Johner groused.

Christie ignored him. "If we're clear, then let's get on it. We'll go by twos."

Just as they started to move out, that flat, dead voice stopped them as Ripley said simply, "We're moving."

"What?" Christie asked, confused.

"The ship is moving," Ripley stated. "I can feel it."

She can feel it? Christie thought, nonplussed.

Wren shook his head. "This ship has stealth-run. Even if we *were* moving, there's no way she could feel it."

She glanced at him, and he moved to put someone else between them.

Before Christie could collect his thoughts, Call looked thoughtful and interjected, "She's right."

"The ship's been going since the attack," Ripley insisted, staring Wren down.

All eyes turned to him. He started to sweat, finally admitting, "It's . . . uh . . . it's standard. I think."

Distephano was nodding, looked concerned. "That's right. If the ship suffers any serious damage, it autopilots back to home base."

Call's jaw clenched and she rounded on Wren. "You were planning to let us know this?"

He drew away, even more nervous, then dissembled. "I forgot!"

Yeah, who believes that? Christie wondered in disgust.

"What's home base?" Hillard wanted to know.

Softly, Wren admitted, "Earth."

Call was furious now, nearly out of control. "Oh, God, you bastard . . . !"

Johner looked thoroughly disgusted. "Earth? I don't wanna go to *that* shithole."

Call was losing it, yelling at Wren. "If those things get to Earth, it'll be . . . it'll mean—"

"The end," Ripley finished for her, sounding totally unconcerned.

Call shook her head as if she couldn't accept it. "We've got to blow the ship!"

"We don't have to do anything," Christie told her, "except get off it." He turned to Distephano. "How long till we get to Earth?"

The soldier was at a console, calling up information on the screen. "Three hours. Almost."

Call had turned on Christie now, realizing she needed to convince him. "Don't you get it? This thing is gonna put down in the middle of a heavily populated base. No one'll have the slightest idea what's coming. We're gonna be rolling out the red carpet for the end of our species!"

Hillard moved into the argument. "That's not our problem."

"Call," Christie told her firmly, "you're not blowing this ship. Not while we're on it. Once we get outta this shit, you can do as you please." He turned to the clone. "You're called Ripley, right? You mind taking point?"

She nodded, and moved to the front, and once again, they moved out.

Now Christie was in the rear. In front of him, he could hear Johner still grumbling. "Earth, man. . . . What a slum."

Actually, Johner supposed, once he took some time to think about it, there were worse things than ending up on Earth. *Yeah, like ending up like Elgyn!* He shuddered, trying not to see in his mind's eye that hideous, buglike thing coming for them.

As they walked warily from hall to hall, with Ripley on point, Johner had to admit a grudging admiration for the tall woman. She must have ice water in her for veins, the way she confronted that thing with nothing but a still-warm corpse between them. Sure, she was a clone, but shit, even clones had *feelings.*

They came to another juncture, and Ripley stopped, poised. Johner moved nearer, every nerve alert. Finally, she said, "Clear."

Johner moved up closer and caught her eye. "You've

come up against these things before?" he asked bluntly.

She was concentrating on the task at hand. "Yes," she replied shortly.

When nothing else was forthcoming, Johner pushed. "So, what'd you do?"

Her reply was matter-of-fact. "I died."

She moved ahead, and Johner hung back, aghast. Glancing at Distephano, he muttered, "That wasn't really what I wanted to hear. . . ."

The soldier just shook his head, grinned, and patted Johner reassuringly on the shoulder. They moved on a little further, until Distephano tapped him, indicating a door.

"This way," the soldier told the group. "Shortcut through here." He moved back, led them in.

It was one of the labs. For once, Johner noted, Ripley showed some reaction, glancing at a big tube with the words "Incubator" on it. *Home sweet nursery, huh?* Johner guessed.

She steeled her face again and moved on, following the soldier.

Then they turned a corner and Johner spied something else. Everyone did, too, tensing when he did, totally in tune with each other. In the back of the room, where the shadows grew dark, the structure of the room changed. The dim lighting twisted, taking on grotesque shapes in the darkness. The floors, the walls, the ceiling—the entire room here had been altered. Reconstructed. *They* had been here, had made this their home for a while. Redesigning this human space to one more to their liking. It was completely Alien, not like anything Johner had ever seen. The walls were no longer smooth, but textured almost like the inside of a body cavity, with evenly spaced ribs, or bones, connected by dark membranes. And up on the walls—

Johner froze, realizing everyone else had, too, standing their ground with guns held ready. Ripley stood like a statue, not moving, not breathing.

Up on the walls were the deathly still bodies of people, stuck there like flies on flypaper. Glued in place with elasticlike strands of membrane stretched to hold them securely. Johner stared, dumbstruck with horror, at the figure closest to him.

Behind Johner, Distephano found a light control, and flipped it on, making the gunman jump. A small reading spot suddenly illuminated the dead man hanging nearest him. It was a researcher, still in his white coat, the name "Kinloch" stenciled on his pocket. His face a mask of agony, forever contorted in his last death throes, his eyes open wide. His white coat was soaked with his own blood. It looked as if something had detonated inside him, bursting out through his chest. *Or maybe chewed its way out,* Johner thought, sickened. Kinloch's lungs and entrails were plainly visible.

Distephano moved the small light, scanning the other bodies attached to the wall. They were all like Kinloch. All dead. All with the same hideous wound. They must've been people who'd worked here in this lab. He spotted a few names on lab coats—Williamson, Sprague, Fontaine. . . . *It wouldn't be so bad,* Johner told himself, *if they all didn't have their names on them. If they were nameless.*

Most of the group reacted with gasps or moans and even Johner, who had thought he had seen it all several times over, had to look away. He knew if he managed to survive this ordeal, this was one scene he would never forget.

Ripley just stared at the bodies, seemingly unmoved, as if this were a sight she'd witnessed so many times it was too commonplace to register with her anymore.

Then Johner spied a cryotube with someone still inside it. *This is one of those hibernators we snatched and delivered.* He moved over to it, saw that the lid was partially opened. He opened it up all the way. There was a woman inside. Her chest was blown out, too, her face all contorted in pain.

"I must be dreaming!" he muttered, but this time, there would be no waking up.

To his own dismay, Johner found himself face-to-face with his own culpability. *You delivered her here for this. You kidnapped her and all the others and didn't ask no questions. Just take the money and run. And now you've brought about your own destruction. Look at her face. And the face of all the others on the wall. That's gonna be you. And you thought you were ugly before.* Johner was suddenly flooded with a nearly uncontrollable need to vomit. He breathed in sharply, turned away from the sarcophagus, and quelled the urge.

Suddenly, Christie was beside him, offering silent support. Johner was glad of it, glad of the big man's presence. "Let's keep moving," Christie said quietly. Johner nodded, pulling himself together.

They continued through the lab, finding it littered with evidence of the Aliens' occupation. His feet alternately stuck to the floor in splatters of blood or skidded in globs of spattered human tissue.

They hit another darkened area and moved even slower. A flickering neon light acted like a strobe, splashing intermittent light and dark over the nightmare landscape of the wrecked and altered lab. Beside him, Vriess raised his weapon, stretching from the chair to tap the malfunctioning light, but that only made it strobe harder.

There was so much equipment in here, so much *stuff,* the place was a warren of hidey-holes and corners, everything lit in alternating shadow and light. It was nerve-racking.

Ripley was back on point, as they examined their

surroundings, slowly moving forward the whole time. Johner scanned everything, straining his eyes. One of those huge black dudes with all its external tubing would look like part of the scenery in here. Johner stared through the strobing light. Pipes, equipment, desks, cubbyholes, pipes, face, more pipes. Johner blinked, had that been a *face* hiding among that equipment? Ripley registered first, swinging back to look, as Johner and Christie saw it next. The light strobed again. There it was. A *face*, a pale, terrified face, eyes wide in panic.

Suddenly, the body attached to the face erupted from its cramped hiding place. The man was holding something long, like a pipe. Screaming, he launched himself at the nearest target—Ripley—and swung. She was off balance, for once, unprepared, and took the blow hard, toppling over.

Instantly, Christie was at her side, blocking another blow.

Johner spun, aiming, and screamed, "DROP IT! DROP IT, DAMN YOU!" He was so wired, it was everything he could do to keep from firing at the offender. His adrenaline was pumping wildly.

The others were all just as focused, just as hyped.

Christie, still protecting the recovering Ripley, yelled, "Calm down! Everybody ease up and calm down!"

The man folded back into his hole, all crouched and small. Miraculously, the neon lights suddenly burst on clearly.

Instantly, everyone froze, the entire company keeping their guns aimed on the cringing man. Ripley shook her head, as if a major head blow like that was just something you shook off. She stood.

"Drop the rod, man!" Christie shouted at the whimpering figure. The stranger was trembling uncontrollably. "Do it!"

The man glanced at them, his eyes huge, the picture of stark terror. "Get away!" he ordered, but his voice was shaking too hard for anyone to take him seriously. The attack had obviously taken every bit of bravado he could summon. The pipe he was holding clattered to the floor. He peered, baffled, from face to face, finally asking weakly, "What's going on?" Slowly, fearfully, he crawled out of his hiding place.

Johner could see the name "Purvis" stenciled onto his coveralls. *Damn. Another one of them sleepers we took.*

Christie moved forward, still tense, still wired. "Purvis, what's going on is that we're getting the fuck off this ghost ship."

Purvis blinked, obviously totally confused. He was sweating profusely, the smell of fear radiating off him in waves. "What ship?" he asked. "Where am I? I was in cryo on the way to Xarem, to be on the work crew for the nickel refinery. . . ."

Christie and Johner glanced at each other, then had to look away. Even Wren was trying to be somewhere else.

Purvis continued. "I wake up, I don't understand. . . . Then . . . then . . . I saw something . . . horrible. . . . It suffocated me . . . !" He looked like he was about to break down in sobs.

Call stepped up, took over, and for once, Johner was grateful. "Look," she said to Purvis, "you come with us. It's too dangerous here for you."

Johner and Christie exchanged a look, then both shrugged. Johner guessed they owed him something for kidnapping him, even though none of them had a clue he'd end up as Alien food.

Suddenly, Ripley moved up beside Purvis. He flinched and cringed away, but all she did was . . . *sniff him?* Johner could smell the guy from five feet away, and he sure wasn't wearing any *perfume.*

"Leave him," Ripley said, as flat-voiced as usual.

Call spun on her. "Fuck you! We're not leaving anyone on this boat."

Ripley's expression never changed. "He's got one inside him. I can smell it."

Purvis started twitching. The man looked like he was on the verge of a total breakdown. "Inside me? *What's* inside me?"

Johner's skin crawled, as if there were a thousand ants marching over him. All of them with silver teeth. He said to Christie, "Shit, I don't want one of those things birthing anywhere near my ass."

Vriess had wheeled up alongside them. "It's a bad risk."

Call was ready to take them all on. "We can't just leave him."

Damn, didn't she ever get tired? Johner wondered wearily.

Vriess tried to reason with her. *Good idea,* Johner thought, since he was probably the only one who could. "I thought you came here to stop them from spreading."

She looked torn by Vriess's words. She turned to Wren. "Isn't there a process, can't you stop it?"

Christie shook his head. "We've got no time for that!"

Wren wouldn't look at Purvis. "I couldn't do it here. The lab's torn apart."

Christie spoke softly to Call. "I could do him. Painless. Back of the head. Might be the best way."

The old softy, Johner thought, looking at the big man.

Call shook her head, upset. "There's gotta be another way. If we freeze him . . . ?"

Purvis was looking from one to the other of them, getting more and more panicky. He stared down at his own chest. "What's in-fucking-side me?"

All eyes were on him, and, Johner realized, they were all embarrassed, even Distephano. They were *all* culpable here, every one of them.

Wren finally said quietly, "A parasite. A foreign element that. . . ."

Ripley moved forward, clearly impatient with all the bullshit. "There's a monster in your chest," she declared. Right in his face, point-blank range. "These guys"—she cocked a thumb back at the *Betty* crew—"hijacked your ship and sold your cryotube to this guy." She indicated Wren with a nod of her head. "And he put an Alien in you. In a few hours, it'll punch its way through your rib cage, and you'll die. Any questions?"

Oh, that is one cold bitch, Johner thought admiringly.

Purvis, wide-eyed, could only stammer, "Who . . . who are you?"

Still looking him dead in the eye, unflinching, she said, "I'm the monster's mother." Then she turned that laserlike stare on Wren until he cringed.

Ripley started heading toward the exit, back on point. She was finished with this issue.

Obviously taking her cue from Ripley's straightforward manner, Call pushed her way past Johner, grabbed Purvis's arm, and announced abruptly, "He comes with us. We can freeze him on the *Betty*, and the doctor can remove it later."

Everyone stared at Wren. He nodded. "All right."

Johner blinked. He couldn't believe they were all going along with this, just like that. He loomed over the small woman. "Since when are you in fucking charge?"

She glared back at him brazenly. "Since you were born without balls."

Before Johner could fire something back, Vriess was between them. "Ease off, people."

Christie had moved over to Purvis and started herding him after Ripley. "Come with us. You might even live. Get twitchy on me, and you'll be shot."

Grumbling about the whole mess, Johner moved with the group as they proceeded through the lab.

10

Cloning storage facility? Ripley read the sign over the final lab they had to traverse, but the words didn't really register. She was still on point.

Distephano went to one of the consoles; his hands moved over the controls. "We're past the moons of Jupiter," he told them.

Ripley knew she should feel some sense of urgency, some compelling sense of action, but the only thing driving her was self-preservation. *Like any animal,* she thought with bitter acceptance. *Just like them.* She moved her mind away from the Aliens, fearing they might sense her if she did. How long would they be too occupied to come for her?

They passed in front of yet another in an endless series of doors, with legends on them that were meaningless to Ripley. But at the next door—

She suddenly froze.

There was something in there. Someone in there.

In spite of the bottomless emptiness Ripley felt— had been feeling since her birth—she suddenly experienced a ripple of fear. Her senses on hyperalert, she turned back to the door. On the glass window inset in the door was a sign.

1—7.

Slowly, she turned and approached the door, staring at the inscription.

Looking down, she pulled the shirt away from her inner arm and stared at the number—*8.*

Just walk away, she told herself. *Just move.* She closed her eyes, a shudder traveling over her body. There was something terrible behind that door, and it had to do with her.

Distephano had moved away from the console and gone ahead of her. "That's not the way," he said helpfully.

Christie stepped beside her, obviously worried by her strange behavior. "Ripley, we got no time for sightseeing."

It didn't matter. They could go on without her. She knew that she had to go in there.

Suddenly, Wren was there. Even he sounded worried. "Ripley . . . don't."

She had to. She opened the door, stood there for a moment, her mind trying to come to grips with what she knew she was about to see.

All this time, she'd worried about her lack of feelings, her lack of *humanity.* And suddenly, she was flooded with feelings, drowning in them.

Pain. Horror. Disgust. Remorse. Heartrending sorrow.

The others hung back in the doorway, confused, but clearly unwilling to go on without her.

Ripley found herself staring at a room full of incubators. No, not incubators, not anymore.

Preservation units. High-tech storage jars. For my sisters.

The first unit held an organism the size of a fully developed human fetus. It was totally deformed, barely recognizable, as it floated in its preservative liquid. It was labeled *Number 1*.

Not "it," Ripley told herself, *she*. She touched the jar reverently, and moved on.

The next unit, marked *Number 2* was the size of a small child. It, too, was grossly deformed, half Alien and half human. Ellen Ripley's face on that terrible, elongated head. Dorsal horns erupted from her back. Ripley twitched her shoulders, feeling the scars alongside her own spine.

Number 3 had a tail and no face. She was about two years old.

Number 4 was about four years old, had an exoskeleton, and the rigid, fanged tongue, emerging from a half-human face that couldn't support it.

Something fell from Ripley's eyes; she touched her cheek. Wetness. *Tears? From a monster?* She almost laughed.

Number 5 had nearly reached adulthood. There were dorsal horns, but they were clearly vestigial. The head was completely Alien, a Queen's head, grotesquely grafted onto a twisted version of a human female body. Her tears were falling freely now.

Eight of us. But how many hundreds, how many thousands of cells were started that never got beyond the eight-cell stage, the sixteen-cell stage? I guess they only labeled us if we reached a certain stage of advanced development.

She thought of all the researchers working on her cells, slaving over them, week after week, month after month, year upon year. All of them dead now, fodder for their own machinations. It didn't make her feel any better.

She came to *Number 6*. Her face again on a bizarre, elongated head, but nearly adult, looking so much like her. The hands the same as her hands, with the same strange long nails. The eyes were open. Her eyes. Seeing—

What? My future? One more monster in the collection?

She moved on, in a nightmare world all her own.

Number 7 was written not on a preservation tube, but on the side of a large, square, opaque unit. Ripley noticed electrical wires going into it. She saw gauges registering—something.

Her sense of dread was overwhelming as she walked around the unit.

It's not a jar at all! It's an ICU unit, complete with hydro-bed, and all the necessary equipment to . . .

She started shaking wildly, her mouth open, her eyes wide in horror.

On the bed was a living being, if you could call what this organism was experiencing, life.

The monster had Ripley's face on a misshapen head that grew only spare bits of brown wavy hair. Twisted limbs were in restraints, held fast, even as myriad tubes fed nutrients into the arms, keeping the thing alive. Bright, intelligent, human eyes stared at Ripley, seeing her.

Recognizing her.

My sister! Ripley thought, aghast.

The mouth opened and silver fangs sat within. Ropes of clear mucus drooled from the mouth as the monster hissed her recognition.

Then she begged. Two words. **"Kill me!"** She begged it from the one creature in all the universe she knew would grant her wish. The human eyes in Ripley's face wept, huge, sticky tears that ran down her face. The monster twisted in her restraints, as if to plead, implore.

Ripley staggered back, repulsed. She uttered a soft cry, and wept uncontrollably. Suddenly, Call was beside her. She was holding something big, something vaguely familiar.

"It's a flamethrower," Call said softly. "Distephano found it in a weapons cache he knew about."

Ripley looked at it, blinking away her tears. It was familiar, she realized. She turned back, took a last look at her sister. The monster in the bed writhed, opening its obscene mouth, dripping ropes of sticky saliva over her chin, the bedclothes. Her eyes said everything her tortured brain couldn't.

Ripley loaded the gun automatically, and fired on the tethered creature. She made herself deaf to the terrible half-human, half-Alien screams, as she fired again, again, again, melting the unit, the tubes, the restraints, demolishing everything.

She started backing out, the weapon in her hand feeling good, feeling right. She fired again, hitting each storage unit as she retreated. Alarms sounded, and the ship tried to defend itself, but there seemed to be no water available to the sprinkler system, and Ripley's destructive rampage went unchecked. One by one the beakers exploded in a mess of plasti-glass and steel, as she kept backing away from her own development.

She stopped only when the lab was a melted, burning mess, and the gun was empty. Ripley dropped the flamethrower at the door, then slammed it shut to contain the fire within.

Her tears were gone. In its place was something far more deadly.

Ripley turned on Wren.

Glancing around desperately, he backed up, looking around for protection. But the others, having seen a glimpse of her hell, moved away from him, letting him know there would be no help for him. Only Call interceded as Ripley advanced on the doctor.

"Ripley . . . don't do it," Call said softly.

She froze in her tracks, then incredible weariness swamped her. She sagged. "Don't do what?" she whispered desolately.

The tension seeped out of the quiet group. Wren exhaled audibly, and actually had the nerve to look a little smug.

At that instant, Call spun on him and punched him hard, right across the jaw, with all the wiry strength in her small form.

Wren's head snapped back, and he collapsed in a heap at Ripley's feet.

Ripley met the younger woman's eyes and something passed between them, some connection. What it was, she couldn't exactly say.

"Don't do *that*," Call said, referring to the sucker punch that now made her flex her bruised hand. Call started on down the hall without a second glance at the crumpled scientist.

Ripley glanced at him on the floor. His hand was on his jaw, he was shaking his head. Christie leaned over him, as if afraid that while he was down, Ripley would finish the job.

"Had it coming, Doc," Christie told him matter-of-factly.

That almost made Ripley laugh. She took hold of her own gun again, and moved on after Call.

Behind her, she could hear Johner, who'd been staring at the burning lab, ask Christie, "What's the big deal? Fucking waste of ammo."

Christie only shrugged, as he helped Wren to his feet.

Ahead of them, Call called back. "Let's get going before anything comes to check out the noise."

Johner was still talking to Christie. "I just don't get it. Must be a chick thing."

With the lab complex behind them, they stood in the dark as Distephano opened a floor hatch. There was some emergency lighting down the shaft, Christie realized, but it wasn't bright enough to see all the way into the tube.

"We go down from here," Distephano said unnecessarily.

Christie turned to the wheelchair-bound man. "Vriess, we got to lose the chair."

"I know," the man said tiredly, pulling coils of rope from some hiding place on the chair.

As Call started down, following several of the others, Christie said to Vriess, "Kawlang maneuver, all right?"

Vriess gave a short, bitter laugh. "Just like old times. . . ."

Christie smiled, too. They had thought that was the end of them then. They had thought that was the worst horror they could ever face. . . .

Now, standing in the corridor of the *Auriga,* Christie thought that Kawlang seemed like a day in the country.

Dropping off the ladder at the bottom of the shaft, Call found herself inside the cooling tower. She was knee-deep in water and wondered why. Distephano and Johner had gone ahead of her and were standing back to back in the water, guns ready, checking things out. They motioned silently for Call to move on ahead as the others came down the ladder.

Call waded down to the end of the room, where Ripley was standing. The tall woman was looking at her hands, which were still shaking badly from the incident in the lab. Her face was etched in pain. Her eyes were red. Seeing her like this upset Call. She'd kept telling herself Ripley wasn't human, that she didn't actually *feel* anything. And now she had to face the reality. Ripley was every bit as human as Call was. She could feel, entirely too much.

Call stopped next to her, feeling awkward, yet needing to say something. "I . . . I can't imagine how that must feel."

Ripley looked at her somberly. "No. You can't."

Call turned away, studying their surroundings. The

dark, pipe-filled chamber was flooded, the water level rising. Water was cascading down from the ceiling, from the cooling pipes. The crew was all assembled again. At Christie's signal they moved on, walking in water up to their knees.

Everyone was still on hyperalert. It was wearing them down: the need to be constantly ready, the lack of rest. Call could see the tension in Johner, Hillard, the twitchy Purvis. Christie's big body waded through the water strongly despite the fact that he was carrying Vriess on his back. They were back to back, the paralyzed man actually tied to Christie with the bonds that had been in Vriess's chair. Vriess was inspecting the ceiling, too.

"Must be the cooling tanks," Vriess said. "Somebody must've opened the valve."

"The nasties couldn't have done it," Johner said, then hesitated. "Could they?"

Hillard looked confused. "What for . . . ?"

They kept going, wading their way through.

Finding themselves at a wall, they halted. There was a short hatchway with a stairwell leading down to the last level. The hatchway was still open, but almost completely submerged.

"We're at the bottom of the ship," Wren told them. "This sector has been sealed off. We have to go down that staircase through the galley, then come back up another short service shaft, maybe twenty-five meters."

Call realized he meant twenty-five meters *underwater.*

Christie leaned back and said to Vriess, "You ready to get wet, partner?"

Vriess gave a short bark of a laugh. "Oh, yeah."

Johner looked around. "This sucks."

Hillard turned to Wren. "Are you sure about the distance?"

The doctor nodded.

Christie looked reluctant. "We should send out a scout. Ripley?"

Call frowned at Christie. But Ripley approached the hatchway and looked it over.

"I don't like it," she said softly.

Christie agreed with her. "There's nothing to like."

Then, fatalistically, Ripley shrugged her shoulders, a bemused look on her face. "Okay!" she announced, taking a gulp of air and diving smoothly underwater.

The tanks must've finally gone dry, because the cascade of water died down to a dribble, then a drip.

No one said anything or moved, just watched the hatch where Ripley had disappeared. How long could any one person hold their breath?

Standing near Call, Distephano took a protective covering from his belt pouch and slipped it over the cylinder of his weapon. Christie was watching him. "You should do like me," he suggested helpfully to the big man and his Siamese twin.

Christie showed him his weapon. "These are disposables. They can take it."

Distephano looked interested. "Disposables. I heard about those. How many rounds?"

"Twenty," Christie said. Suddenly the pirate and the soldier were just two guys talking about a common interest. "Split points, give you good hole even at the smaller caliber."

Distephano nodded admiringly. "Cool."

Christie went on, as if the chatter were helping him relax from the terrible tension. "They're big with hitters. 'Cause you throw 'em away after the job. Nobody likes throwing away a weapon they're attached to. You know?"

That was when the big man must've realized that no, Distephano wouldn't know, that he'd gone too far. This was a career soldier. Might for right. All that patriotic stuff.

An embarrassed silence set in. The men had nothing more to say. Vriess, from his perch on Christie's back, busied himself inspecting the ceiling.

The only noise Call heard now was the last of the water trickling down. Nervous about Ripley's long absence, Call dipped her hand in the cool water and splashed some on her forehead.

Suddenly, behind them, a rash of bubbles rose to the surface of the water. Everyone turned and tensed, weapons aimed at the spot. Seconds passed. The last bubble popped, but nothing more happened. Everyone turned back to the hatchway.

Suddenly, Ripley emerged from the water in front of them. They all jumped. She was gulping air frantically.

When she could find her voice, she gasped, "There was a door that was blocked about twenty meters ahead. It took me a while to get it open. I didn't go any farther, but I could tell the surface was really near."

Call looked around at the others. "Do I have to tell everyone to take a deep breath?" A few of the guys smiled at her.

"Christie," Vriess said teasingly, "do me a favor. When we hit the surface on the other side—no backstroke, okay?"

The big man chuckled, as the crew took in as much air as they could handle and one by one followed Ripley as she dived back under the water to lead the way.

Hillard and Johner were the last two to submerge. The visibility underwater was bad. The water was clear, but there were few lights still functioning in the galley, so everything was dim. Hillard didn't like it, but she didn't know if she would've liked bright light any better. The galley was vast, which limited visibility even more. She watched Wren, who was ahead of her, swim off toward the other end of the room. She didn't trust him, and he had an advantage on them, since he evidently knew the layout of the ship.

They rounded a corner. Still a long way to go. Hillard was starting to feel the pressure on her lungs to breathe. She resisted it. At her side, Johner swam doggedly on. Suddenly, he glanced behind them, then looked again. He slowed, falling behind, and Hillard looked to see what he was seeing.

And nearly gasped. Two Aliens were swimming furiously after them, as agile as eels, their tails undulating effortlessly under the water.

Johner's eyes went wide in panic. Quickly, he loaded his weapon and fired, the force of the recoil pushing him through the water.

The projectile shot through the water toward the beasts, hitting one of them dead center, blowing it up. The sound was muffled underwater, sounding like a heavy thump. The second Alien just kept on coming.

Johner was in a righteous terror now, and shot off through the water like a rocket, passing Hillard, passing Ripley. It made the cloned woman turn around, and she spied the monster. Some of the others turned also, and suddenly there was general panic in the group. Except for Ripley. She gestured strongly at Hillard, urging her on, as if the pilot needed any urging.

She's not having any problem down here at all. It's like she doesn't even need to breathe! Hillard thought, kicking frantically, feeling that heavy-pressured hum in her head that kept screaming, *Air! Air! Give me air!*

Hillard realized Purvis and Distephano were taking on water, choking in panic as the monster gained on all of them.

Ripley was still gesturing at the swimmers, hurrying them. Hillard realized they were all drawing away from her—that she was lagging behind.

I'm losing it! I need to breathe. This thing's gonna catch me!

She struggled not to think about it, just put all her waning energy into kicking, swimming, hurrying. She made the mistake of glancing back.

It was so close! Two arms' lengths and it would be on her. It bared its teeth and for Hillard, the dim light in this nightmare underwater world was all reflected back from those shiny fangs. She saw its tail lash faster.

Panic set in, and suddenly she choked in a mouthful of water. *NO!* She kicked harder, more frantically.

Powerful, inhuman fingers suddenly grabbed her ankle.

She screamed involuntarily, releasing all the air from her lungs, then sucked in hard, desperately searching for air to fuel her shouts for help. But nothing entered her lungs except water. Huge, forceful hands gripped her legs, her waist, her torso, until she was trapped in death's embrace. She flailed and kicked to no avail, watching the others trail away from her in the murky water as she turned to face the terror of her underwater lover.

Hillard's gone! She's gone! Call mourned as she passed through the door and saw the light from the elevator shaft beckoning her on. How many more would they lose to those bastards? Would they be picked off one by one until none of them were left? And with the ship still heading toward Earth, was there anything— *anything*—they could really do?

She couldn't afford to give up hope now.

Take it one step at a time. Get to air. We gotta have air.

She kicked hard, rocketing up toward the looming surface of the water. But just before her head emerged into the air and the light she hit something hard, something flexible and transparent.

What—?

She pushed against it, felt it give a little but not enough. The air was still a tantalizing six inches away. It had to be something the Aliens had spread, some kind of transparent web. But why? Out of breath, Call struggled against the transparent stuff, kicking her legs.

The others were beside her now, fighting the web, struggling to break through. Some of them were getting stuck to it, using up the last of their strength.

Call peered up at the tantalizing air just out of reach. There was an elevator twenty meters overhead, the bottom of it as shiny as a mirror. And then Call saw them, reflected in the elevator's shiny bottom. At the edge of the pool, a collection of eggs laid out along the edge.

Call couldn't think about what lay ahead, she only knew that every one of them would die if they didn't get to the air. She popped her damaged stiletto, still hidden up her sleeve. The melted blade still had a sharp edge. She stabbed at the web with the steel, poking a small hole into it, sawing at it wildly, widening it centimeter by painful centimeter. Johner and Christie shoved their huge hands in the hole, pulling, rending it, trying to force it to tear, but it barely budged.

Out of the corner of her eye, she could see the soldier, Distephano losing it, growing limp in the water. And somewhere behind them was that *thing*. . . .

Suddenly Ripley shoved her way through the group. Grabbing the web with two hands, she heaved, and ripped it apart. The crew bobbed to the surface, their mouths opened wide, gasping and gulping and coughing huge lung-fulls of the wonderful air. Beside her, Ripley, too, sucked in air, and Call was grateful that she finally showed that small bit of human need.

As Call blinked the water out of her eyes, she glanced up at the bottom of the elevator. Her eyes opened wide as one of the eggs slowly, wetly, opened. In a sharp, explosive move, something multilegged and grotesque catapulted from it. Before anyone could react or try to get out of its way, it landed with a sickening plop right onto Ripley's face. Purvis screamed shrilly as Ripley disappeared under the water. Call tried to follow her descent, but could only see her for several minutes before she was lost in the gloom. Her last image of Ripley was of her struggling with the thing wrapped around her face.

"Holy shit," Johner hissed, looking up at the elevator. In the mirror-bright bottom, they watched as other eggs opened with that same slurpy sound, and spider-like legs could be seen emerging from inside.

"It's a trap!" Johner shouted. "They set another goddamn ambush! Everybody dive! Dive! Dive!" And he disappeared beneath the water.

Everybody followed him without a second thought.

What kind of a trap drowns you—? Call thought, then realized. *Either we broke through the web and came up sucking air, our mouths wide open, or we passed out under the web and they plucked us like flowers. Either way, we'd be theirs.*

Underwater once more, the crew looked around desperately, not knowing where to go. Call couldn't see Ripley anymore, but she could make out, in the distance, the Alien who had killed Hillard swimming toward them. Seeing them under the water, it speeded up.

Christie spied it, too. Then he looked up at the freight elevator and the image of the eggs just sitting, waiting for them.

Christie grabbed his grenade launcher. Everything was happening in silence, with only the burbled, muffled water sounds to accompany their actions. Christie adjusted the range of his weapon, pointed the gun upward, and aimed at the reflection of the eggs. He fired.

The grenade shot through the water, ricocheted off a pipe near the ceiling, then fell back onto an egg with a slurpy splash. There was a beat, then an explosion that rocked them even underwater.

Christie had already fired another, then another, then another. One after another the deadly grenades destroyed the waiting eggs, blowing spider-monsters and egg tissue everywhere. Then Christie gestured to them when it was over, letting them know it was safe to emerge.

Call could still see the Alien approaching them. He seemed to be watching something, but what? And where was Ripley?

Call found that the thought of losing Ripley, especially to one of those terrible face-huggers, was more than she could handle. As she hit the surface and helped Christie and Johner pull the unconscious Distephano out of the pool, she couldn't help but call Ripley's name, until Vriess told her to pipe down, before she called down all hell on them.

She bit her lip and obeyed, turning her attention to pounding the water out of Distephano's lungs, her eyes blurring.

"Everybody," Christie snapped, "quick. That thing's comin' up right behind us. We gotta get up that ladder."

Call looked up the shaft, saw the ladder going straight up the side, past the elevator, all the way up through the center of the ship. She looked past Distephano as he coughed and gasped, conscious once more, and stared into the pool.

Vriess, still riding Christie's back, touched her shoulder. She looked up at him, everything she was feeling about the cloned woman showing on her face.

"Okay, Call," he said softly. "That's enough for now. The soldier's okay. We gotta go."

She could only nod and follow them with one last look behind.

* * *

Ripley tore at the creature on her face, even as it fought to shove its implantation tube into her mouth. It couldn't get past the barrier of her clenched teeth, but that didn't stop its single-minded effort. It had but one aim in life, one purpose, and even as she ripped its legs off, it struggled to achieve its end.

Fighting with all her strength, she felt herself settle to the bottom of the pool, ripping and tearing at the monster. Its legs were destroyed, but its tail was still coiled tightly around her neck.

Clamping her teeth around the fibrous, ridged tail, she bit down hard and ripped it off, tearing some of the skin on her throat in the process. Once it was free of her face, she tore the creature into pieces with unfettered fury. But just as she convinced herself that thing was finally and truly dead, she looked up and realized the Alien that had been stalking them underwater was after *her* with a rage as pure as her own.

Without hesitation, she pushed off the bottom of the pool with a powerful thrust, rocketing through the water, shooting ahead of it as fast as she could.

As soon as she broke the surface, strong hands grabbed her roughly, hauling her from the pool. Ripley gasped air roughly and stared, surprised, into Johner's wickedly scarred face.

"It's right behind me!" she spat.

He shoved her toward the ladder. "Then let's haul!"

She turned back, saw the creature emerging, as she hit the ladder running. The iron rungs were a three-sided affair wrapped around a pole, and she and Johner scrambled to catch up to the others.

Glancing back, she was amazed to see the Alien dropping down below the water, submerging like a submarine, until it had disappeared. Under the circumstances, though, that was little comfort. Ripley scurried to catch up to the rest of the team. She wondered at her own urgency, then realized that she wanted to let Call know she was all right.

* * *

Call wasn't surprised when Wren was the first one to hit the crawl space ledge. Distephano had told them which floor they needed to get access to, and Wren made sure he was there first. At this point, it hardly mattered to Call. They all needed to get as far from that Alien as possible, as fast as possible. If he knew how to get the door open, all the better.

Wren balanced on the narrow ledge, next to a maintenance access door as Call climbed up behind him. He kept glancing down at the others, still climbing up, as he punched codes into a small keypad beside the door.

"Hurry!" Call urged, unable to see if the Alien was pursuing them.

"It's jammed!" Wren yelled. He slammed his fist on the pad in frustration. "Shit! Weapon!" He held out his hand to her, not even looking her way, the way any surgeon would for an instrument he trusted his assistant to provide.

Call glanced down again, wishing she could see more, and automatically handed him the small weapon Vriess had given her. She didn't even think about what she'd done until she looked up and found the muzzle pointed directly at her.

How could I have been so stupid? she thought disgustedly. She'd been too distracted by Ripley's disappearance, by the oncoming Alien.

Wren's expression was one of smug satisfaction as he took aim and fired, at point-blank range. Call took the projectile right in the chest, and instantly clutched at the wound, staring at Wren in shock. Her extremities went numb, her brain stopped processing, as every organ in her body desperately fought for life. As her consciousness grew dimmer, she fell, plummeting down the long tube of the elevator shaft.

Dimly, she heard Vriess screaming, "NOOOO-

OOO!" as she fell past him and Christie, fell past
Johner, fell past Ripley—

Ripley? Ripley? You made it . . . ? Then she hit the
water hard and sank, drifting right past the submerged
Alien who watched her drift by without making a
move.

Call's last conscious thought was, *Ripley made it.
Ripley made it.*

Ripley watched Call fall past her and went numb with
shock, then felt surprised that she felt that way. She
watched as Call's body hit the water and went under,
watched as the other woman sank to the bottom,
watched as Call drifted right by the shadow of the
Alien still beneath the surface of the pool. Something
was tugging at the recesses of her mind. Something—

*A little blond girl, walking in waist-deep water, call-
ing her name. "Ripley! Ripley!" Racing to save the girl,
racing against time and monsters. "I'm coming! Hold
on! I'm coming!" But when she got there, to the water,
there was nothing. Nothing but a plastic doll head sinking under the waves, just like Call was sinking. And
she was sobbing, screaming, "I've got to save her! They
won't kill her. You've got to understand, they won't kill
her. . . ."*

She remembered sobbing, she remembered feelings
so strong they tore at her, feelings like those she'd had
in the lab when she saw her sisters.

She watched Call's disappearing body, remembering a plastic doll's head disappearing below the
waves. . . .

Ripley looked up. Looked at Wren. Wren who had
created her for his own ends. Wren, who had killed
Call in cold blood. Colder than the Aliens. The coldest
blood of all. The doctor was reworking the code on
the keypad that would open the door. Ripley stopped

analyzing her feelings and started moving, racing up the ladder, passing Johner, passing Purvis and Distephano, passing Christie and Vriess.

Vriess started screaming hysterically, **"WREN! YOU BASTARD! YOU MUTHA-FUCKER!"** Crazed, the paralyzed man loaded his gun and started firing at the doctor, but his position on Christie's back hampered his aim. The bullets ricocheted around the doctor, but the door opened then, and he disappeared inside, just as Ripley got to the ledge.

She lunged for the door, but it slid shut in her face. She jammed her hands between the panels, just before they sealed together and fought them, trying to force them back open, but finally had to pull her fingers free. The doors slammed tight. Ripley screamed, the same scream of fury she'd screamed over the dead Alien. She pounded the door in frustration.

Some distant part of her mind wondered if she hadn't been better off before she'd found these feelings.

"Vriess!" Christie shouted to the enraged man on his back, "VRIESS! Quit firing, man! You're gonna hit one of us! Quit, man!"

Somehow the words got through to the paralyzed man and Vriess stopped. Christie felt Vriess sag against him, spent. "Oh, shit, Christie," he choked, "that bastard killed Annalee. Little Annalee. . . ."

"Yeah, man," Christie said, feeling his throat tighten up. "She was a fighter. A hell of a woman. I'm sorry, man." Vriess trembled against his back, and Christie hoped he wasn't crying. If Vriess lost it now, Christie was afraid that after all they'd been through, he might, too, and he couldn't afford that. Not while he was still carrying them both.

Suddenly, Vriess tensed. "Oh, shit, Christie. Move it, move it, MOVE IT!"

The big man glanced down in time to see the Alien from the pool suddenly spring at the ladder and start clambering up like a monkey. A monkey on joy juice! Dammit, could that thing move!

Christie went into overdrive, pulling him and Vriess up the ladder hand over hand. "Do somethin', will ya?" he barked at Vriess.

He could feel Vriess jerking his gun around, wrestling with it. "I'm *jammed,* dammit!"

One handed, Christie tried to fire down on the pursuing monster, but couldn't fire low enough with Vriess on his back. The bullets passed harmlessly above the Alien's head, ricocheting off the opposite wall.

The Alien clambered up higher, then halted. Christie glanced back at it, only to see the creature open its silvery jaws and spit a gob of venom at them, like a monstrous cobra.

The Alien's aim was perfect; the noxious stuff hit Christie hard right in the eye. The shock and surprise and searing, burning pain were so sudden, so unexpected, that Christie screamed and lost his grip. The two men plummeted toward the creature waiting for them, while all Christie could do was shriek and claw at his dissolving face.

They jerked to an abrupt halt, forcing Christie to focus on something else besides his own agony. Somehow, Vriess had managed to snag a rung as they fell. The paralyzed man's upper body was incredibly strong, much stronger than his smaller size would imply, but was it strong enough to support them both? Trying to force his mind to concentrate on their survival, instead of the acid still eating away at his skin and face and ruined eye, Christie realized what a liability he'd just become to Vriess. This was pitiful, really. Totally pitiful.

Vriess managed to grab the rung with his other hand, but Christie could see with his good eye that their feet were dangling temptingly just above the monster's head. With a grunt of effort, Vriess started pulling them up the ladder, but suddenly the Alien's hand shot upward and grabbed Christie's leg in a viselike grip. The big man moaned, repelled by the inhuman touch and all that it implied. He thought of Elgyn. And Hillard.

The Alien pulled, its strength equal to that of five men, maybe ten. Christie heard Vriess moan, felt him cling to that rung for all he was worth.

Christie had a sudden memory of Kawlang—

—of him bending over Vriess in some horribly swampy place, seeing the shrapnel sticking out of his spine. He remembered Vriess sobbing, screaming, "Get out of here! Leave me! You'll all die if you don't leave me!" He remembered Elgyn snarling, "Vriess, will you shut the fuck up?" and nodding at Christie. He remembered Hillard tying the broken man onto his back, with Johner grousing the whole time. "If we all get killed, you bastard," Johner swore, "I'm gonna haunt you, mutha-fucker." They were almost out of there clean when they caught that ambush, and Johner got that scar on his face. He blamed Vriess for "losing my damn good looks!" and things were never the same between them.

But all Christie could remember now was packing Vriess out of there on his back, feeling the solid presence against him, telling Vriess over and over, "Man, don't you die on me. You gotta watch my back, partner. Just keep watchin' my back."

Funny how the mind could work so fast when there was no time to spare.

The Alien gave a casual tug, and Christie could swear the beast was smiling at them, toying with them. Vriess gasped, still clinging to the ladder for all he was worth.

My turn to be back here now, Christie thought,

watchin' your back. But, buddy, I think we just ran out of options. And man, I ain't never hurt like this, not this bad, not ever.

The Alien tugged again, and Vriess groaned. Christie felt his partner's hands start to slip almost as if it were his own on the ladder.

Johner couldn't believe it when he saw Vriess grab the ladder rung and stop their fall. It was an amazing move, but it looked like the cripple and Christie just ran out of luck. He could see the Alien grappling with them, toying with them. And Johner could see the tortured expression on Vriess's face as he clung for his own life and his old friend's.

Without a second thought, Johner spread his arms, snapping a weapon into each palm. Hooking his knees over a ladder rung like an aerialist, he dropped upside down with the ladder at his back, leaving his hands free as his legs held him in place. Aiming for the huge black skull perched beneath his crew mates, he fired at the monster.

The bullets flew down, past the two struggling men, and impacted solidly with the massive Alien head. There was a momentary pause—

Then the beast's head exploded with a *whump,* and a huge spattering of blood and tissue. Some of it landed on the ladder, which started to sizzle, but Vriess and Christie seemed to escape without further damage.

"Got you, you bastard!" Johner shouted, then swung back up to continue his climb.

However, as soon as he righted himself, he came face-to-face with something on the ladder, something horrible. His face contorted in fear and loathing, and he nearly fell back down, as he discovered two rungs covered in a massive web with a hideous, huge spider-like . . . thing . . . crouching smack in the center of it.

With a high-pitched scream, Johner brought his gun up, and blasted the damned insect. Then, realizing what he'd done, how he'd overreacted, he just clung to the ladder and started to shake.

"Is it dead?" Vriess gasped, still clinging to the ladder.

"Oh, yeah," Christie wheezed, barely able to get the words out past the pain, "it's dead all right." His agony was nearly all-encompassing, but he was still aware of the lifeless creature that still clung to his ankle. He couldn't shake it off. It swung, a dead weight, permanently fastened to him. Vriess was losing his grip. They were plainly out of options.

Vriess must've glanced down, realized what had happened. He was muttering a litany of "Oh shit, oh shit, oh shit. . . ."

You got that right, ol' buddy, Christie thought, delirious with pain. He felt Vriess's grip slip a little more. Out of options.

From high above them, the others must've realized what was happening. He heard, dimly, Distephano cursing, heard Ripley suddenly yelling. Maybe they were on their way back down—but they'd never make it in time. Christie knew what he had to do.

Fumbling in his side pocket, Christie pulled out his knife.

Ripley's voice drifted down, shrill, demanding. "CHRISTIE, DON'T! DAMMIT, DON'T!"

How 'bout that! the injured man thought, as he slipped the knife under the bonds that tied him to Vriess. *I didn't even think she knew my name.*

Behind him, Vriess realized what his friend was about to do. "Man, what . . . what the hell are you . . . ? Christie! No! Nooooo!"

Stop yellin', man, and save your strength! Christie thought, annoyed. He was so weakened by pain and the

unyielding pull of the dead weight on his leg that he
barely had strength enough to saw through the bonds
that held him to his friend. But he had to. Or they both
would die. He closed his eyes and forced himself into
one final effort.

He heard his name shouted by his friends, women
and men alike, as the ropes suddenly gave. Christie and
the Alien plummeted down the elevator shaft, crashing
brokenly onto metal beams and the edge of the pool
before finally sliding away under the water.

As the terrible weight of his friend and the monster
attached to him dropped away, Vriess gripped the ladder with all the strength left in him. Christie had died
to save him; he couldn't dishonor his friend by giving
up now. But, yet, how could he go on? Elgyn. Hillard.
Call. Now, Christie.

But Christie had died to save *him*. He had to live. To
live as a tribute to that sacrifice.

Hand over hand, Vriess climbed the ladder by sheer
force of will, crying all the way up.

11

Ripley stood on the narrow crawl space that ringed the shaft and tried to figure out what their next option might be. Christie's sacrifice, coming so close after Call's death, had shaken her complacency. But she had no time to feel, to grieve, even to acknowledge that she was having such feelings. She could sense yet another warrior on his way to take the place of the one Johner had killed. She redoubled her efforts at the keypad, trying to get the doors open. Had Wren sabotaged the portal somehow?

Thinking about Wren, even briefly, fueled her rage. No doubt, he was on his way to take the *Betty* and escape, leaving them to negotiate with the Aliens.

Distephano and Purvis were both watching her, waiting for her to come up with some answers. She sighed in frustration and wondered why they thought *she* might have the answers. Then she wondered when she'd started caring about what *they* thought.

To compound the matter, Johner finally got to the top of the ladder and, to her dismay, looked right at her and asked, "And now what do we do?"

Not him, too!

Before she could respond that the door was locked, and that she was out of ideas, the portal began to beep loudly. Startled, Ripley nearly lost her balance. She turned and realized that the keypad was flashing some intermittent signal, and then lights began to blink on the sealed shaft doors.

Everyone froze, then brought up their weapons all at once, aiming for the doors. No one breathed.

Did Wren have second thoughts and come back for us? Ripley wondered, then dismissed that ridiculous notion. Especially when there was another, more likely scenario. *They've learned how to open the doors, something I can't figure out.*

She was weaponless herself, and just stood frozen on the narrow crawl space, hugging the wall, waiting for the bad news. *What else could it be?*

She glanced at the doors and realized that there was water seeping under the seal. *Water . . . ?*

Then, finally, the doors opened with a *whoosh*, and Ripley stared, disbelieving. As did everyone else.

Call? No, that's not possible. . . .

The small woman was drenched, dripping wet from head to toe, but other than that, she seemed none the worse for wear. She wasn't even breathing hard! She looked at them all hanging in the shaft, staring wide-eyed at her, and said, matter-of-factly, "This way."

But no one moved. They were all too stunned, totally uncomprehending. They stood rooted, their guns still absurdly aimed at her.

"Get on!" she snapped at them, trying to motivate them.

They finally responded as a group and scrambled over the crawl space one by one to get through the doors. The group went out the other side, emerging into the ship's corridor.

Vriess had finally reached the top of the ladder and

Purvis and Distephano grabbed his arms and hoisted him the rest of the way. Vriess sprawled in the hallway, with the others semicollapsed around him, leaning on walls, taking a minute to catch their breaths.

Vriess regarded Call with stunned surprise. "Baby, am I glad to see you! I was *sure* that asshole got you. Are you hurt?" He held a hand out to her, and waited for her to take it.

But she only turned her back on them all, muttering, "I'm fine."

Ripley glanced at each of them in turn, and they met her eyes with the same questions she had, even Vriess.

Quietly, Distephano asked, "You got body armor on?"

"Yeah," Call said dismissively. "Come on."

But Ripley wasn't buying it. She'd seen Call with her vest open down at the bottom of the shaft. Her thin, wet T-shirt had clung to her ribs clearly. There'd been no body armor. She moved over to the woman.

"You took it in the chest," she said softly. "I saw."

Call stared at her defiantly. "I'm fine!"

Ripley met the dark eyes with her own piercing gaze, looking for the truth, looking for the answers. Call couldn't hold her stare. Her chin quivered slightly, then suddenly she completely broke down, and the tough mechanic started crying like a lost child.

Her tears touched Ripley in a very visceral way. Even so, she gently opened and spread the ends of Call's sealed vest.

She'd taken it directly in the chest, all right—but instead of showing blood and bone and lung tissue, the ugly, gaping wound revealed a confusing tangle of computer parts, manufactured organs, memory components, and synthorganic wiring and tubing.

"A robot," Ripley said, dead-voiced.

From somewhere deep inside her, a memory flashed. *I prefer the term 'artificial person.'* She closed her eyes wearily.

"Son of a bitch," Johner muttered, amazed. "Little Annalee's just full of surprises."

Ripley dropped her hands, talking now almost to herself. "I should have known. All that crap about being *human*. There's no one so zealous as a *Born Again*."

Distephano had drawn closer and seemed to be examining the blue and white liquid Call used for blood. It was splashed over her chest and clothes, but she'd obviously gotten it under control. She must have. She was still functioning.

"I thought synthetics were supposed to be all logical and shit," Johner said to the group. "She's a big ol' psycho!"

Ripley had to stop herself from rolling her eyes. How easily Johner recognized one of his own.

"A terrorist?" Purvis said nervously. "Then she wasn't here to protect us?"

Ripley tried to find answers in Call's eyes, her expression, but the woman—the *robot*—wasn't giving her any.

Vriess's voice nearly broke. "You're a Second Gen, aren't you?"

Ripley searched her memory, but couldn't find any references for that term. After her time, and *before* this one?

"Leave me alone," Call said tiredly, having gotten her tears under control. Her tears, perhaps, but not her voice. Her vocal track was slipping, revealing the effects of the damage. Her words were a bit slow with a strange, mechanical echo. It was eerie.

"Call . . . ?" Vriess pressed, wanting his answer. Feeling, perhaps, that he deserved it.

Bitterly, she whispered, "Yes."

"Second Gen?" Johner barked, laughing. "Shit, that explains a lot."

Ripley didn't recognize the term. But she didn't ask questions, just listened and waited.

"You're an Auton, aren't you?" Distephano asked. He sounded oddly curious, not condemning. No doubt, he was remembering how Call had saved his life in the mess hall when Johner would've cheerfully killed him in cold blood.

Distephano must've noted the confusion on Ripley's face and realized she'd have no way to follow any of this. He explained to her, "Robots designed *by robots*. Highly ethical and emotional. They were supposed to revitalize the synthetic industry. Instead—they buried it."

Ripley looked back at Call. She thought of Bishop. Then, she thought of Ash. She understood now. "They were too good."

Distephano nodded. "They didn't like being told what to do. The government ordered a *recall*." His voice grew soft. "Fucking massacre. I'd always heard there were a few that got out intact, but, *man* . . . I never thought I'd see one."

Ripley observed Vriess from the corner of her eye. He looked disappointed and sad, nearly broken, like a man who'd lost everything.

Purvis glanced from one to the other, nervous. "Great. It's great. She's a toaster oven. Can we leave now?"

The rude remark was the slap they all needed to shake off this latest surprise. Everyone seemed to stand a little straighter.

"How much time till we land?" Johner asked the soldier,

"Under two hours," Distephano told him.

"And we're already off track," Johner mumbled. "We should go now."

Call had turned away from the group, ostensibly to effect more repairs in her cavity. The men suddenly all started talking, interrupting each other. Once more, Ripley stood apart from them, observing them, feeling the group dynamics shift once more. Only now, Call, like herself, was outside the group, separate from them. Never to rejoin.

She remembered Call handing her the flamethrower in the clone lab.

In a sudden lull in conversation, she noticed Vriess glancing over in Call's direction. He still looked sorrowful, disappointed. She heard him mutter disgustedly, "Jesus. . . ."

"Yeah," Johner agreed, "get your socket wrench. Maybe she just needs an oil change. Can't believe I almost fucked the thing."

Vriess looked at him with contempt. "Yeah, like you never fucked a robot."

They were falling apart, thinking individually again, no longer a unit. Ripley didn't want to assume the leadership, but she couldn't see any other way. Christie was dead. Stepping forward, she asked, "Where are we exactly, Distephano?"

"Upper decks," he said. "Storage . . . . The chapel's up here, not much else."

"Can we get to the ship from here?"

"It's down a few levels," he said, thinking. "It's doable."

Johner had a thought, a negative one. "What if the good doctor reaches the *Betty* first?"

"Shit!" cursed Vriess.

Ripley looked at the soldier. "Another way? Faster?"

He thought about it. "Uh . . . yes. Through the wall. We'll have to unblock the door. It'll take awhile." He glanced down at Vriess. "You got tools?"

They all remembered the abandoned chair.

Vriess shook his head. "Tools, yeah. But no torch."

"Just blow the door!" Johner decided simply.

Distephano pointed to the ceiling. "We're at the top of this shaft. That's outer hull."

"And if Wren gets to the computer," Ripley realized, "he can really screw us." *And would. Without hesitation.*

"We've gotta find a terminal," Johner announced.

"There's no console on this level," Distephano explained. "We have to go back."

Back? Ripley stared at him. "No way."

The soldier sighed, disgusted. "And I don't have Wren's access codes."

What else? Any more bad news? Ripley ran a hand through her hair distractedly, thinking, trying to come up with —

She turned and looked at Call, standing apart, still fiddling with her cavity. She took a step nearer the robot. "Call."

The robot never looked at her, never indicated that she'd heard. Her voice sounding a little clearer, she said, "No. I can't."

Johner seized on it. "Bullshit! She damn well can talkie machinie."

"Shit," muttered Vriess. "That's right. You're a new model droid. You can access the mainframe on remote."

Call shook her head resolutely, still not looking at them. "I can't. I burned my modem drive. We all did."

Vriess leaned toward her. "You can still patch in manually. You know that." His voice had gone soft again.

That tone must've touched something inside Call, because she finally looked up, staring at each of them. Her expressive, oh-so-human-face showed contempt, anger, disgust. She knew she had no choice. It was an agreement of sorts. Ripley felt bad that she'd been forced to make it this way.

Like any of us have had any choices in this?

"There's ports in the chapel," Distephano said, flatvoiced.

Ripley placed a gentle hand on the robot's shoulder. "Come on," she urged quietly. Realizing the others were all staring at them, she looked over her shoulder. "You," she addressed the rest of the group, "get started on that wall."

They immediately set to work as if she'd lit a fire under them.

As Ripley and Call entered the small chapel, Call wondered at the difference in Ripley and how it might be reflected in the difference in herself. Even after she'd decimated the clone lab, Ripley's cold distance had remained unthawed, or so Call had thought. But clearly, all the difficulties they'd been through, their swim through the flooded kitchen, then the climb up the elevator shaft, had finally touched her. Maybe those experiences had finally resurrected the real Ripley. Perhaps this clone of the woman who'd fought so hard to destroy the Aliens was now fully human.

Resurrected just in time to save her people again.

At least she has a people to save, Call thought bitterly, remembering, now and forever, the look on Vriess's face when he saw her wound, realized what she was. She wondered distantly what Christie would've thought if he'd lived. *Poor Vriess. He's lost everything, everyone he ever cared about, even me. He'll never look at me the same way again.* . . . Losing his regard meant more to her than she ever thought it would.

Oh, Ripley, she thought, *you were better off when you didn't give a shit about anything. I wish I could find those connections inside myself and turn them off.* But she was hardwired for that—*human emotional sympathetic response.* Big words to explain away a robot's genuine heartache.

She looked around the small room. It was a classic

chapel, scrupulously clean and very small. There was an altar, a variety of religious symbols that could be interchanged for the denomination being represented—a Star of David, a plain silver cross, a green banner with a crescent moon, a Wiccan staff of rowan, and—ironically—the white dove of peace. It almost made her laugh to see that symbol here on a military vessel whose sole purpose was to master the most deadly bioweapon ever discovered.

The only religious symbol missing is a computer chip with divine rays coming out of it, for those like Wren and Perez who only worship technology.

Behind the small altar was a false stained-glass window, bolted to the wall and lit by lights. The last service here must've been Christian, because the cross was perched before the window on the altar. Without thinking about it, Call crossed herself.

Ripley blinked in surprise. "You programmed for that?"

Call just gave her a bitter glance. *No, I'm not programmed for it. I have a working brain. I've examined the topic. I happen to believe. But there's no point in discussing that with you. You haven't been alive long enough to develop philosophy, clone.*

She immediately felt guilty. Who was she to disparage any *real* human being, any one who possessed a *true* soul? When she was finally terminated, there would be no afterlife experience for her, any more than there would be for a lightbulb!

Call looked around the pews and found a Bible. Pulling it out of the rack, she flipped the electronic device open. Under the fake leather flap of the cover was a small screen. It read: "HOLY BIBLE. PRESS START." Reverently, Call touched the screen, thinking how much comfort some of the words in this book had been to her after she'd been told about this mission, after she'd decided to take the assignment, regardless of the risks.

Though I walk in the valley of darkness, I shall fear no evil. Thy rod and thy staff shall comfort me. . . .

Leaning over, Ripley pulled the cord from the Bible's port, and held it out to her.

"Don't make me do this," Call whispered, her voice still uneven.

"Don't make me make you," Ripley answered.

Both their voices were low, respectful. After all, they were in church.

Call dared to meet the clone's eyes. The sympathy there nearly undid her. Still, she protested. "I don't want to go in there. My insides are liquid. It's not as if they're real."

What she wanted to say is, *I've been pretending to be human for so long, I've been accepted as human for so long, I don't remember what it's like to be Auton! And this will remind me. It will make me a machine again! I don't think I can face that.*

Ripley gripped her wrist, her face growing determined. With a shock, Call realized that she finally *looked* human. She finally looked like the *real* Ellen Ripley who'd died over two hundred years ago.

"Get over it," Ripley said gently. Then she added the one thing calculated to get through to Call in spite of her damage, in spite of her loss. *"You can blow the ship.* Before it reaches Earth. Kill the Aliens. Kill them all."

It was the reminder Call needed, why she'd come here in the first place. Her mission. Her purpose.

"Just give us time to get out first," Ripley added as an afterthought.

This is why it was you, Call realized. *This is why you always survived, why you always defeated them. Your focus. Your determination. Genetics? Environment? Personal fortitude? Doesn't matter. You are Ripley. You.*

Call nodded, feeling as if some of Ripley's

strength—Ripley's humanity—was in her now. She pulled up her sleeve, found a beauty mark on her forearm, and opened it like a little hatch. Under it were two ports.

Taking the cable from Ripley, she plugged it in, then waited for the automatic connections to start their dance. At first, nothing happened. *Had the Aliens actually sabotaged the main computer? No, that wasn't possible.* She cocked her head, listening, waiting, feeling. "Dammit," she whispered.

"Anything?" Ripley asked, concerned.

"Wait a minute. . . ."

When it happened, it happened all at once.

One instant she was still Annalee Call, outwardly human, if damaged, and the next instant, she was the *Auriga.* Massive. Moving. Invaded. Yet, strangely unable to care. It was as impersonal to her as it would've been to the core memory of Annalee Call that had been created in a robot factory. While Call had had feelings and ethics *implanted* in her, she'd had to be *taught* how to use them like any newborn child. The ship did not have to deal with that issue, it only had problems and solutions to contend with. All issues were black and white, no gray areas. Invasion was just a problem to solve. A problem it had yet to solve. But it was working on it.

As the *Auriga,* she knew all, saw all, heard all. She could see herself, her Annalee self, sitting next to Ripley in the Chapel. Call looked like an abandoned doll, her eyes wide and unseeing, the pupils hugely dilated. Beside her, Ripley looked concerned, worried.

It touched her somehow, that this woman, this human, would worry about her. Of course, Ripley wasn't really *human.* . . . No, her matrixes dismissed that notion. Ripley was totally human. Her blood type, her fingernails, her ability to last underwater, her strength—all of it meant nothing in the long run. Rip-

ley was human. And hurting for Call. It touched the
ship in a new, startling way. The ship would have to
think about that.

In the meantime, it scanned itself for information,
wanting, needing to know *everything*.

Ripley said softly, "Call? What's going on?"

The ship responded immediately. Ripley did not
have any access codes, but Call overrode that require-
ment. She proceeded to tell her *everything* as fast as
she could.

"Breach in sector seven, sector three. Sector nine
unstable. Engines operating at eighty-six percent.
Ninety-six minutes until earthdock." There was more,
so much more, that the ship spoke faster and faster,
trying to get it all out.

Finally, Ripley touched her arm, and the warmth of
that human contact jolted the ship, changed it. "Easy,
Call. Can you come back now?"

The robot blinked, separating from the intelligence
of the ship, and became just Call again, a badly used,
slightly damaged Auton. She blinked, and said to Ripley, "We burned too much energy. I can't make critical
mass. I can't blow it." She had feelings again, and they
were the most desolate she'd ever experienced.

Ripley was still watching her, that level, intent gaze
unnerving. "Then crash it," she said decisively.

As everyone worked feverishly on unblocking the
sealed door—with Vriess offering some semblance of
leadership, even though his heart wasn't in it—Larry
Purvis tried not to spend any time thinking about the
bizarre circumstances that had brought him to this
juncture. If he thought about it, his rage at everyone
he was working beside would erupt into something he
couldn't control. It was a terrible irony that his only
possible salvation resided in the very hands of the peo-

ple who had done this to him, but that was the reality of it. And Purvis was a realist.

He worked harder than he ever had in his life, and didn't let himself think much. Trying to pry up the corner of the door, he jammed a rod into the corner to get some leverage. He grunted, leaning on the thing, waiting for his weight to move the seemingly immovable door.

A sharp, stabbing pain in his upper abdomen made him gasp, and clutch his chest. Everyone else stopped instantly. In spite of his pain, Purvis was all too aware that Johner and Distephano had brought their weapons to bear.

No! No, it can't end this way, so pointless, so stupid! NO!

He gritted his teeth, waited it out. Then, as quickly as it started, it faded. Purvis took two deep breaths. It was gone. Nerves, maybe. Stress? Yeah, stress.

He grinned feebly at the others, who were staring at him warily. "I'm okay. I'm okay. Really. I feel good." He nodded vigorously, as if he could convince them with false cheer and too broad a grin. The weapons were lowered, and everyone went back to working on the door.

But Purvis knew they were all watching him from the corners of their eyes.

Ripley watched as Call zoned out again, her eyes unblinking, the pupils dilating, first one, then the other.

"Ground level recalibrated. . . . New destination seven sixty, four-oh-three. Uninhabited quadrant. Braking systems off-line, acceleration increase. Time until impact now forty-three minutes, eight seconds."

"Try to clear us a path to the *Betty*," Ripley reminded her. "And start her up."

Call blinked once, as if to acknowledge the taller woman, then went back into her trance.

* * *

The *Auriga* checked the corridors that were on the path
to the unofficial ship. It opened four hatchway doors in
succession to give access to the ship. It hooked into the
Betty herself, and turned her on. Aboard the *Betty,*
lights went on, screens and indicators lit up, the engine
hummed awake, then the pirate vessel began her own
self-diagnosis prior to warm up.

Back in the chapel, the ship told Ripley through
Call's body, "Ship in prep, fuel on line. . . ." The ship
paused. Something. "Tracking movement in *Auriga,*
sublevels six through nine. Video is down. Attempted
rerouting nonfunctional, wait, partial visual in waste
tank, unauthorized presence. . . ."

Beside the body of Call, Ripley asked, "Unauthorized?"

"Nonhuman," the ship specified.

Ripley's voice changed. "How many?"

"Please wait," Call/*Auriga* said. "Emergency override in console forty-five vee, level one. . . . Handprint
ID. . . ."

Call blinked, turned to Ripley as Call once more. In
her own voice, she said, "It's Wren. He's almost at the
Betty."

Ripley raised an eyebrow. Imitating Wren's patronizing voice and manner, she said to Call, "And how do
you feel about that?"

Dr. Mason Wren came to another locked hatchway
door. The doors slowed him up, but with his top, top
security access codes, they had yet to halt his progress.
And at this moment, he was only five doors away from
the *Betty.* Once he was aboard the small pirate vessel,
he could use his knowledge of the *Auriga* and his codes
to gain access to the ship's computer and control the

big vessel from the outside. He'd be able to stop the military ship, then put it in safe orbit around the nearest planet. Once it was stable, he could contact the military brass and they'd send everything they needed to repair the ship along with enough troops and supplies to gas the entire ship and knock every Alien out until they could contain them. Then he'd be back on track, with more specimens to work on than he'd ever imagined.

But first things first. And his first priority was to get aboard the *Betty* and get her underway.

He still regretted losing the Ripley clone in the process, but at least he'd gotten to study it for a while. And now he'd have more specimens of the Aliens than he could ever want, so he certainly wouldn't need to clone it again. Not that he couldn't. They had plenty of samples of its current body on ice. It would be simple now to clone hundreds of Ripley's, each with a Queen growing inside it.

Wren stood in front of the locked hatch and tapped in his access. The lights on the keypad flashed for a moment, and then the red "locked" light turned green. With muffled clunks, the locks in the door opened.

Father's voice announced, "Emergency override validated."

The huge door began to rise. Wren glanced around himself nervously, still keeping a close eye open for Alien activity. He was so close now—

Only inches above the floor, the heavy door suddenly froze in place. It was way too low for a grown man to squeeze under. Wren frowned, punched in his codes again. But this time *Father* did not respond.

As he was about to input the codes one more time, every light in the corridor suddenly went out. Now he was standing in near darkness, only the faintest glow coming from the instrument panels and emergency lights.

Wren could actually feel the color draining from his

face. He glanced about nervously, swallowing a hard lump in his throat. Wetting his dry lips, he said quietly, "*Father,* reboot systems on forty-five-vee. Authorization 'starling.' "

He was met with a thunderous silence. Wren broke out in a heavy sweat, despite the fact that he felt chilled. *Could the Aliens have done this? Caused a power breakdown so vast, or a computer failure so complete that . . . ?*"

"*Father,* locate power drain. Report." More silence. "*Father?*"

The voice that answered him from the computer's speakers was young and feminine. "*Father*'s dead, asshole."

He recognized it instantly. It was the voice of that little terrorist, Call, the one he'd discovered in Ripley's cell. He spun around, trying to see her. But the voice was everywhere, just like *Father*'s always had been.

The door he'd been trying to open suddenly slammed back down, narrowly missing his toes. The locks clicked back into place. The sound was final, irrevocable.

Wren just stood there, staring stupefied at the door, at the entire ship that had just become his sworn enemy.

Behind him, a different door opened. He could see the emergency light pulsing along toward him, like an arrow pointing in his direction. Dammit, that was the wrong door, the totally *wrong* door. There was no way he could get to the *Betty* through *that* door.

Call's voice echoed throughout the ship. "Intruder on level one. Intruder on level one. All Aliens please proceed to level one. Dr. Wren is there."

Wren gasped in panic, then turned away from the door and began running back down the corridor.

* * *

Ripley watched as Call pulled the cord out of the port in her arm. "You've got a mean streak," she said offhandedly. "I like that."

Call avoided her gaze. "It's done. That should hold—" Her voice track slipped again, sounding more mechanical. "Dammit!" She dug around in her chest cavity, trying to fix it.

Ripley leaned over, thinking she might help. "Let me see—"

Call flinched away, still not facing her. "Don't touch me."

Stung, Ripley sat back, putting space between them. The rejection hurt, and it angered her that it did.

"You must think this is pretty funny," Call grumbled, her voice still off, sounding strange. She lifted her face, met Ripley's gaze. Call's was defiant. Angry.

Ripley sighed, suddenly very tired. "Yes. But I'm finding a lot of things funny lately. And I'm not sure they are."

Call glared at her, suddenly furious. "Why do you go on living? How can you *stand* it? How can you stand . . . *yourself*?" Her mechanical voice, still slipping, sounded more and more bizarre.

Ripley shrugged. "Not much choice." She'd never really had choices, not from the moment she'd been roused prematurely from cryosleep on a ship called the *Nostromo*. Anyway, Call was really only talking about herself, not Ripley at all.

Call turned her attention inward again, fighting with whatever parts of her controlled her vocal mechanisms. "At least there's a part of you that's human! I'm just— I'm just . . . Fuck. Look at me. . . ."

Ripley did then, stared at the hole in her chest, the white oozing mass of torn and sticky fibers. There was something so familiar. . . . She blinked, remembering Bishop, his courage, his *humanity*.

"I'm disgusting. . . ." Call complained bitterly. Her

voice was slowing down, sounding low and eerie like a badly recorded overdub. Ripley knew the problem was mechanical, but to her ears it sounded just like despair.

"Why weren't you destroyed along with the others?" Ripley asked.

Call faced her squarely. "To kill *you,* remember?" She paused for a moment, then went back to repairing herself. "Before the 'recall'—before everything fell apart for us—I accessed the mainframe. The *Defense* mainframe. Every dirty little covert op the government ever dreamed of was in there. Even this one. The plans, Perez's involvement, the Aliens, you. . . . Even the plans to hire the *Betty* crew. And I knew, if they succeeded, it would be the end of them." Her voice was clear again, the right timbre, the right speed. "The End Of Humanity."

Ripley felt herself smiling. There was something terribly funny in all this. "Why do you care what happens to *them?*"

"Because I'm *programmed* to, okay?" Call snapped.

Ripley started to laugh. "Are you programmed to be such an asshole? Are you the new asshole model they're putting out?"

Call couldn't help herself, she started smiling back, then laughed along with Ripley. But then she sobered again, and when she spoke, this time, there was a level of caring that she hadn't been willing to reveal before.

"I couldn't let them do it," she told Ripley. "I couldn't let them annihilate themselves. Does that make any sense? Do you understand?"

Ripley thought about that. "I did, once." She looked around the chapel, seeing flashes of faces, names, and events that were more a jumble in her head than coherent memories. "I . . . I tried to save . . . people. . . . Didn't work out. There was a girl. A little blond girl. She had bad dreams. I tried to help her . . . and . . . and she died. . . . And I can't remember her name."

Call patted her hand, then pulled away again.

Just then Distephano entered. "I guess we're almost there."

"Right," Ripley said.

As the soldier left the chapel, the two women walked toward the door after him.

"Do you dream?" Ripley asked, curious.

Call hedged. "I . . . we have neural processors that run through. . . ." She stopped, started over again. "Yes."

"When I sleep," Ripley said, closing her eyes, "I dream about it. *Them.* Every night. It's like they're all around me. In me." She remembered the little girl saying, *I don't wanna sleep. I have scary dreams.* "I used to be afraid to dream, but I'm not anymore."

"Why?" Call asked.

Ripley stared at the stained-glass window for a moment. "Because no matter how bad the dreams get . . . when I wake up, it's always worse."

Ripley wondered what kind of supreme being might listen to the prayers of a robot, then she wondered whether it would mind listening to the prayers of a clone as well. . . .

The two of them quietly left the chapel. As they did, the ship's computer voice—now permanently programmed as Call's voice—calmly sounded over the intership P.A.

"Ventilation systems stabilized. Oxygen at forty-three percent."

Call seemed surprised. "Is that *my* voice?"

Ripley nodded. "Ships are supposed to be female anyway."

12

They walked hurriedly, if cautiously, through the halls, Johner on point, Distephano and Call carrying Vriess, Purvis behind them, and Ripley taking the rear.

Ahead of her, Ripley heard Distephano tell them, "Not far now."

Purvis sighed. "God, I'm so tired. . . ."

"Yeah, well," Johner snapped, nerves frayed, "we'll sleep when we're dead."

That was when Ripley felt something squish under her foot. She stopped, looked down. There was a clear, gel-like goo under her booted toe. The others discovered it, too, when they stepped in it.

She fought the urge, then yielded, bending to touch it with her fingers, making sure. The mucus dripped stickily from her hand. *Yes. Them.*

Purvis glanced at them. "Uh, this is bad, right?"

Ripley looked back the way they'd come, then ahead again. "We must be near the nest." Instinctively, she *knew* the Aliens were gathered there, though she didn't know why or how she knew.

"Well," Vriess said impatiently, "then we go another way."

Distephano nixed that. "There isn't one. This is it."

Johner was nearly twitching with fear. "*No*! Okay, now, fuck you! 'Cause I ain't goin' in there!"

"Soldier's right," Call said, sounding subdued. "I did a diagnostic on the ship. This has to be the way. . . . Unless we go all the way back."

"I can live with that," Vriess announced. "We could go back. . . ."

"We don't have enough time," Call said simply, in that same subdued tone. She looked at Ripley.

"We got near ninety minutes!" Johner insisted.

Call paused, then shook her head, "Not anymore."

"What are you saying?" Distephano asked.

Johner caught the look going back and forth between the two women and nearly exploded. "What did you **do**, Robot?"

"Forget it!" she ordered Johner.

But Johner was beyond listening to her. He moved forward, threateningly, pointing at Ripley. "Hey, you wanna die here with your little brothers and sisters, that's fine. But I plan to live past today and if **this** hunk of plastic is pulling some shit"—he jerked a thumb back at Call—"I'm gonna kill her."

He rounded on Call next. "**Kill you!** Does that fucking compute? Or do you want me to . . ."

Ripley was on him before he could finish, before he could draw another breath. Her hand shot out and grabbed his moving tongue as her other hand anchored his jaw in place. He froze, unable to move, unable to speak. Ripley got nose to nose with his ugly face.

"It would make a hell of a necklace," she purred, tugging threateningly on his tongue. Then she released it.

Johner shut his mouth with a snap, and was silent.

Ripley turned to Distephano. "How far to the docks?"

"Hundred meters," the soldier estimated.

As one, they all looked down the forbidding corridor. It looked empty, but . . .

"So, what's the plan?" Vriess said tiredly.

Everyone glanced at one another. The feeling in the air was clearly, *No choice.* Again.

Without discussing it, Call and Distephano picked up Vriess, and every one of them burst into action, running down the corridor as fast as they could. It was the only thing left to do.

Ripley brought up the rear. She was running along with the others, watching behind them. Then, all of a sudden, it *hit* her. *Them.* Behind her eyes. In her brain. In her *soul. Them.* Coming for her. She staggered, tried to keep going, but couldn't. She fell to one knee.

Call must've handed Vriess off to Purvis, because suddenly she was standing over her, shaking her. "Ripley? Ripley? What's wrong?"

The terrible, insectile buzzing in Ripley's mind nearly made her deaf to Call's words. She shook her head, clamping her hands around her ears, grimacing in pain.

She tried to gasp out a warning. "Mistake . . . ! Mistake. . . ."

"Ripley!" Call yelled.

"I can hear them," the clone gasped, nearly weeping. The pain, the horror of it, was overwhelming. She was losing herself, her identity, her very humanity. They were overwhelming her. "The hive. . . . It's close. We're right over the hive. . . ."

They were both so focused on Ripley's problem, neither of them saw the rivet drill itself out of the floor, right by Ripley's foot.

"I can hear them," Ripley choked, every word a razor in her throat. "So close. . . . So close."

"Jesus!" Call said, pulling at her nervously. "Come on!

But Ripley was glued in place, in too much pain and horror to move. "I can hear them. . . . The Queen!"

A second rivet popped out of the floor, still unnoticed.

"The what . . . ?" Call asked.

Dimly, Ripley realized that Call didn't know anything at all about the *family* structure of the Aliens. And she was in no condition to explain details. "She's in pain . . . !"

Awareness of her own danger hit Ripley suddenly, as she heard something move beneath her. Glancing down, she saw an Alien hand shoot up through the grillwork, grab the floor panel, and yank *down*.

As the floor was pulled out from under her, Ripley staggered, then slid downward. She scrambled for purchase, lurched to grab the edge of the floor in front of her. She saw Call reach for her frantically, but it was too late. With a sickening plunge, Ripley fell.

Call nearly pitched headlong into the hole that had suddenly opened up in the floor as she reached for the disappearing Ripley.

"Ripley!" she screamed into the darkness under the floor. "RIPLEY!"

"What the fuck's goin' on?" Johner barked, running up beside her.

"I don't know! I don't know!" Call was frantic.

"Oh, Christ!" Johner moaned.

Vriess pulled himself up to the hole, grabbed the shoulder of her shirt as she leaned in. "Annalee, you'll fall! Get back!"

She didn't even register the concern in his voice. She was focused on only one thing, the black hole Ripley had disappeared into.

"Here!" Distephano said, slapping a flashlight into her hand.

She leaned back over the hole, but all she could see was a dim, distant glow. She could hear something screeching from far away, but it wasn't Ripley.

Call flicked on the small lamp.

What it illuminated was a vision straight from hell. At first Call thought she was staring into a bottomless snake pit, a viper's nest, but then realized that everything she was seeing, all the black, gleaming, moving parts all belonged to *them*. Aliens. Countless numbers, all working together, side by side, back to back. It looked like a huge tangle of tails, skulls, arms, all shining and moving like serpents entwined as they thrashed under the light of her lamp.

And in the center of that writhing, sticky, living mass, was Ripley, trapped, held, on her back, her arms outstretched. Call had the sudden image of the cross in the chapel and had to blink. She almost called out to Ripley, seeing the woman's eyes were wide open and staring up, but then realized Ripley wasn't seeing her. She was seeing only one thing—her future.

As Call and the others stared into the hole in horrified fascination, Ripley began to sink beneath the mass of moving Alien bodies, slowly, as if in quicksand. . . .

. . . Until she completely disappeared, smothered under the bulk of the creatures who had claimed her at last.

At first Ripley felt shock, then horror, then revulsion as she landed in the midst of the lurching, undulating mass of Aliens. Then there'd been a terrible, bottomless panic as they moved against her, embracing her, accepting her, collecting her as one of them. But soon that dissipated, as the part of her that wasn't truly Ripley began to surface. And as the warmth of their bodies surrounded her, as she sank under their collective mass, she felt a great lethargy overwhelm her.

In the stillness of that moment, her eyes drooped, her body sagged, and she slipped into sleep unawares. And then it was there, waiting for her. . . .

*Her longing for the steaming warmth of the crèche,
the strength and safety of her own kind. All this time,
she had suffered the aloneness of her individuality.
Only in sleep could she join them, rejoice with them.
The time was here. They had built the crèche. It was
time for her to join with other warriors and serve the
Queen. It was why she lived.*

*In her sleep, the warrior, Ripley, lashed her tail,
transmitting everything she thought and planned and
felt to her Queen. And her Queen sent her love and
approval back to her warrior. And her need. It would
happen soon.*

Call felt moisture on her cheeks, and realized with
some remote, logical part of her brain, that her tear
mechanism still functioned. She felt crushed, defeated.
It hurt worse than being shot.

Had it all been for nothing, all Ripley's courage, all
her fighting to regain her humanity, her *self*? If so,
what could one damaged robot do to change anything?

*The warrior moved toward the steaming warmth of the
crèche. The strength and safety of his own kind. He
was no longer burdened with the aloneness of his special individuality. He had been honored by the Queen,
selected because of his cleverness. He had been the
first to escape, to free the others, to capture the first
wombs, the first food. And so, he'd been chosen to
serve his Queen once more. He had taken the Ripley
away from the prey and carried her now through the
nest to the crèche.*

*There were warriors enough to protect her there,
where they had constructed the perfect crèche. There
humans, those pitiful, soft humans, waited to be food*

for the Queen's young, and host to the new brood. It would happen. It would happen soon.

But the warrior was burdened with memories. Of unexpected chaos. Warriors screaming and dying. And fire. And the Ripley, standing firm, holding her own young in her arms. Causing death and destruction to the crèche.

The sweeping pain of loss—sickening, irretrievable loss—flooded his mind, his entire body. It meant nothing—it meant everything. He searched for the connection to his own kind, and found the strength and safety of the crèche.

That had been a different nest, a different time. He would not think of it now, when his Queen called for his service.

In spite of their guns, in spite of their restraints, the humans had once again fallen to them. They fed them, and gave birth to the Queen's young. They had taken them by force. As they always had. As they always would. With the purity of their drive and their ferocity.

Our structural perfection is matched only by our hostility.

The big warrior lashed his tail, transmitting everything he thought and planned and felt to his brothers and his Queen. His Queen, his Mother, sent her love and approval—and her need. Her need for the Ripley he carried so very carefully in his arms. His Queen sent her love and approval back to her warrior.

And this shell that was human, this Ripley, was the mother of them all. The first womb. The first warrior. And she would live to know it all, to share the glory with them. The Queen had seen to it, and the warrior had made it happen—for Ripley was the keystone of the hive. The nurturer of the crèche. The foundation of the Newborn.

The Ripley twitched helplessly in her sleep, making soft sounds of protest and pain. The warrior breathed on her face, giving her air and warmth. Nurturing she who had nurtured them all. The Queen approved.

* * *

Call stood frozen over the open floor panel, unable to accept what had happened. She was aware of the others looking at one another, and realized what had happened had changed them. Somehow Ripley's strength, her courage, had knit the group together—but now Ripley was gone and they were on the edge of unraveling.

Even Johner was still, his throat working as if he were trying to swallow something too big.

Vriess was looking at her with so much sorrow in his eyes, so much sympathy for *Call*, that she knew if she met his gaze she'd fall apart.

Distephano glared, his jaw tight. He clutched his gun, his knuckles white.

But it was Purvis, again, who found the words to break the tableau. Dimly, Call realized this was not the first time he'd done that. It was a good thing they'd brought him along, for all their sakes.

"We've got to be moving, miss," Purvis said quietly. "Best gift you can give her right now is a quick death."

That's what it would be for Ripley when the *Auriga* impacted with Earth. Finally, Ripley would go home.

Call still couldn't move, couldn't leave the last place she'd seen her. "It's not right. . . ." The words caught in her throat, but there was nothing wrong with her vocal mechanism now.

Purvis slipped a hand under her arm, urging her to move forward. The others went ahead, as Purvis led Call on, toward the *Betty*.

"It's not right—" Call insisted, shaking her head.

Purvis sighed. "I've been saying that all day."

* * *

Wake up. Be quiet. We're in trouble.

She paused, listening, sensing. Something was happening. Not a dream. Something real.

Ripley lay still in the arms of the beast. The light was minimal, but that did not hamper her. She breathed quietly, absorbing the breath of the creature. The warm wetness around her said safety, but chaotic dream images flickered across her faltering consciousness.

The cold comfort of cryosleep.

The driving need to protect her young.

The strength and companionship of her own kind.

The power of her own rage.

The warmth and safety of the steaming crèche.

The images were meaningless and meaningful at the same time. She recognized them on a level beyond consciousness, beyond learning. They were part of her, part of who she'd been, what she'd been. And now they were part of what she was becoming.

She floated in the humid, comforting warmth, wanting to hide. There were murmuring, distant sounds that were outside of her. Inside of her. They came and went, the sounds, meaning nothing, meaning everything. Distantly, she could sense the Queen and her terrible need.

Then she heard the inside sounds again, one stronger than the others. The one she always listened to. The one she tried so hard to remember. It whispered—

My mommy always said there were no monsters—no real ones. But there are.

That sound insisted she wake. But once she woke, the dreams would all become real. She was tired, so very tired—But when she slept . . .

I don't wanna sleep, the tiny voice said. *I have scary dreams.*

They touched her in her sleep. All the monsters, the real monsters. Moving, breathing, seething—dreaming, planning. . . .

She shuddered.

They were a perfect organism, with only one true function.

Its structural perfection is matched only by its hostility.

She moaned softly, despondently.

An idealistic young woman had shown her the shadow of what she had once been. What fate had made her. But what was she now? Was she Ellen Ripley, or a changeling as grotesque as . . . as . . .

At least there's a part of you that's human! I'm just— I'm just . . .

I prefer to be called an artificial person.

Slowly, she registered a dim sensation. Something outside herself. Something happening to her self. Her eyes moved around as she gathered information.

Her terrible children had finally come for her. They were everywhere, carrying her, welcoming her.

But the others were gone. The humans. Those she'd fought so long and hard to protect and save. She'd been separated from them, taken from them. Part of her felt enormous relief. Part of her felt tremendous rage. She vacillated between the feelings as she lay in the arms of the beast.

A cartoonish picture of a blond child wavered in her mind, gradually replaced by a clearer image of a real child. Her child? No, not hers. . . .

Yes, mine!

Her mind swam with chaotic memories.

The steaming warmth of the crèche. The strength and safety of her own kind. The aloneness of individuality. And the driving need to find—

Small, strong arms wrapped around her neck, small, strong legs wrapped around her waist. There was chaos. The warriors screamed and died. There was fire.

I knew you would come.

She blinked, confused, her mind a sudden shambles

of fragments, memories, instincts she could not sort out. The sweeping pain of loss—sickening, irretrievable loss—flooded her mind, her entire body. It meant nothing—it meant everything.

My name is Newt. No one calls me Rebecca.

I'm coming, Newt! I'm coming!

Mommy! Mommy!

Ripley searched for the connection to her own kind, she searched to find the strength and safety of the crèche, but it was not there. And in its place was nothing but this pain, this terrible loss. She was hollow. Empty.

Dimly, she looked at the huge warrior holding her and longed to ask him the same question she had asked the others, the humans. The question no one would ever answer.

Why? Why?

As the memories of Newt's voice ricocheted around her brain, she determined she would have the answer. She would take it from them. In spite of their size, their strength, in spite of their ferocity and hostility. She would take it by force.

Nervously, the survivors of the crew traveled the rest of the way to the *Betty* quickly, but without racing. They saw no other signs of Aliens, no slime, no acid damage, nothing. Everything was amazingly still.

As Vriess was carried into the ship, he felt an overwhelming pang of homesickness, then a sorrow so gripping, it surprised him. As Johner and Distephano carried him to the copilot's seat, evidence of Hillard's occupancy was everywhere, as was Elgyn's around the pilot's chair. He shook off the memories, promising himself he'd deal with them at a more convenient time, once he got their asses safely outta here. Assuming he *could* get their asses outta here.

As Vriess securely strapped himself into place, Johner asked, "How long till we can get airborne?"

Vriess punched up some schematics and a quick flight plan, looked at the image of Earth filling up their screen, getting closer by the second. "I'll need Call to patch in to the ship again, open the hatch, release the magnets, like that."

"We hit atmo in a few minutes," Johner said urgently. "Only gonna make it harder."

Vriess nodded, hands flying over the board. He didn't want to think about how little time he'd spent piloting this ship. He didn't want to think about his lack of experience. They'd always had Hillard or Elgyn to fly the *Betty,* with Christie as backup. Vriess was a *mechanic,* for chrissakes, and Johner was muscle. They were so used to their roles they rarely had occasion to step outside them. He wouldn't think about that now. Today he was a pilot. He had to be.

Call moved up beside him, distracting him from his worries. He stopped, met her eyes. From the first moment they'd met, she'd never looked at him like a cripple. Never stared at his legs. Never saw the chair. She only ever saw him, Vriess, the man. He looked at that fine-featured, pretty face and told himself that the least he could do was the same. See Call. Not the wire-festooned hole in her chest. Not the mechanical port in her arm.

She gave him a weak smile. "Need my help?"

He nodded, immensely relieved. "If . . . if you wouldn't mind . . . Annalee."

She started at the sound of her first name, then nodded briefly. "Sure. No problem." And went about connecting into the computer brain as though she'd always done that in front of him.

He didn't pay any attention to the way she plugged in. He just watched her face. Her small, pretty, human face.

* * *

Ripley swam back to consciousness slowly. She was swamped with a feeling of vertigo, a dizziness she couldn't seem to overcome. She kept her eyes shut for a moment. She heard wet sounds, dripping, splashing. She heard moans, human moans. She heard a humming, like insects. And the smell—

Blood. Offal. Death. All of it as wet and hot and humid as a tropical swamp.

Slowly, she tried to move, her body almost too languid to respond. Was she drugged? Hypnotized? She was lying on something firm, rigid, solid. Suddenly, something sticky plopped onto her face from above. She frowned, the dizziness unabating. Finally, the unpleasant dripping sensation was too much, and she opened her eyes.

The stuff dripping over her face oozed off her cheek and onto the floor, and started hardening immediately, pinning her head in place. She reached up, pulled it off, then wiped her hand on the floor without thinking. Even as she performed this automatic task, she blinked, looking around, trying to think, trying to understand where she was, what was happening. She knew she should be anxious or alarmed, should be worried about her own welfare, but her mind wasn't clear enough for that.

She looked around in the dimness. She was not alone. There were other humans, at least eight of them, standing over her on some kind of ledge nearby. She squinted, trying to see better. Finally, her gaze sharpened and she realized the others weren't standing on a ledge at all. Their arms and hands and legs were all fastened down, glued with ropes of exudate to the walls of a huge cylindrical room. Vaguely she remembered Call's mechanical voice saying something about activity in a waste tank and wished she'd paid more attention.

The eight people she could see were all trapped against the walls of the circular tank. Soldiers, researchers, all stuck like giant flies, half cocooned.

She remembered a similar scene. . . .

All the colonists from Hadley's Hope, cocooned to the wall, growing chest bursters. Most of them had emerged. But everyone here is still intact.

She touched her own chest, but she hadn't been reinfected. She'd know if she had been. She would be able to *feel* it. Were these people being held here to be infected? The thought terrified her, but as she looked around, she realized there were no eggs in the tank. Yet the image of the eight people trapped like insects in a spider nursery would not leave her.

Ripley pulled her gaze away from the trapped humans and looked around, finally seeing *them.* Aliens. They were floundering in the deeply sloping bottom of the waste tank, like alligators in a swamp, only their swamp was a sea of human blood, offal, and their own secretions. Ripley was perched where the floor met the wall, at the highest part of the flooring, the very shoreline of the fetid lake. Lying there, hesitant to move, she watched the warriors, wondering if they were there to tend to the cocooned humans. Would they be bringing eggs to infect these people?

Ripley frowned, looked around again. Then she saw her. The Queen.

The huge creature was directly across from Ripley, but the image she presented was so confusing, it took Ripley a few moments to sort it out.

Ripley clearly recalled seeing the Queen and her massive ovipositor once before. Then, the huge reproductive organ had been tethered in place to support its terrible weight and size as she deposited egg after egg after egg on the floor of the atmosphere refinery at Hadley's Hope. But that was nothing like what Ripley was seeing now.

This Queen was tethered in place all right, but not by her ovipositor. She *had* none. Apparently, that part of her had already been discarded. The Queen *herself* was partially cocooned against the floor of the waste tank, in the sea of blood and waste. It was either a shallow part of the tank, or the Aliens had supported her by an invisible sling constructed of the same material as the underwater web. Ripley realized now that the Aliens half submerged in the chemical soup below were taking care of the Queen, tending to her. They were completely ignoring the human prey they'd secured in the tank.

Ripley continued staring, still trying to understand what she was seeing.

The Queen was trapped on her back, her legs, tail, and arms half submerged. Her head thrashed back and forth, her extremities waving feebly. Was she *in pain?* And what was that on her abdomen . . . ?

Then Ripley realized the true horror of what she was seeing. The Queen had a huge, distended belly, fleshy looking, with thick black veins snaking over it. The belly moved, as with a life of its own. The Queen's huge mouth opened, and she hissed furiously.

Ripley stared, whispered, "No eggs. Just . . ."

An oddly familiar voice spoke up excitedly. "Our greatest achievement!"

Ripley was afraid to turn, afraid to see the owner of the voice, but she was compelled to. As she looked up, she saw Dr. Gediman, cocooned neatly among other researchers and soldiers. His eyes were wide, glowing. He was clearly poised on the edge of sanity—with his toes hanging over.

"A secondary reproductive cycle," he babbled cheerily. "Asexual. Mammalian. No host!"

Ripley almost moaned. "That's not possible."

Gediman grinned hugely. "We thought we could alter its reproductive system. Obviate the egg-laying cycles. But the beast doesn't trade." He giggled. "It just added a second cycle. It's wonderful!"

A keening shriek from the Queen shook Ripley, as she glanced back at the creature. She was thrashing, obviously in unrelieved pain. The Aliens tending her backed off slightly, chattering wildly, their insectile hum almost musical to Ripley.

"But how . . . ?" Ripley muttered, confused.

"Genetic crossover," Gediman supplied helpfully. Then he looked at her, eyes wide, grinning maniacally. "From the *host DNA.*"

"*No . . . !*" Ripley couldn't, wouldn't accept that.

"Look at it!" he chortled, gleefully. "It's you! *It's you!*"

She could barely stand it, but, fighting back tears of horror and frustration, she forced herself to look at the Queen. In despair, all she could think was, this was *her* terrible child.

The bulge in the Queen's belly grew noticeably larger, then started moving, rippling.

Ripley found her motivation. Struggling to rise from the floor of the tank, she found her body traitorously slow, sluggish. She didn't care; she pushed up from the floor, swearing, "I'm getting out of here. Goddamn it, I'm getting out of here!"

Gediman was still watching her, grinning. As Ripley watched, the last glimmer of his sanity vanished. "Don't you want to see what happens next?" he asked joyfully.

13

Call unplugged herself from the *Betty* and watched as Vriess prepared to separate them from the *Auriga*. She felt terrible about Ripley, but they still had to get the rest of them to safety. Vriess smiled at her once he had his flight plan in place, and she allowed herself to smile back tentatively.

There were still things to do. She moved away from the command console to join Johner and Purvis. Looking up at the scarred man, she murmured, "Johner, take Purvis to the freezer."

Johner was clearly relieved to be safe aboard the *Betty.* Agreeably, he patted Purvis's back, and said, "All right. Nap time, buddy."

Purvis, looking incredibly tired and drained, nodded and followed along.

Call moved ahead of them to help Johner with the cryomix. It'd be faster if she did it, and they were on borrowed time with Purvis already. She started down the dark hallway, waiting for the lights to go on ahead of her, but they didn't. She frowned. She hadn't noticed any mechanical problems while she'd been plugged into the ship, but she hadn't really gone looking for anything minor, either. Still, these lights should've come on when they first entered the vessel. She turned to Johner, concerned.

Before she could speak, a hand appeared from the darkness near her, light glinting off the barrel of the gun it held. A deafening explosion in the small space rocked Call as the gun went off. Purvis took the bullet in the shoulder. He screamed, and hit the floor.

As Johner reached for his own weapon, an arm snaked around Call's throat roughly, and the hard metal barrel of the still smoking gun was shoved into her cheek. She froze.

Who . . . ? What . . . ? How . . . ?

As the man holding her shoved her forward, out of the shadows and into the light, she heard a familiar voice.

"You move," the man said to Johner, "and I put a bullet where her brain is!"

Wren!

Call saw Vriess spin in his chair to face them, his expression one of rage and frustration as he sat there, trapped, unable to help.

Johner was tense, collected. This was a conflict he understood, an enemy he could deal with. The scarred man stood with his feet apart, hands away from his sides, trying to appear nonthreatening. But Call had seen Johner in action. If Wren had any understanding of men like him, the doctor would kill him now, with no discussion. Call also suspected that Wren's knowledge did not lie in those areas.

"Distephano!" Wren barked at the soldier. "Take their weapons."

Call looked right at the soldier. Would he? She'd saved his life in the mess hall riot. Would he turn on them now?

Distephano stood tall, as if ready to salute. "Begging your pardon, sir, but . . . fuck you." He made no move to yield his own weapon or disarm Johner.

Wren pulled her harder against him, strangling her. She could feel the terrible tension in his body, his trembling as he grew more desperate. He ground the gun muzzle harder into Call's face. "Drop it!" he screamed at the others. "Drop it, or we all die together!"

A sudden, high-pitched shriek made them all turn. Purvis jerked upright, eyes wide, grabbing at his chest.

No one moved, not even Wren.

Frantically, Ripley tried to figure out how to escape from the waste tank, but from where she knelt she could see no doors, no exits of any kind. They'd gotten her *in* here, there had to be a way *out*!

The Queen was thrashing more wildly, shrieking steadily. The other Aliens were more and more agitated, humming, twittering, darting through the muck.

One particular cry from the Queen was especially piercing, and Ripley froze in place. The Queen's belly heaved, alive, something clearly writhing inside it.

Ripley tensed as a memory surfaced.

This happened to me. I gave birth. I was a mother once, a real mother. I lay in my own bed, and my husband was there. And a nurse, and doctor. I cried out as my belly heaved.

She could *feel* it now, the memory was that strong. Instinctively, her hands rubbed her own belly.

I was sweating hard, but I didn't want drugs, even when my husband begged me to take them. I was worried about all those years of cryodrugs, and wouldn't take anything as I delivered. In my own bed. My own home.

She watched the Queen thrash and scream in the slime and the muck and this travesty, this obscene parody of her own experience, made her sick.

I had a girl, a beautiful little girl. She looked like both her parents. We called her Amy.

Ellen Ripley blinked at the flood of human memories crashing in on her, while she remained trapped here in Alien hell.

You told Amy you'd be back for her eleventh birthday. You promised. That was the first time you defeated **them.** *But your escape pod wasn't found for fifty-seven years. Amy died never knowing why you didn't come home for her birthday.*

Ripley closed her eyes for a moment, her daughter's face clear before her. Other memories surged up.

Newt.

Hicks.

Even Jonesy. . . .

All of them gone, lost to the years.

Beside her, Gediman watched, amazed, wide-eyed, grinning like a lunatic, chuckling with a low "he-he-he" that was almost as disturbing as the Aliens' sounds.

The Queen screamed again, and reached toward Ripley, as if the clone, her own "mother," could somehow help her through this experience, somehow coach her birth. The Alien female bellowed, struggling to pull herself out of her fetid bed.

Remembering her own pain, Ripley moaned along with the Queen, her gut contracting in reflex.

And inside her, inside her genes, she felt the Queen's pain on a visceral level. The telepathic link forced it on her, forced her to be the Queen in her terrible travail. The swollen, rippling belly, the tearing, burning pain, the inexorable pressure. The complete rebellion of her body forcing her to perform a function she no longer wanted to perform. Ripley moaned along with the Queen, suffering with her out of effort and sympathy.

At the same time, she could feel the concern of the warriors as they moved closer to the helpless Queen.

She could feel their anxiety. All of them—her husbands, all—longed to help their Queen, but not one knew how.

Suddenly, a spout of blood spurted like a geyser from the Queen's heaving belly. The blood dribbled and seeped from that first eruption, tracing acid rivers over the rotund mound of flesh. Ripley tried to turn away, not wanting to witness this any longer, this ugly mockery of human birth.

Then the Queen shrieked again, lifting her head, staring at Ripley, as if she were her midwife. Ripley curled in on herself, gripping her own stomach, and screamed in concert with the Queen.

The writhing creature collapsed back into the mire, and the warriors surrounding her suddenly backed off, as if sensing something imminent.

Ripley blinked wearily, dazedly, staring at the pulsating stomach. Another gout of blood spurted, and then something pressed upward against the thinning tissue of the Queen's belly. It kept pushing up, up, until the flesh took on the shape of the form beneath it as it resisted.

Ripley blinked. It looked like a skull—a *human* skull—was struggling to emerge from the torn belly of the Queen.

The baby. . . . Ripley thought distractedly. *The baby's crowning. I see her head. . . .*

There was a final shriek, a terrible tearing sound, and suddenly The Newborn emerged, unfolding itself from the cramped confines of its mother's womb. The creature was pale, not black, its skin looking more like human flesh than the hard silicon exoskeleton of the Aliens. Its head had the classic, elongated skull, but the face . . . The face. . . .

Beside her, Gediman babbled, weeping with mad joy. "Beautiful! Beautiful butterfly. . . !"

The Newborn's face clearly had something human about it, all too human. It looked like a skull, with massive eye sockets, long, gleaming white teeth, a chiseled jawbone, and the hollows where a human nose belonged. The Newborn's face was the very image of Death.

"So beautiful," Gediman muttered.

Ripley glanced at him. He looked beatific, as if he'd given the universe the finest gift science could bestow.

Ripley felt like she was on the verge of joining him in his madness. She turned away from the scientist and tried to get a grip on her seesawing emotions.

The Newborn uncurled its massive body from its mother's innards.

The Queen, no longer in such immediate pain, moaned softly now, her thrashing slower. She reached for her child with a trembling hand. Ripley envisioned herself making that same gesture, remembered her husband lifting their daughter and resting her on her mother's stomach. She remembered bursting into tears, then near hysterical laughter, as all of them rejoiced in the wet, squalling, healthy baby.

As the Queen reached for her child, the Newborn turned toward her.

It's not even full grown, Ripley realized, not knowing how she knew. *It'll double, maybe triple in size, all within a day. And its appetite is boundless. As is its ferocity and hostility. The perfect organism.*

As the Newborn extricated itself from the womb, Ripley saw its hands. They were as strong and massive as the Aliens' hands usually were, but there were only five fingers. The long nails and pale skin made the thing's hands look. . . .

. . . *Just like mine!* Ripley thought, sickened.

In a parody of human tenderness, the Newborn crawled up its mother's body to her head. The Queen was making soft, cooing sounds now, maternal sounds, examining her young, clearly proud of what she'd accomplished. The Newborn drew nearer, and for a moment it looked as if the young might actually kiss its mother.

Then, in one massive, abrupt movement, the Newborn slapped out with a huge hand and ripped the Queen's head off, sending blood spraying everywhere.

Ripley, still connected telepathically with the Queen, felt the Alien female's death screams deep in her marrow.

The Newborn didn't stop, but attacked its mother's quivering body with its massive teeth, ripping the Queen to shreds, devouring huge chunks of her. Immune to the acid blood, the Newborn feasted on its parent's flesh.

Ripley felt the Queen's death as the telepathic link was severed. It was a painful break, as sharp as a broken bone, its jagged edges grinding horribly in her head, her soul. Her brain reached out, fumbling for more contact with the warriors, *needing* the link. But the connection with the warriors was fraught with terror and confusion as the Aliens milled frantically, not knowing what to do as their Queen, their entire focus, was destroyed.

Ripley felt as if she were surrounded by the screaming souls of hell as the Aliens whistled and chittered in pain as the Newborn continued to devour its mother. Then Ripley realized it wasn't just the warriors who were making noise. She turned. Gediman was still gibbering to himself, and his whimpers quickly dissolved into terrified screaming.

Gediman's eyes widened and he began to thrash, then flail, harder, more wildly. He began shrieking hysterically, fighting frantically with the resin holding him prisoner.

Ripley sagged back against the tank, trying, again, to summon the strength to escape, but she was so *tired*. The loss of her telepathic link with the Queen made her feel empty, disoriented.

The Newborn, covered in its mother's blood, suddenly froze, then cocked its head as if listening. Slowly, it turned, and Ripley had her first chance to really look into the creature's face. Deep within the depths of its massive eye sockets, the human saw two eyes, not unlike her own, shining out.

She stared. *Amy had my eyes, too*, she thought, feeling a bubble of hysterical laughter welling in her chest.

Gediman saw the eyes, too, shining in the terrible Death's head of the Newborn, and screamed louder, more frantically.

Awkwardly, the Newborn rose.

It's bigger already! Ripley realized.

Standing on two spindly, shaky legs, the two-meter-high baby took its first steps as it toddled toward the scientist.

As the Newborn drew near him, its massive, terrible appearance made Gediman grow still. He snapped his mouth shut, and froze, his eyes bulging, his awareness of his danger pushing him clearly beyond terror. The Newborn sniffed the man, and Ripley could see his frame trembling as if in a seizure.

Then the Newborn's massive jaws opened, and opened, wider and wider. Like a snake about to devour its prey, the powerful jaws seemed to unhinge themselves as they loomed over the trapped man. Ripley could see no fanged tongue in this creature, just the massive jaws, and horribly long, shining white teeth.

With shocking suddenness, the Newborn struck, sinking its massive fangs into the top of Gediman's skull. The man found his voice again, shrieking more horribly than before, as rivulets of blood ran down his forehead into his eyes, his ears, his own mouth.

Oh, God! Oh, no. NO! Ripley thought, praying that she could connect with the Newborn and somehow stop what it was about to do. But the creature ignored her.

With a sickening wrench and the crunching sound of bones breaking, the Newborn ripped off the top of Gediman's skull as easily as a human would pop the top off a hard-boiled egg. His brain was exposed, glistening pink and throbbing.

Ripley moaned in horror and turned away. She could hear soft tissue tearing, the wet sounds of chewing, swallowing, along with the dying researcher's moans and gurgles. She smelled the metallic scent of fresh blood as the man finally went limp, still suspended in his prison of resinous tendrils. The last of his blood dripped into the morass below him.

The only thing Ripley could do was shut her eyes.

She did not see the Newborn turn, stare meaningfully at her, then hungrily lick its bloody teeth with a long, serpentine tongue. . . .

Purvis was in agony, so much agony, he could barely isolate what hurt worse. His shoulder was on fire, in terrible pain from the bullet lodged there. It throbbed so bad he could barely think. But the pain in his gut— God, the pain in his gut was really horrible. It was like something was walking around in there, moving like a snake, like it was looking for a way out. He felt sick, nauseated, and in so much raw *pain*—

In spite of his agony, he managed to focus on the tableau in front of him.

Wren, freaking out, was gripping Call so tight she was nearly choking. Her chest wound glittered and blinked bizarrely where telltales had been exposed. Wren was shoving the muzzle of his gun hard into Call's face. Purvis knew he was hurting her. Call, who'd tried so hard to save them all. Especially Larry Purvis.

Wren was shouting. "This synthetic bitch is going to plug back into the *Auriga* and land it according to standard operational procedures."

Call struggled to speak, her voice gritty. "No, she's not!"

Distephano confronted his superior officer. "You're nuts! You still want to bring those things back to Earth?"

"Have you been paying any attention today?" Johner asked sarcastically.

Purvis felt something uncoiling inside him and moaned, both arms wrapped around his stomach.

Wren was losing it, that was obvious. "The Aliens will be contained by the base quarantine troops." Suddenly, Wren swung his weapon, aiming at the others, pulling it off Call's face.

"For about *five* seconds," she growled.

The doctor swung the gun back, shoved it roughly into her cheek, making her wince. "Shut up!" he screamed. "I said *shut up!*"

Just then, Purvis felt a horrible *tearing* in the center of his chest, just below his rib cage. He looked down at his own belly. A spot of blood blossomed against his shirt, and he stared at it, uncomprehending.

Everyone else stopped, too, even Wren.

Then Purvis understood. The thing inside him. It was time for it to be born. He hadn't been frozen in time and now it was too late. This monster was going to rip its way out of his body and *kill him*. And this son of a bitch Wren, this motherfucking scientist, was responsible. The *Betty* crew might've done the kidnapping, they might've delivered him here, but this entire project of spawning these hell creatures inside living human hosts was *this* man's doing.

Purvis's rage boiled up in him, stronger even than the Alien who was killing him. Purvis lunged upright, glaring at Wren.

Wren must've recognized some of what Purvis was feeling on his face, because he swung the gun away from Call, aiming it now at Purvis. Not that Purvis cared. It was just a gun. All it could do was kill him and it would be a gift if it did.

Purvis forced himself to his feet, lurching like a zombie. He staggered toward Wren, who was frozen with horror. It pleased Purvis inordinately to see that expression of terror on that smug bastard's face. Purvis jerked forward, fighting his agony—literally, a man possessed.

Terrified, Wren fired.

The bullet hit Purvis hard in the other shoulder, knocking him back a step, but not stopping him. The creature inside him was moving so frantically now, chewing itself free so urgently, that Purvis couldn't feel anything else, not even bullets hitting him at point-blank range. He was dimly aware of blood seeping over his belly, over his shoulders, down his back. But he was too focused to care. His entire universe had narrowed, and there was only Wren. . . .

Wren fired again and again, hitting Purvis each time. The doctor's grip on Call loosened, and in one quick, practiced move, she slammed an elbow into his chest, at the same time as she grabbed the pinkie of the hand holding her and wrenched it back so hard it snapped with an audible crunch.

Wren screamed and released her, and as she fell away from him, his next shot went wild, thudding into a padded chair.

Then Purvis was on him, driving a fist full into his face so hard he could feel the nose shattering beneath his knuckles. The gun went flying, and dimly, Purvis was aware of Johner diving for it to keep it out of Wren's reach.

Purvis somehow found the power to hit that hated face again, again, again, until blood flowed freely from the nose, the mouth, the split lips, the broken teeth. Then he hit him some more.

Struggling to escape the ferocious blows, Wren fell,

and flipped over onto his stomach, trying to crawl away from Purvis's unrelenting fury. Purvis straddled his back like a demon obscene lover, and grabbed a fistful of Wren's hair, yanking his head up.

"NO!" Wren screamed. "No! No! NO!"

Purvis used the grip on Wren's hair to pound his face into the floor once, twice, three, four times until Wren was sobbing, moaning, helpless in his hands.

Vriess suddenly shouted, "Call! Johner! Soldier! Heads up!" and tossed the crew rifles that had been secreted beneath the command console.

Clinging to Wren's hair, and slamming his face into the flooring, Purvis felt the terrible pain in his gut cresting. Burying both hands in Wren's hair, he gripped the feebly struggling doctor's head hard, harder than Wren had ever clutched Call.

The scream started deep in Purvis's gut, and he wondered if it was the creature's scream, the scream of birth, as the sound pushed its way up through his body and out of his throat. He felt the thing moving, chewing, fierce little teeth eating him from the inside out, gnawing through his organs, up through his diaphragm, his lungs, cracking his very ribs.

His chest bulged outward, the bloodstain on his chest blooming, growing, erupting in a rush of blood and bones and organs. With one massive, final effort of hatred and vengeance, Purvis yanked Wren's head against himself, pinning it to the bloody spot on his chest. Now both of them, Purvis and Wren, were shrieking.

Wren swung his arms, trying to dislodge his captor, but Purvis was inexorable in his death throes.

Purvis felt his ribs snapping outward. He held Wren's head tightly, knowing it was almost over. It would end here. But his way. One thing would end his way.

Purvis felt its birth. As his lungs were destroyed, he

stopped screaming, but Wren's voice was loud enough for them both. The Alien embryo burst out of him, slamming into the back of Wren's skull.

With his last gasp of consciousness, Purvis watched something small and snakelike burst from Wren's forehead right through his brain. The scientist's screams scaled up and up, resounding like the combined shriek of every hibernator that had been kidnapped, every soldier who'd been captured by the Aliens. To Purvis, Wren's screams were a sweet anthem of vengeance.

The birth of the Alien sprayed the onlookers with blood and tissue and they recoiled. The translucent creature writhed in Wren's face, trying to free itself from the tight prison of Wren's skull. It shrieked defiance at the armed crew. Wren's scream was a terrible echo.

Just as everything before him went dim, Purvis watched the *Betty*'s crew engage their weapons. He wished he could say "thank you," as they opened fire.

The four survivors pumped round after round into the dying men and the screeching Alien, making the bodies jerk and dance, spattering the interior of the *Betty* with blood, both human and Alien.

But then, finally, the silhouettes of Wren and Purvis collapsed, and the Alien chestburster had been so totally disintegrated there was nothing left of it.

Call walked over to the bodies, openly sobbing. She kicked the dead Wren out of the way savagely, wanting to shoot him a few more times, but resisting. As Johner would say, it would just be a fucking waste of ammo.

Then she knelt by Purvis, and touched his face gently. "He . . . he looks almost grateful. . . ." she sniffled.

Johner's big hand gripped her shoulder. "He was, Annalee. He knew we were trying to do him a favor. He trusted us to do it."

She looked up into the scarred man's face. It had grown soft just for this moment. She patted his hand and nodded.

"Come on," Distephano said gently. "We gotta get out of here. We can ditch the bodies when we're free of the *Auriga*."

Yeah, Call thought dismally. *If we can get free of the Auriga.*

14

Gediman swung slowly in his webbing, back and forth, back and forth. He looked bizarre, still dripping random fluids into the grisly mire beneath him. His missing skullcap and brain made his face appear inhuman through the streaks of blood. The doctor's eyes were open, but the only thing they might be seeing would have to be the afterlife, if there were one for bastards like him. After all, he'd already died in hell.

While the Newborn had been devouring his brain tissue like so much pudding, a small chestburster had exploded from Gediman's rib cage—to the Newborn's complete indifference—and skittered off into the pool of blood while Gediman thrashed and twitched in his death throes.

It was a scene Ripley knew she would never forget. Not in this incarnation, or—she fought back the urge to laugh hysterically—the next.

Ripley still crouched on the floor of the waste tank, trying to make herself small and unnoticed. She knelt there quietly, perfectly still, as still as the remaining cocooned humans who were, luckily for them, still unconscious. Ripley envied them.

She didn't move a muscle, afraid to blink, afraid to breathe. She remained motionless, waiting for the Newborn's attention to turn elsewhere, now that it was finished with Gediman's corpse.

The creature looked about the tank, at the milling Aliens, at the rendered corpse of its mother, at the still swaying Gediman. And then the massive head turned slowly and grinned hideously—at Ripley.

Slowly, the Newborn approached, spider-agile, creeping along the waste tank wall, using the resinous fibers for hand and footholds.

Ripley struggled to control her breathing, her fear. The closer the monster drew, the more clearly Ripley could see its features—which was not an advantage. The being's face was spattered with blood and pink brain matter, some of it stuck in its massive teeth. As it breathed into Ripley's face, the woman could clearly smell the fresh blood.

The monster was barely a handbreadth away from her face now. Ripley trembled, fighting to contain her fear, her instinctive urge to panic and bolt.

Part of her couldn't believe it had come to this. All the struggling. All the fighting. Would she have to go through it yet again, in some other incarnation? Would the malign thug of a God who'd ruled her various lives insist she keep getting reincarnated into the same nightmare over and over? Hadn't she earned a second chance in some other lifeform after all this?

The Newborn's mouth opened, and it extended a long, sinuous tongue. Ripley tensed, trying not to think about having her skull ripped off, her brain consumed.

The tongue snaked out, then ever so gently touched Ripley's face, cleaning off some resinous goo that had fallen there. The woman blinked, waiting for the inevitable. The creature licked her again, like some monstrous cat, over and over, cleaning her face, her neck, her shoulders of some of the waste and offal that had been smeared on her. Tenderly, the Newborn cleaned her. It moved slowly, careful not to pull at tender skin, or tug at strands of hair. Even its clawed, terrible hands were gentle where they touched her, as if checking for wounds, or to ensure that she was safe. The gestures were reminiscent of a faithful pet, a dog greeting its master at the end of the day, a cat begging to be petted.

And as the monster cleaned her face, and touched her body, as it denied her the death she had imagined, Ripley looked into eyes that were her shade of brown and saw something there.

That was when the telepathic connection slithered through, touching her mind, whispering to her of genetic bonds she could not deny. And then it was all right there. Her longing for the steaming warmth of the crèche, the strength and safety of her own kind. Just a moment before she had suffered the aloneness of her own individuality. But now she was given the chance, again, to join them, *rejoice with* them. *She was in the crèche. She could reunite with the warriors, and serve as the Queen, nurturer of the Newborn.* That *was why she had lived.*

Because this shell that was human, this Ripley, was the mother of them all. The first womb. The first warrior. And she had lived long enough to know it all, to share the glory with them. Ripley was the keystone of the hive. The nurturer of the crèche. The foundation of the Newborn.

This was the answer to the question she'd been asking. Why? This *was why.*

She gazed into the liquid brown eyes that could have been her own, and reached out a hand, placing it on the Newborn's skull. Her hand slid over the long, Alien head, patting it as she once had done to Amy's, stroking it as she once had done to Newt. This was her child, just as they were.

The Newborn uttered a soft mewling sound, and

gazed at her, and Ripley felt the telepathic connection deepen, grow stronger. It was so different from the others, yet the same. But there was something more in this contact, something undeniably **human**. It was like being connected to a part of herself, a warped, malevolent part that was bonded to all her fierce self-preservation, all her intense determination.

The perfect organism.

Perfect for—?

And then a voice touched her from her memories, the memories the Aliens themselves had inadvertently given her. And she heard Newt's voice, just as she'd first heard it in the incubator.

My mommy always said there were no monsters—no real ones. But there are.

Ripley shuddered, still bombarded by the intensity of the Newborn's telepathic contact, at the terrible Alienness of the creature wanting her allegiance.

The Newborn parroted Newt's words. *I knew you would come.*

To hear that loving phrase from this travesty of a living being made her ill.

Then she heard Call's distorted, mechanical voice. *"Why do you go on living? How can you stand it? How can you stand . . . yourself?"*

"Not much choice," she'd answered, believing that. She'd never had any real choice, not since she'd awakened from cryosleep on the **Nostromo** in the wrong part of space.

But she had a choice now. For once, she had a **real** choice.

She had asked Call, *"Why do you care what happens to them?"* meaning humans. But now Ripley wondered herself, why did **she** care? What had they ever done for her to make her care so much for them? Maybe Ripley was the new asshole model. . . .

She searched for the connection to her own kind,

trying to find who and what she was, so that she could make the right choice. She searched to find the strength and safety of the crèche, but it was not there. And in its place was nothing but pain, and terrible loss. She felt hollow. Empty. The way she'd felt since her birth.

As she reached out telepathically, she heard deep inside her the voice of children, two girls, **human** children, calling to her from across the years, *Mommy! Mommy!*

Ripley stared into the watery, reptilian eyes of the Newborn and moved her hand away. With a groan of loss, she made her choice.

She had her answers. They were locked in her very genetics. In spite of the lure of the Aliens, in spite of their power and strength, their purity of purpose, she knew she would have to endure. To save humanity. That was her purity of purpose, made stronger by the infusion of their genes.

She was Ripley. It was who she'd always been, the only thing she could ever be. Ripley. She would destroy them. She would do it by force.

Taking a deep, steady breath to calm her nerves, Ripley stood cautiously, straightening up. She kept her mind clear, watching the Newborn, thinking kind thoughts toward it and the suddenly leaderless warriors who were trying to figure out what to do, now that their Queen was dead.

The Newborn stepped away from her now that she was erect. Ripley reached up, seizing strands of the webbing that draped everywhere on the walls of the tank. As she gripped some of the stronger, more elastic ropes of webbing, she kept an eye on the Newborn, as the half-Alien creature cocked its misshapen head, trying to understand Ripley's actions.

The woman looked down into the pool of blood and waste below her. She wet her lips, and another memory surfaced—*a molten cauldron of white-hot lead.* So, okay. . . . She'd jumped into worse things—but not this time.

Wrapping the webbing around her wrists, Ripley used it like an acrobat, swinging up, clambering against the walls, finding handholds and toeholds, even as her eyes searched the ceiling. All the while, the Newborn watched curiously as Ripley kept her mind calm, and her thoughts neutral.

As Ripley moved higher up the wall of the tank, the Newborn waded out to a spot where it could watch Ripley better. Two warriors approached the Newborn, moving through the liquid like crocodiles, tails undulating, as though they, too, were curious.

Slowly, so as not to startle the Aliens, Ripley clambered higher and higher, searching for a telltale seam of light. She was dripping with sweat as she finally spied it, struggling all the while to keep calm. She began to hum a song she suddenly remembered to keep her mind from betraying her to the Newborn.

"You . . . are . . . my . . . lucky . . . star—"

Finally, she saw what she'd been searching for. She climbed, moved forward, touched the ceiling of the waste tank and found the handle that released the trapdoor there. As she shoved the trapdoor open onto an upper floor of the *Auriga*, Ripley jerked around to face the Newborn.

In her head, she could feel the shocking surprise of her betrayal in the beast's mind. The monster drew itself up as tall as it could, stretched its arms threateningly, and screamed its challenge at its betrayer.

The monster leapt onto the nearest wall and began scrambling after the woman, but Ripley was too far ahead of it. Shoving herself through the trapdoor, Ripley slammed it shut behind her and latched it, praying it would hold the enraged monster.

Even through the closed trap door, Ripley could hear the creature scream in fury, as she scrambled to her feet, turned, and ran.

* * *

"We ever gettin' outta this thing?" Johner asked, and Call could hear the edge of panic in his voice.

"We'll make it, son," Vriess said calmly, but Call could hear the edge in his words as well. "Just keep your pants on."

The planet Earth filled the entire view screen. It was still a predominantly blue world with a scattering of clouds across its surface. But almost two-thirds of it was obscured by a giant orbiting latticework of metal, part of the extensive space operations run by corporations and the planetary government in cozy cooperation. The grid was like a partial shell that rotated slightly faster than the planet itself. Call knew how many people lived there—and could access the minute-by-minute update anytime she wanted—but she didn't like to think about those kinds of numbers. About the only people who actually *lived* on Earth were the disenfranchised and unemployed. Most meaningful work now was in space and on the colonies. It wasn't hard to pick a location on the planet that was completely uninhabited to crash the *Auriga*. Johner hadn't lied; Earth really was a slum.

She talked to the *Betty* through the port in her arm, working out the timing of their ejection from the *Auriga*. She'd already set the big ship up to avoid the grid completely, and hit the surface of the planet in the most remote part of the central Australian outback.

It wouldn't be long now. They'd be leaving soon and all this would be behind them.

Call sighed. She still hadn't accepted leaving Ripley behind as well.

Outside the ship, the *Betty*'s wings rotated up as the ship prepared to separate from her berth.

Call looked over her monitors even as the *Betty* fed her information through her arm.

Both she and Vriess were monitoring a flood of information on the *Betty*'s current condition. The stabilizer in the cargo hold was doing its job, indicating that the repairs she and Vreiss had done before docking with the *Auriga* were holding. There was some slight problem with hydraulic pressure in the airlock doors' system that might be caused by a small leak. Must've been something that happened when they shot up Purvis's Alien embryo—either a bullet nicked a line, or a small spray of Alien acid caused a pinhole leak somewhere. In a ship this size, any loss of pressure could affect the systems throughout the vessel. Well, the airlocks were all sealed, so it shouldn't stop them from getting free of the *Auriga*—

"Call," Johner snapped, his nerves fraying, "is the *Betty* prepped?" Earth was growing much bigger in the view screen as the planet pulled the *Auriga* down into her final embrace.

"She's hot," Call said, still calculating. It was going to be close. She found herself wishing Hillard was here. "I'll shut the docking bay airlock." She didn't look at Vriess as she said to him, "Pull the holding clamps on your mark." She was *one* with the ship, she was *Betty*. It felt weird, but good, too.

There was a long pause from Vriess, too long, and Call glanced over at him. He was scanning his equipment, looking around nervously. "Right . . ." he muttered. "Just need to . . . find, uh . . . the vertical thrust lock. . . ."

Distephano leaned over the engineer and asked worriedly, "You guys *can* fly this thing, right?"

Ripley raced through corridors as fast as she could, finding her way to the *Betty*'s dock almost by instinct. Call's voice—the voice of the *Auriga*—was repeatedly telling her to evacuate, that impact was so many minutes and seconds away.

In frustration, she yelled back at the voice, "Dammit, I'm moving as fast as I *can*!"

As she rounded the last corner, she saw the massive airlock doors leading to the *Betty*'s dock begin to shut, as the ship, with Call's voice, told her, "Airlock doors closing. Stand clear."

"NOOOOOOOO!" she bellowed, hurling herself forward with a burst of speed.

The doors were sliding shut before her. Throwing herself full speed at the narrowing space, she slipped through just in time, the sealing doors nearly catching one of her heels. She fell hard against the deck, and gulped air desperately.

Then Ripley heard the resounding clang that indicated the first docking magnet was disengaging.

"NO!" she shouted, as if anyone in the small ship could possibly hear her.

Lunging to her feet, Ripley raced the length of the dock toward the *Betty*. Another magnet disengaged with a huge clang. Speeding across the platform, Ripley moved faster, faster, until she could see the ship, the last magnet still in place. Five meters away. Three. . . .

A flurry of activity in one of the *Betty*'s video monitors suddenly attracted Call's attention. She glanced over and saw—

"Shit!" she yelled, unplugging herself and bolting out of her seat to lean over Vriess's shoulder. "It's Ripley! She's coming! She's almost here!" She reached past him, took hold of the *Betty*'s airlock controls.

"Call, dammit!" Vriess yelled, confused. "We're almost disengaged! We're out of time. We can't wait!"

"We're not leaving her behind!" Call shouted back, as she slammed her hand against the cargo bay door control mechanism.

* * *

Screaming in the rage of its abandonment, the Newborn finally managed to squeeze through the small
trapdoor in the waste tank ceiling. The beast fell onto
the upper deck of the Auriga in a tumble of limbs, the
new, small wounds it had just earned seeping onto the
surface, raising smoke from the quickly melting flooring. The acid blood had helped the Newborn widen the
hole it had just crawled through, making it large
enough for the being's huge body.

The Newborn looked around as its wounds stopped
bleeding and started to mend. It saw the Ripley disappearing down the hallway, running fast. But the Newborn could still find her, could still follow the human
clone through the link in its mind. Pulling back its lips
and grinning with teeth that were part Alien and part
human, it loped after its ancestor down the darkening
hallways of the doomed ship.

The last magnet was still in place as Ripley raced hard
for the ship. The loading platform and all the ramps,
however, had already been withdrawn, and the ship sat
over the abyss of the docking tube, waiting for her final
tether to be released so she could descend out of the
bay.

As Ripley worried how she might gain access to the
interior, the cargo bay airlock suddenly opened invit-
ingly. Without hesitation, Ripley reached the edge of
the platform and jumped, flinging herself off the platform like a diver going for the gold. She sailed through
the air, three meters, five, seven—then landed hard on
the solid floor of the Betty's cargo bay. The landing
knocked the wind out of her and she gasped for air as
she waited for the doors to close behind her.

Ripley counted down in her head, but nothing happened. She had a sudden flash of *déjà vu* of waiting somewhere, somewhen, for another set of doors to close and keep her safe, but the memory was too insubstantial to capture.

As she looked back down the *Auriga*'s corridor at the sealed airlock she'd narrowly gotten through, she saw the massive doors suddenly shudder as a huge force slammed against them.

Then again.

And again.

She closed her eyes, not wanting to feel the contact, but knowing it was there all the same. Because *they* would never let her go, never release *their* claim on her. Not in this life. Maybe not ever.

Glancing around the cargo bay, she recognized certain pieces of equipment as critical for the ship's functioning. It startled her to realize how *familiar* it all seemed, all the things associated with operating a spaceship. It had been so *long*. Another lifetime. A different body. She snapped out of her reverie, dealing with the problem at hand. This place was never meant to be exposed to vacuum. They'd never survive descent if they couldn't get those doors shut. Did the crew know? Could they monitor this area? She looked around but couldn't decide if there were small cameras in the hold or not.

Forcing herself to move, to react, she staggered to her feet. The ship rocked in her berth and Ripley nearly lost her tenuous footing as she grasped the manual override controls to the *Betty*'s airlock. Gripping the handholds and using her greater-than-human strength, she tried to force the overrides to close the doors.

Suddenly, with a squeal, the doors began to close slowly. There was so little time left. . . . Trusting the airlock to do its job, she abandoned the controls, and bolted for the access stairway that led to the cockpit.

The squeaky, descending doors masked the fact that

the pounding of the Newborn on the sealed corridor airlock had suddenly stopped.

"**We** got her!" Vriess told Call as Ripley landed in the cargo bay. "She's in. Now, let's get the hell out of here." He fumbled with the controls that would prepare the *Betty* to start her descent through the *Auriga*'s long docking bay. As soon as the ship reached the halfway mark, Vriess could open the *Auriga*'s outer airlock. The big military vessel was already in the ionosphere. They were cutting it close. *Too close,* Vriess thought, really feeling the pressure now. As soon as the cargo bay doors sealed shut, he'd start their descent.

Vriess and Call watched the monitor, seeing Ripley stand up slowly and brush her hair away from her face with a hand. The woman forced the manual override to respond, then left as the doors began to drop.

That was all Vriess needed to see. He switched the monitors from the cameras back to the critical readout screens he'd need to manage their escape from the falling *Auriga*. Quickly, he glanced over Call's flight plan as it scrolled over the screen. *Lookin' good,* he thought, and signaled the ship to start her descent.

That was when the screen turned red and the bottom of the readout flashed a message Vriess really didn't want to see. He rapidly tried some overrides, but the message never changed.

"Call," Vriess said quietly, but the concern in his voice was plain. "I can't get the damned doors to close."

"You *what*?" Johner snapped from the seat behind them. "We can't hit atmo with those doors wide open!"

"Ripley nearly got them closed by using the manual override," Vriess told them, still reading the bad news on his screen, "but they stopped again halfway down. I can't get them to budge."

"Let me try," Call said quickly, plugging her connection back into the ship. Muttering, she begged the ship, "Talk to me, *Betty.*"

In the docking bay, the ship's exhaust caused steam to condense throughout the tube. Some of the steam had followed Ripley into the cargo hold, creeping around the equipment and cargo like the low-lying mist that shrouded graveyards. As the docking bay prepared to allow the *Betty* to depart, the air currents suddenly changed, and blew the steam away into a different pattern. The clinging strands of gray water vapor that trailed around the cargo bay airlock doors were whisked away in a sudden gust.

All that was left behind was a solitary figure.

As the Newborn pulled itself through the narrow space between the doors that had once stood between itself and the ship, it saw the magnets disengaging. And it saw the Ripley standing inside the ship. Determined to wreak its revenge on the being who betrayed it, betrayed the Queen, betrayed the entire hive, the Newborn growled a vow of vengeance. Waiting until the condensing steam once more enveloped it in camouflaging grayness, the Newborn crept on all fours toward the ship.

The gray death's head of the Newborn grinned as the creature stealthily approached its newest home. It didn't know what this place was, only that its mother— who was trying so hard to abandon her orphan child— had led it here.

The other four people already on board the *Betty* turned as their newest passenger rushed into the cockpit.

"Ripley!" Call called, turning in her seat. For some

reason, she just needed to *see* her to be sure she was there.

"Hi," the woman gasped breathlessly.

As she passed Distephano, he grinned at her. "Man, I thought you were dead!"

She nodded distractedly. "I get that a lot."

"Glad you could make it," Distephano told her. "I'd say it was good to see you, but Jesus, woman, you look and *smell terrible*!"

Ripley leaned over Vriess's shoulder, scanning the monitors. "Why are we still here?" It was obvious from the readouts how little time they had left.

From her seat behind him, Call glanced at Vriess. He was sweating hard, distracted, clearly overwhelmed at the task ahead of him. He stammered, "I'm just . . . uh . . . trying to find . . . the, uh, manual override. . . . Is that it?" He reached hesitantly for a switch.

Johner leaned forward as if to assist when Ripley shoved the big man out of her way, and slapped Vriess's hand. "Oh, for chrissakes . . . !" she muttered disgustedly as she hopped into the second pilot's chair, the one right beside Vriess.

Elgyn's chair, Call remembered with a pang.

Johner looked furious. "What do *you* know about flying these . . . ?"

Ripley cut him off impatiently. "Are you kidding? This piece of shit's older than I am." Her hands flew over the controls unerringly, hitting buttons, flipping switches. She wasn't even looking at half of them. "Just open the *Auriga*'s goddamn airlock," she ordered Vriess.

He seemed happy to yield control of the ship to Ripley except for the monitor he couldn't stop watching. He nodded toward it. "We've *still* got breach! Look! The hatch!"

"I shut it," Ripley told him calmly.

Johner leaned over her chair, pointing to Vriess's screen. "The goddamn hatch!"

Her eyes were drawn to a flashing screen that told the same story.

Vriess's hands were once again moving efficiently over the control board. This was a problem he understood. "It's this piece of shit again! We've lost pressure in the hydraulics. How did that happen?"

Johner was leaning over Vriess's shoulder now, reading the panel. He stood and turned toward the cargo bay. "Maybe I can wrestle it closed."

"I tried that already," Ripley told him. His expression told her he knew he could do no better.

Call stood, rapidly disengaging herself from the communication port. At this point, they really didn't need her here. "I got it!" She started to climb from her seat, then stopped for the briefest instant as she realized Ripley was watching her.

The intensity of the older woman's gaze seemed to say, *Of course I know who let me in.* Ripley's gratitude was clear in her expression. The robot nodded once.

Ripley barely managed a wan smile as she turned her attention to the monitor in front of Vriess.

The readouts on the screen told them the *Betty* was slowly pulling out of the dock. Call wouldn't have much time to shut the doors before the outer lock opened. But she was the only one who might be able to survive back there once it did. Rapidly, she wove her way past the seats toward the back.

As the cockpit door closed behind her, Call took a second to look over the area. The cargo bay airlock had been sitting open less than a minute, but those *things* could move incredibly quickly. Could one of them have crept in here while they were all messing with the controls?

The very thought made her feel edgy, made the short hairs on the back of her neck stand straight up.

The hoists and chains hanging overhead swayed and jingled as the ship moved, seeming to echo her nervousness.

Cautiously, she approached the emergency override controls. Grasping the lever, she used all her strength to yank the handle down, hoping this would force the closure of the lock in spite of the faulty hydraulics. The telltales flashed red, then green, and with painstaking slowness the doors began to lower, only to jam once more about a half meter from the floor.

"Call?" Vriess's voice on the intercom startled her so badly she jumped. "Call?"

She started to answer him but before she could, a shadow flickered behind her. She froze instantly, every sense on hyperalert. The shadow moved, flickered again. Sensing a presence, Call turned slowly, ready to face whatever might be there.

"Call?" Vriess called over the intercom. "Call?"

Ripley handled the ship ably as it passed through the first set of docking bays as it descended toward the *Auriga*'s massive airlock. But even as she controlled the *Betty*, her attention was inexorably drawn to the monitor that indicated the cargo bay airlock was still open.

There's nothing there, Call thought irritably, wondering if the damage to her body from Wren's gunshot was affecting her sensory reactions. She peered around the vacant cargo bay and decided it was only the constant jostling of the hoists and chains that lent a sense of activity to the quiet area.

Need a lever, she told herself, forcing herself to focus on getting the lock sealed. Looking around the dimly lit bay, she saw, for the first time, all the complicated shadows cast by the various shapes of equipment and cargo. Suddenly, they all looked like hiding places.

Get the lever! she ordered herself sternly, annoyed at her imagined terrors when the real one they were facing was scary enough. Spying a long iron bar, she reached for it, picked it up, hefting its weight and strength. *This'll do nicely.*

There was a sudden creak of equipment as the ship shifted slightly and the sound made her jerk to attention and look around the bay. The chains jangled together harshly, jostling each other in the dimness.

Get on the door! she reminded herself, turning her back on the cargo bay. Slipping the iron bar into the manual override grip, she leaned on the end of the bar to force the jammed handle all the way down.

A sudden sense of *Otherness* was suddenly so strong, Call could no longer deny it, not even for the airlock. There was a *sound* like a hissing breath, the sense of heat as if from expelled air, the feeling of something near, something dangerous—

Tensing, she turned, every sense wired, the mechanism she used for a heart accelerating wildly.

This time, it was there, really there, right behind her, and it was *huge. And* hideous. From the darkest shadows rose the most nightmarish vision Call had ever seen—and she was no stranger to nightmares. Whatever this thing was, it wasn't your garden-variety Alien. This looked like a horrific cross between the typical beast and the Angel of Death. Its skull-like face leered at her, its parody of human teeth grinning. It was bigger than the other Aliens, and the slight hint of humanity about made it seem that much more grotesque.

She had never seen anything like it, not in the history books, and not on the *Auriga*. It was related to the original Aliens, yes, she could recognize that, even in her terror. But the difference—Could this be Wren's last gift . . . ?

The human traits of the creature are unmistakable. Oh God . . . Ripley's genes . . . !

She had to get out of here. Had to get away from it.

And then it moved toward her, reaching, reaching with arms impossibly long.

She felt as if she'd grown roots into the deck. She couldn't move. She couldn't think. Everything was on overload in her brain as she stared at the terrifying thing reaching for her.

But its hand moved right past her, grasping, instead, one of the crossbeams on the jammed airlock door. Then, to Call's dazed surprise, the creature helpfully shoved the door to the floor, sealing it shut.

"**S**he's got the doors, man," Johner told Ripley, as the warning message on the monitor turned green and changed to an all clear. He slid into the chair Call had vacated and switched the monitor there to an outer view of the *Betty.* "And *we've* got no time left. Open the docking bay doors before we kiss the ground."

Ripley was aware of him only peripherally as she manipulated the ship's controls, taking over, she imagined, for the things Call might've done much more easily through her port.

"Go full thrust on the downdraft!" Vriess called to her. "We can still get clear." He glanced at Ripley. "But it's gonna be close. And it's gonna be a bumpy ride."

She nodded, surprisingly reluctant to turn her attention away from the monitor. But Call had the doors secure. She was all right. There were more important things for Ripley to do. She worked the controls and, at the same time, managed to strap herself in securely. She could hear Distephano and Johner doing the same. *So familiar,* she thought tiredly, handling the heavy harness that encircled her waist and shoulders. . . . Just like the controls of the ship. All so strangely familiar.

The computer voice of the *Auriga,* sounding just like Call, suddenly announced through the *Betty*'s intercom, "Warning. Procedural interruption. Ship not leveling for vertical drop. Braking system disengaged. Collision imminent."

"No shit," groused Johner from behind her. Distephano was silent.

Ripley sat back in the chair and relaxed, as if this were some kind of pleasure cruise.

"Almost there. . . ." Vriess said quietly.

Everything jelled. All at once. The *Auriga*'s descent rate. The speed of the *Betty*'s ejection. Everything worked.

"Now!" Ripley called, and hit the switch for maximum power. The *Betty* jerked hard and everyone braced.

Vriess wasn't worried about Call right now; he had much bigger issues on his mind. Some of *Betty*'s systems weren't up to par, since he'd never been able to make the repairs he'd scheduled. To get truly free of the *Auriga,* the ship would have to respond quickly, have to use real power. He had his doubts as to whether she was up for it. Especially without Hillard at the helm. . . . He glanced over at Ripley, trying to figure out how she came to be there, how she knew so much about the *Betty*'s controls, her foibles, her abilities. . . .

Ripley suddenly yelled out, "NOW!" and hit the controls.

And Vriess watched the monitor, which showed—

—The exterior of the massive *Auriga,* its myriad lights winking against the darkness of Australia's night sky, as the ship raced recklessly toward earth. Suddenly, the *Betty,* looking like a toy next to the huge frame of the military vessel, shot out of the airlock, nearly smashing into the bottom of the bigger ship as it ejected. Vriess thought it looked like nothing more than a tiny piece of trash hurled out of a speeding plane.

"Look out!" Johner warned.

"I am!" Ripley assured him, as she maneuvered the little ship in a tight arc away from the behemoth threatening to crush them.

The *Betty* swerved, zigging and zagging to avoid the bulk of the big ship, until she was finally clear. She leveled out and sped away, as the *Auriga* continued plunging to her death. Vriess checked again, just because he knew Call would care. But this part of the Outback was all open space, no cities, no people, just dark, desolate land for miles. The crater the *Auriga* would leave would be the most interesting part of the landscape for years to come.

Vriess and Ripley fought together to control the speeding *Betty*, pushing the ship and all her aging parts as hard as they could to save them.

Call hadn't been this afraid when she'd fled the robot purge. She couldn't think, couldn't process, merely react.

The monster was between her and the cockpit door. But that hardly mattered, the only thing that mattered now was escape. Anywhere. Anyhow. Escape.

The Newborn took one step toward her but as it did, the ship jerked hard suddenly, and they were both knocked off balance. It was just the slap of awareness Call needed. Suddenly, she was *motivated*.

Dodging the creature's outstretched arm, Call ran as fast as she could move. The thing was right behind her, nearly stepping on her heels, as if toying with her before the kill.

The creature hissed, and she felt its claws brush her leg. Swerving sharply to the right, she lunged at the last second for the crawl space under the stabilizer. As the huge Alien realized its prey was about to evade capture, it bellowed a protest and leaped, but Call had already disappeared beneath the belly of the big machine.

Making herself as small as possible, she rolled over and over until she hit the back wall. Spinning in place, she faced out at the three open sides, searching for her pursuer, fully expecting the creature to be scrambling after her.

But it was gone!

The Alien warrior had followed the Newborn out of the crèche, just to be near the young one. His Queen was dead, and the warrior was adrift. He'd thought that the Newborn would use the Ripley to center them, to give them their purpose, but the Newborn had been unable to hold the Ripley. Why, the warrior didn't understand. Now the Newborn was gone, sworn to kill the Ripley, devour her.

The warrior had followed the young one on its quest because he needed a focus. But the Newborn's focus was not his and he was floundering. The last of the young had emerged from the hosts and were growing. The crèche had been completed. There might be a new Queen in some of the last young who had hatched, but the warrior wasn't sure.

Without a Queen to guide him, he had no focus, no ambition, no purpose. Perhaps it would be best to hibernate now.

The ship they rode on was empty of the prey, having nothing aboard it now but warriors, dead hosts, and young. The corridors were strangely vacant. This was no longer a viable nest. Not without new hosts. But without a Queen to direct them, the warrior feared they might not ever find new hosts.

A voice spoke from inside the ship, and the warrior lifted his head, hearing the voice.

"Collision in six seconds. Five. . . . Four. . . ."

The Newborn was no longer aboard. Yes, the warrior thought, curling into a tight ball, this would be a good time to hibernate.

The voice of the ship said softly, "Here we go—"

Aboard the *Betty*, Distephano could see enough of Vriess's monitor to know what was about to happen. He glanced over at Ripley, who seemed completely in tune with a ship she should have no knowledge of. Her mouth was a grim line, as her eyes moved back and forth, missing nothing. *Man, you are one strange lady*, he thought sympathetically. Still, he admired her ability to handle the vessel and everything else that had happened. As accustomed to space flight as he was, this was one hell of a rough ride, and it wasn't over yet.

Call's voice from the *Auriga* said softly, "Here we go—" and they all watched the giant ship impact like a meteorite, smashing into the ground, exploding into a massive fireball that lit up the night sky for miles around.

The *Betty* was safely away, watching from a very discreet distance. Not that the ship herself was safe yet, not by a long shot.

"Wow!" Johner said for all of them, as the gigantic explosion filled the sky. The impact, Distephano knew, would be felt on seismographic instruments all over the planet. Let them try and figure it all out. The thundering firestorm raged on, consuming everything the *Auriga* was, everything it stood for. Too bad they were all too tired and preoccupied to cheer.

He glanced over at Ripley. Her expression showed many things—relief, satisfaction, sadness, a bone-weary exhaustion coupled with intense concentration.

So Distephano cheered her silently. *You got them, lady. Once again, you got them.*

He felt pretty good. As soon as they stabilized the ship, they'd get ready to land on Earth. The *Auriga* was destroyed. They were *safe*.

Then he realized something.

"I only had three weeks to go," Distephano said wistfully. "Wonder if they'll believe my story, or if they'll can me for telling the truth?"

"Hey, man," Johner called over cheerily. "You're welcome to hang with us. We ain't real organized, but you're a resourceful guy. You'd fit in fine."

He and Johner laughed lightly, way too tired to enjoy the humor.

"Where's Call?" Ripley said anxiously. "She should've been back here by now."

"You're right," Vriess decided. "We sure could use her. We've got questionable readouts in half a dozen areas. If she plugged back in, she could nursemaid the old girl long enough to let us land." He hit the intercom switch, and said impatiently, "Call, where the hell are you?" At the same time he flipped the monitor over from the smoking ruin of the *Auriga* back to the cargo bay.

With Ripley in the way, Distephano had to lean over to look past the woman's shoulder, but he couldn't see Call in the monitor. Just then, the ship shook furiously again as Ripley wrestled with the controls.

A panel sparked suddenly, then a hose ruptured and steam hissed out near Johner.

"SHIT!" the big man shouted, unbuckling quickly, and wrestling with the hose.

"This thing is gonna fall apart!" Ripley hissed through clenched teeth.

Vriess was doing a quick scan, and evidently didn't like what he saw. "Pressure's unstable!"

Johner looked over at Distephano. "Go get Call back there, will ya? We need her up here *now.*"

As the soldier unbuckled from the chair and reached automatically for his rifle, he heard Johner mutter disgustedly, "What is wrong with that chick?"

Good question, Distephano thought, as he headed out to help her.

From beneath the stabilizer, Call could hear the tone chime that indicated they were free of the *Auriga*'s docking bay. In the cockpit, Vreiss and Ripley would be totally preoccupied with getting the ship as far from the pull of the bigger vessel as they could. There was still too much risk that they could be dragged down in the crash trajectory with the massive military ship.

She wondered if Vriess—if anyone—had seen the invading Alien in the camera, if they knew what she was dealing with back here.

Call lay totally silent and motionless under the stabilizer, wondering where the Alien had gone. Was it lying in wait for someone to come rescue her?

A sudden sharp scrabbling on top of the machine made her tense, but she never uttered a sound. *It's on top of the machine!* she realized. Then that small bit of noise stopped and there was nothing. Call froze in place, waiting. Worrying.

All at once the creature slammed itself against the floor, trying to flatten itself into the small space under the stabilizer. Its arm and part of its hideous head squeezed under the machine as it clawed the floor in a desperate attempt to reach her.

Terrified, Call pressed back against the wall, wanting to disappear into it, but she could go no further. The clawed hand gouged the thick, tough, shock-absorbing flooring of the cargo bay, pulling ribbons of it up in dense, black curls. The Alien roared its rage, reaching, groping, shredding whatever part of the floor it could reach. Call plastered herself against the back wall and sucked in her gut.

Squirming, lashing its tale, scrabbling like a crab, the creature fought to reach her, squeezing itself further into the restricted space, until the long, deadly claws were flailing right in front of Call's face. The Alien was berserk with rage, but its head was simply too big, too inflexible to squeeze under the machinery. Still it fought against the physics of the space, convinced if it just tried harder it would finally reach its goal.

On the next swipe, the claws nearly touched Call's nose.

15

The longest finger on the Alien's hand nearly touched Call's face. She couldn't breathe for fear of putting herself within reach of the thing, and didn't know how much longer she could evade it. It was growling at her, terrifying her with its threatening sounds. And worst of all, she could smell it, with its terrible human/animal stench.

How long could she hold out, how long could she stay just out of reach? And how long would it take before someone in the cockpit missed her?

Suddenly, Call's sole focus—the reaching hand of the Alien—became secondary as she saw a pair of booted feet enter her range of vision. She blinked. Military issue. Distephano!

From where he'd entered the cargo bay, the bulk of the stabilizer would be hiding the Alien from him. Did he even know it was after her? Had he seen it on the monitor? It wasn't like the damned thing was staying put.

Suddenly, the Alien was also aware of Distephano's presence. Call could tell because the claws groping for her suddenly stopped moving, and the entire body of the beast froze.

Distephano moved cautiously into the room, searching, not assuming anything. It was dim in here. Spooky. Equipment hid most of the floor space and the chains hanging from the ceiling created a soft jangling sound that made it hard to think. So where was his favorite robot anyway?

"Call?" he called softly. The weird ambiance of the cargo bay seemed to call for quiet. Caution. "Call? You in here?"

And where else would she be? he asked himself. It wasn't like she could've slipped past him.

Distephano moved on, sweeping the area carefully, methodically, like any good soldier.

As Distephano moved around, the Alien slowly, silently began to withdraw its hand from under the stabilizer.

Part of Call felt tremendous relief, but that was immediately overridden by her own internal imperative. It would go after Distephano. It was a hundred times faster, a thousand times more deadly.

Beneath Distephano's feet, the *Betty* shook hard, as he imagined Vriess and Ripley fighting the controls, manually trying to force the ship to their will, because Call wasn't up there, plugged in.

Finally, Distephano stopped in his tracks. He felt a chill race down his spine and found himself wondering—could one of those *things* be in here? Could it have gotten Call? What else might've stopped her from returning to the bridge? He stared disbelievingly around the cargo bay. There were hundreds of hiding places here. He felt an almost animal terror at the thought, but then got a grip on himself. He was a soldier. A member of General Perez's handpicked crew.

Calmly, with an almost detached air, Distephano armed his rifle.

Distephano took another step forward, stopping near a big piece of equipment that dominated the room. With that same detached air, Distephano lifted the rifle, sighting cleanly down the weapon.

If one of those things, if one of them is here in this hold. . . . He considered that for a moment. *Those things killed every last man on my ship. If one of 'em is in here, I'm gonna blow it to hell and back. I owe them that much.*

Then he glanced at the big piece of equipment nearest him, the piece that largely blocked his view of the rest of the bay. *This has gotta be the stabilizer!* he realized. *This isn't the Auriga—it's just a small ship. There's got to be a ton of stuff back here that's critical to our survival. And those things have acid for blood!*

As that sank in, Distephano paused. He couldn't shoot it. Not in here. But he might have to. . . .

As Distephano weighed his minimal options, he cautiously eased around the side of the stabilizer.

Call had just come to the same conclusion. *Acid for blood. If Distephano shoots that thing—*

She stared at the nightmare vision of the grotesque face. It was smiling again. The Alien's grinning maw suddenly dripped a glob of mucous. And then, before she could shout a warning, it struck. Desperate to do *something*, Call scrabbled out behind it.

The creature lashed out, reaching with its impossibly long arm, as one of its hands grabbed Distephano's face even as the other knocked his gun aside almost casually. His scream was a short, hoarse, "NO!" as he fell back hard. The rifle flew out of his grip, clattering away uselessly.

The Alien's big palm covered the soldier's face, but it didn't stop him from screaming now in rage, surprise, and sheer terror.

As the gigantic creature pulled itself off the floor, dragging the flailing soldier with it, Call clearly heard the *crack* of Distephano's skull as the young man's cries rang with pain. The creature bit into his scalp, popping his head like a clamshell to devour his brain and drink his blood.

That was deliberate! Call thought, aghast. *Deliberate—and human!*

Then the Alien turned to her, the huge, lipless fangs looking more and more like a terrible death's head grin. Then the creature *laughed*—a breathy, staccato laugh, as Call stood rooted in place, stunned.

Ripley was only dimly aware that behind her, Johner was still trying to splice together the damaged hoses.

She didn't pay much attention either when Vriess yelled back at the big man, "Patch it through the servo!"

"Hey," Johner yelled back, "this is supposed to be *your* job. I mostly just hurt guys!"

Ripley paid much more attention when Vriess hit the intercom button and shouted, "Call! Get back up here!" There was no answer.

That was what was distracting her. Call should've been back long before this. She'd be able to feel the ship bucking back in the cargo bay. The robot would know she was needed in the cockpit. And Distephano had been gone way too long as well.

Then Ripley felt it. *The contact. The telepathic touch of her last living child.*

She shuddered, then unstrapped and bolted from the chair.

Behind her, she heard Vriess and Johner both shout her name as Vriess grabbed the abandoned controls and fought the lurching ship.

There was a part of Ripley that realized they were hurtling toward earth in a ship that was almost completely out of control, but she shut that part away. That wasn't important to her now.

Theoretically, it wasn't possible, but at this specific moment Call's brain simply could not process. She stood in the shadow of the mutant Alien, having just watched it devour Distephano's brain, and couldn't move, couldn't think, couldn't do a single thing to save herself.

The huge beast seemed to grow taller as it loomed over her, but all she could do was stare at its frightening face, at the brain matter speckled on its teeth, and smell the stench of blood on its breath.

It snatched her up before she could react, before she could move, gripping her shoulders and pulling her up, up, toward its face. The huge mouth opened, the teeth moved closer.

Can it do that? she wondered dazedly. *Can it devour processors and microchips?* Maybe not, but the destruction of those units would bring about her end as efficiently as if she had had an organic brain.

Call closed her eyes, and mumbled one final prayer.

As if in answer, there was a bang as the cockpit door shut with a slam, the loud retort deafening in the small space of the cargo hold.

Call heard a voice shout, "Hey!"

The creature holding Call tensed, then turned, growling in annoyance.

Ripley stood with the cockpit door closed securely

behind her. She stood tall, steady, her legs shoulder width apart, her stance as confident as Call remembered. But the robot's eyes were keen, and she could see the weariness etched on the woman's face. She'd been through so much. It was clear she was at her limit.

The Alien's growls lessened as she stared at Ripley.

Quietly, the woman said to the creature, "I can't let you do that."

The big animal's tail lashed in impatience, and suddenly it spun, still hanging securely onto Call. The small woman found herself held as a shield, her back pressed tight against the monster's front. Call blinked, trying to regain her sense of self-preservation. This was such a *human* thing for the beast to do.

Ripley stood rock steady, her eyes meeting Call's.

There's got to be something you can do to help her, Call thought frantically, even as the creature gripped her tightly. In the distance, she glanced at Distephano's abandoned gun, lying where it had fallen. Could Ripley get to it?

We're far enough from the stabilizer, Call thought, *still there's so much shit back here. . . .* What would happen if Ripley spattered this thing to kingdom come? The trembling of the ship told her they were fighting atmosphere, approaching land. Could they make it with severe damage? Suddenly, she didn't know. She didn't know anything.

The Alien's tail lashed wildly, and it hissed angrily, its hot breath rushing by Call's ear.

Ripley's eyes quickly scanned the area, glanced over the military weapon, then returned to Call's face.

She knows, the robot realized. *Sure, she's flown ships before. She's remembering. Maybe she even recognizes some of the equipment.*

But then the taller woman only looked doubtful.

That seemed to snap Call out of it. They were on their way to Earth with this monster in their hold. What did it matter if they were all destroyed, as long as the Alien was? But she knew, instinctively, that Ripley would have trouble shooting *through* Call even to kill this beast.

Galvanized, Call strained forward, needing to convey everything to Ripley, to make her understand.

"Shoot!" she shouted frantically. "Come on, shoot! I'm used to it!" She didn't care if the bullets ripped her to shreds, as long as they destroyed the nightmare holding her. This was, after all, her mission, wasn't it? To save humanity from the beast. Remembering that helped.

But Ripley only looked anguished, and to Call's dismay, made no attempt to retrieve Distephano's gun.

The ship rocked and the three of them, locked in their bizarre tableau, struggled to stay on their feet.

In the cockpit, Vriess was frantically working switches, struggling to keep the *Betty* from shaking completely apart. His eyes were everywhere on the board, trying to keep track of too many things at once. He didn't dare even glance at the monitor that showed one of those *things* holding Call as a hostage. He couldn't let himself think about it.

Beside him Johner was working just as furiously, gripping the controls, fighting to manually steady the crazed ship.

They passed from nighttime into daylight, the sunlight stabbing its way into the cockpit.

"We're shorting out. . . ." Vriess warned his copilot.

"I've got it," Johner reassured him.

"Ten minutes until impact," the computer voice announced calmly. For the first time, Vriess realized the voice belonged to Call.

* * *

As the Newborn hissed and screeched and clutched the terrified Call to its body, Ripley realized that the only way she could kill it now would be to do as Call had wanted, to snatch up Distephano's gun and shoot the monster repeatedly through the robot's body. But Ripley could no sooner do that than she could have done it to Newt. No, shooting the beast was clearly not the answer.

But what *was* the answer?

Ripley stared at the creature and struggled against her own creeping despondency. Everything hurt, *everything*. She was so spent, so exhausted, she just wanted to lie down and die. Oh, God, why couldn't she just lie down and *die*?

Maybe I'm really a robot, she thought crazily. *A robot with only one programming—no matter what, just keep going. God, I hate this.*

The Newborn screeched its fury, its teeth grazing the top of Call's head—but it didn't strike. Had it figured out that Call wasn't human, that Call had no organic brain, no hemoglobin in her blood? Had it finally smelled the Alienness of Call's robot body?

Ripley had a sudden shocking memory of Bishop being torn in half by an enraged Queen and knew that the Newborn could just as easily damage Call. Ripley had not been able to save Bishop then, and—since Call was the only one of her kind in this time period—she would be unable to salvage Call, either.

She had to do something—wasn't that always her fate? With a sigh of despair, Ripley held her hands out in a gesture of surrender, Ripley forced herself to once again search for the telepathic contact she'd felt back in the crèche.

There's something . . . tenuous . . . guarded . . . but something. . . . I feel it—

It was inhuman, repellent, but somehow familiar. It was everything Ripley could do not to shudder. She made herself meet the creature's gaze, meet the eyes that were exactly her color.

The contact was cold, but hungry. Enraged, yet achingly lonely.

The crèche was destroyed. All the others gone. The Newborn was truly alone now. The only one left that had even some small spark of connection to it was the human woman standing before it.

Ripley understood that suddenly, and realized it was the only card she had left to play.

Well, baby, she thought ironically, *I'm the only mother you've got!*

She held her hands out in supplication, and filled her mind with comforting thoughts, with the connectedness that had once existed between them. Mentally, she saw the image of herself holding Newt, small, blond, trusting Newt. She saw the child's arms and legs entwined around her, clinging, knowing Ripley wouldn't let her go, wouldn't release her. Newt, who understood with a child's unshakable trust that Ripley would come back for her. She held the image in her mind as she murmured, "Come on. Yes."

Slowly, the Newborn grew calmer, stopped lashing its tail and began relaxing its grip.

Ripley watched Call watching her. She could clearly see the confusion on the smaller woman's face. Call didn't move. Couldn't move. When the Newborn finally released her, she was so unprepared, she collapsed on the floor. Ripley couldn't afford to meet Call's gaze, or try to answer the question in her eyes. Her eyes stayed locked on the Newborn, luring it, willing it to abandon the robot and come to her.

As the huge creature shuffled toward Ripley, she saw, in her peripheral vision, Call silently creep away from them.

Yes, Ripley thought, *yes!* She was nearly distracted by a memory of herself hissing at Newt, *Run! Hide!* If she dared, she would've shouted the same to Call, but she was still too close to the Newborn.

Without looking at Call, Ripley said to her quietly, "Get out." Then Ripley moved toward the Newborn, meeting it halfway.

"Come on," she bade the monster, holding out her arms.

Two steps, three. The Newborn loomed over her now, close enough to touch, as Call crept farther and farther away. Ripley continued to stand with hands open, mind open, showing the monster the motherly image in her mind. She thought of the Alien Queen reaching out to touch her mutant child just before the Newborn ripped her head off. Could this thing even understand a concept like comfort? Trust? Forcing herself to maintain that one single image in her mind, Ripley held her place, offering a gesture of submissiveness with her posture, her stance. She held her breath as the creature drew closer.

Then the Newborn made a small sound, as if it were in pain, in need. The childlike noise startled Ripley, made her look up. The death's head face left little room for emotion, but she thought she could sense the creature's aloneness. Remembering her own gesture to the Newborn in the crèche, and the tenderness Ripley had shown to Call—the robot who'd come to kill her—she reached up now, and slowly, gently, stroked the Newborn's elongated head.

Behind her, still crawling toward the cockpit door, Call stared back, horrified and fascinated by the interactions of the two beings that were both Alien to each other, yet genetically bonded. As Ripley stroked the Newborn gently, the monster's long, serpentine tongue reached out and lapped the sweat trickling down the side of Ripley's face.

As the creature cleaned her, Ripley's eyes scanned past it, searching the cargo bay, even as she kept her

mind firmly on the image of loving motherhood that
had pulled the beast to her. Directly behind the Newborn, she spied a moderately sized porthole that
showed the dark, Australian night sky now brightened
to dawn as they moved farther and farther away from
the impact site and closer to land.

Ripley continued stroking the Newborn's head, running her hand tenderly over the wide eye ridges, down
over the jaw, forward toward the chin. The lips drew
back automatically in the death's head rictus she was
so terribly familiar with. Her fingers found the massive
teeth, touched them cautiously. Still lapping at her
face, the Newborn opened its mouth, permitting Ripley's curious examination of its human/Alien teeth.

Slowly, Ripley ran her palm along the edge of the
monster's teeth, then pressed down sharply, not even
allowing herself to wince.

When she pulled her hand away and looked at it, her
palm filled quickly with thick, red blood. Her blood.
Human blood. *Mostly.*

Her eyes met the Newborn's, her face still calm, her
mind still controlled. With a sudden gesture, she waved
her arm, flinging the palm full of blood directly at the
porthole.

The glob of blood hit the center of the port with a
splat. At first there was no reaction, but then, seconds
later, the porthole began to sizzle where the blood
touched it. Then it began to smoke. Then melt.

In her mind, along the fragile link, Ripley sensed a
change in the creature's attitude. The sense of childlike
trust, the chilling aloneness was suddenly gone. In its
place was one emotion: *betrayal!*

Immediately, the creature drew itself up tall, hissing
as if in warning.

The Newborn watched the Ripley's *defiant gesture with
surprise. The only thing it had any interest in right now*

*was the slow, painful death of this one frail being who
was standing before it. Even though this place they
were in trembled and shook, even though the Newborn
suspected they were in grave danger, it did not care.
The Newborn would not be distracted.*

*It loomed over its victim and contemplated the joy it
would feel when its teeth broke through this skull. The
Newborn would devour this brain slowly, savoring it,
and wondered if it would be able to absorb the Ripley's
memories by doing so. It would be wonderful that the
Ripley's blood would feed its burning, eternal hunger.*

*Slowly, so as to enjoy the moment, the Newborn un-
furled its tongue.*

Ripley froze, keeping the sudden flood of fear off her
face.

The Newborn opened its huge maw, and its slithery
tongue—the same tongue that had so gently cleaned
Ripley, the tongue that made this creature so different
from the Queen who bore her—slithered out obscenely. Ripley watched in sickening dread as it stiffened, grew rigid, just like its forebears. As the tongue
metamorphosed, small, sharp teeth appeared at its tip,
opening and closing as if trying out their new abilities.

Ripley groaned. The Newborn leaned over her,
ready to drive its rigid tongue right through her forehead. The woman couldn't even make herself shut her
eyes as she stared in horrified fascination at the creature's change.

Oh, God help me! Ripley thought, realizing that this
was the first prayer she had ever uttered in this lifetime.

Tiny, white teeth gnashed at the end of the tongue
as silvery mucus dripped off it. The tongue advanced,
approached her face—

The woman shuddered uncontrollably, but wouldn't
allow herself to retreat, knowing that would cause the
predator to pounce.

Distantly, past the Newborn's shoulder, Ripley spied Call creeping along the floor, reaching finally for Distephano's lost gun. Then her gaze moved up—

To see the viewport directly behind the Newborn. In its center, the blood she'd spilled bubbled and melted away, filling the air with that unique burning plastic scent. They were in the stratosphere, she guessed. Almost home.

Ripley stared in fascination at the port, knowing the view of the disintegrating window would keep her from seeing the gnashing teeth in the tongue edging toward her face.

Suddenly, in her mind, the image of herself holding Newt safely in her arms changed—

There were memories. Of unexpected chaos. Warriors screaming and dying. And fire. And herself, Ripley, standing firm, holding her own young in her arms. Causing death and destruction to the crèche.

The Newborn leaned closer for the final kiss—and was suddenly startled by the change in the mental contact. There was no submissiveness in the Ripley now, no fear, no remorse. Only defiance! The memory of her destruction of the crèche rang through the link, enraging the Newborn. Mocking it.

The Newborn growled before striking, then—

There was a loud sound and a powerful, lurching pull, as if the Newborn had been grabbed by some invisible force. The pull grew stronger, until the Newborn was drawn inexorably back, back, away from its prey. The creature didn't understand! How could this be happening?

The Newborn screamed in rage, as the Ripley moved farther out of reach. The beast flew backward, faster, faster, then slammed into something hard, sticking to it. Roaring in fury, it reached wildly for the Ripley with

its claws. The Newborn could not believe that it was
trapped, not when its prey was still so close.

There was a sudden *BANG* as the security of the window was breached by the acid eating away at the port, and smoke and small objects began hurtling around the hold in the instant windstorm.

Ripley saw Call react quickly, grabbing hold of the ends of some hanging chains and straps, which she unclasped from where they were tethered and secured around her own chest.

Dozens of small objects were being sucked through the hole in the port, while Ripley's acid blood kept eating away at the edges. The hole grew bigger and the power of the decompression was greater. Even as its arms reached for Ripley, the Newborn was drawn back, sucked away from Ripley and yanked toward the port at the same time that Call latched onto Ripley's jumpsuit to keep her from being pulled forward.

The Newborn hit the window with a crash, and screamed in rage and pain as its body was held in place by the force of the rushing atmosphere.

The sudden cessation of the decompression caused Ripley to fall to the floor, out of Call's grip. The robot held out her hand and yelled at the woman, *"COME ON!"* as Ripley clambered to reach her.

The Newborn fought the pull of space, its great strength actually allowing it to push away slightly from the drawing window, and the resulting rush of decompression pulled Ripley back toward it.

The deafening screech of the Newborn grew louder as it fought to capture its ancestor. But all its rage was futile against the power of the rushing atmosphere. Ripley could sense the beast's growing fatigue, its confusion, and realized that for the first time in its short, horrific life, the Newborn was actually *afraid*.

Afraid to die? Ripley thought at it. *Well, get used to the idea!*

She started to laugh and wondered when she would stop finding humor in such strange things.

Then, finally, the Newborn lost its futile struggle against the force of the decompression, and it was pulled against the still-widening hole with a loud *THUMP!* The impact ruptured the creature's skin, and Ripley could see its acid blood explode into the upper atmosphere.

The insectile shriek of the monster rattled through Ripley's bones, and she screamed a cry of pain of her own, as she scrambled on the floor to reach Call, as if attaching herself to the robot was the only way she could cling to her own humanity.

It was true; Call was *only* a robot. But the whole purpose of the original robot program was to use the androids in places where it was too dangerous for human beings. The only reason they existed was to save the lives of real people.

Through the years, came the whispered memory. . . .

I prefer the term 'artificial person.'

I can't lie to you about your chances . . . but you have my sympathy.

Bishop and Ash—only robots. One nearly sacrificed his own life to save her and her child. The other would've happily killed her for interfering with his plans. . . .

Ripley closed her eyes as the crowded, conflicted memories chattered so loudly in her mind she couldn't think.

At first the Newborn was aware of nothing but the inexorable, terrible vacuum, pulling it away from the Ripley, the creature it was determined to destroy. But then it hit the porthole hard and felt the burning, freezing

*cold. The skin over its back and kidneys began to solid-
ify, then suddenly burst outward in an abrupt, terrible
explosion of tissue and blood. It screamed shrilly, grimacing in hideous agony as acidlike blood, organs,
and entrails blew out into space, freezing almost instantly while still connected to the creature.*

*It was dead, really, but its brain would not accept
that. In a desperate fight for survival, the Newborn
plastered its palm against the glass, struggling to pull
away. But the port was partially dissolved there, too,
and the original hole grew bigger still as the Ripley's
acid blood—and now the Newborn's, too—continued
to eat away at it. As the Newborn pushed frantically,
the original hole melted into this weakened place, and
the whole area dissolved. Its arm was immediately
sucked out into space, freezing solid and breaking its
shoulder almost at the same time.*

*The Newborn opened its eyes wide in horror, the
pain more excruciating than anything it could ever
have imagined, and stared helplessly at the Ripley. It
could not speak, could only scream, but surely this
being would understand what it wanted. How could
the Newborn's own mother watch it die like this and
not help?*

*So, with eyes that matched Ripley's, it pleaded
with her.*

***KILL ME! KILL ME! FOR GOD'S SAKE, MOTHER,
KILL ME!***

In the cockpit, Vriess watched the earth loom nearer
and nearer as he fought the ship's controls. The count-
down continued in Call's voice, reminding him with
every second that she still wasn't there, that Ripley
hadn't returned, that he was alone in his futile battle
with the ship's aging systems. Alone. Inadequate. Crip-
pled. He'd never be able to control the *Betty* now as
she plunged wildly toward the planet.

Suddenly, Johner threw himself in the seat Ripley had vacated and wrapped his hands around Vriess's own, lending the mechanic his own brute strength. Together, they wrestled with the bucking ship.

When the terrible suction stopped as the Newborn hit the window, Ripley sagged, exhausted, against the floor. She heard Call screaming her name, but could barely think, barely react, even to save herself. Call was reaching for her with one arm even as the robot clung to the apparatus of the ship with the other. Slowly, Ripley forced herself to crawl toward the smaller woman.

The Newborn's screams grew louder, shriller—scaling up into panicked hysteria. The creature clawed the air desperately, its face, its eyes riddled with terrible pain. Ripley looked back, even though she didn't want to, but she was unable to hear the sounds of fear without feeling something.

The Newborn looked straight at her, hissing, mewling painfully.

She shook her head. Her last terrible child. It was appropriate that she be here to mark its passing. She needed to witness. *Just to be sure.*

She felt Call's fingers latch onto her clothing, haul her closer, then tie some kind of strap around her waist, then her chest, but she was unable now to pull her gaze away from the flailing, crying creature that was still tied to her genetically. Ripley sobbed as the Newborn stretched its arm toward her, pleading with its eyes for her help.

It ends here, Ripley thought at the creature. *All of it. Forever. No more incarnations.*

The Newborn writhed in torment, whimpering.

Okay, Ripley thought, as if trying to ease its pain. *It won't be long. Easy now.*

With a sudden jerk, the outstretched arm was sucked

into the creature's body, the bones flying through the hole into the air. The Newborn bellowed in agony, writhing against the hole that held it as fast as a glue trap pinned a fly. Then its belly hollowed, as its entrails erupted out of the window.

Its piercing scream ripped right through Ripley's brain, hitting her like electricity. She sagged, grabbing her ears, trying to block the terrible sound of her offspring's death rattle. She screamed with the Newborn as the sound tore through her like razors. Ripley felt the warm stickiness of her own blood seeping through her hands as her ears bled. She huddled on the floor, crying out, as Call pulled her nearer, clinging to her, holding onto her with all the strength the robot had, as if to save Ripley from this last attack.

As the women watched in shocked terror, one of the Newborn's legs retracted sharply into its body, disappearing into its torso, as huge bones and muscles were sucked out into the void.

Then the Newborn's other leg contracted into its body so fast, Ripley feared the port wouldn't last much longer. But she couldn't tear her eyes away from the horror of the melting Newborn. The creature looked back at her as the second arm retracted. The Newborn's head sank into its grotesquely misshapen body.

Oh, God, tell me you're dead by now. You've got to be dead! Ripley begged for it to be true, but then the living eyes of her terrible child said no. Its lungs had to be gone, and its terrible screams had finally stopped, but its mouth kept moving, the frightening teeth opening and closing. Ripley knew the Newborn was still connected to her.

And silently begging, *Help me. Help me.*

Then suddenly, with a final, terrible rush, the creature's skin tore, wadding around the remnants of its body like so much clothing, then slipped out the port bit by bit as the Newborn's living flesh was sucked into space. Ripley could see fingers of one hand still wiggling near the being's eyes.

I've got to get out of here, she thought, fearing she'd lose her mind if she didn't. *I've just got to get out*—But those eyes, those damned eyes that were just like hers were still *alive* and Ripley felt trapped by them.

Even as the ship shook and rattled around them, the inexorable destruction of the monster, piece by piece, continued. Everything happened much faster now, as the last of the Alien's skin peeled off its body and flew out into the stratosphere. Ripley let go of her bleeding ears, and found herself hugging Call's head, as if trying to keep a young child from seeing something horrible. But they were both watching it, unable to pull their eyes away.

Ripley felt the tenuous telepathic link try one last desperate time to capture her. She shuddered under that inhuman contact, and mourned it at the same time. It was part of her, after all, and it was dying. But she could not allow it to take her with it.

The Newborn's head jerked suddenly, and finally, mercifully, Ripley realized the back of its skull had exploded outward, taking its brain.

As the head erupted and extinguished the Newborn's life, Ripley felt the grasping mental touch evaporate like a sigh and found herself weeping, half in relief, half in grief.

Oh, thank God, it's dead, finally dead! Ripley thought, wanting to just break down and sob. But there wasn't time as the decompression continued, pulling everything not nailed down toward the grisly remains of the Newborn.

More sucking noises, and suddenly the skin on the Newborn's face ripped completely away, pulled out through the eye sockets. There was a momentary pause, as if they'd reached the calm center of the hurricane, as the Newborn's eye sockets got plugged with its last mass of skin, but then one socket blew free, once again acting as a suction hole. And suddenly, the women were back in the wind tunnel, as the vacuum pulled them toward the hideous, grinning skull.

It was too horrible to consider, that they might get yanked out into space through the Newborn's head.

The two women clung together desperately, fighting the terrible pull.

"We're not gonna make it!" Johner swore, even as he battled the controls. The ground was coming up fast. The decompression in the cargo hold was tossing them around like a paper airplane.

"Oh, yes we are!" Vriess barked back at him, waging his own war.

Call's voice maintained a bizarrely calm level, as it counted down the seconds until impact.

As the ship trembled violently around them, and cargo and machinery were flung about the hold, Ripley and Call clung to each other for safety. But as Ripley wrapped her arms tightly around the robot's torso, Call kept attaching more safety webbing to them, snapping the end clasps to metal handholds bolted into the cargo bay walls. The straps bit into Ripley's body as they fought the pull of space, but she hardly noticed.

Inside her, in spite of the terrible jarring, in spite of the fact that they were probably plunging to their deaths, Ripley found herself amazingly placid. She remembered the drop ship from the Sulaco and the violent ride down to Hadley's Hope. She remembered Hicks sleeping as if it were just a pleasure cruise, and that made her smile. She held Call against her, wishing she could convey the image, convey her tranquillity. Nothing mattered now. Earth would be safe. *They* were all dead. All of them. And she had outlived them, if only for this little while.

At last, the leering skull of the Newborn shattered into a thousand pieces and disappeared through the breached port.

"This is it, man, this is it!" Johner yelled.

"We're gonna make it, I said," Vriess argued, as both men still wrestled with the helm.

Without warning, the ship gave a final shudder, then suddenly calmed. Ripley felt the cool rush of natural air as it blew wildly around the hold, whipping papers and debris around like a whirlwind, only now it was blowing *into* the hold, not sucking everything out of it.

She blinked as she drew in the cool, crisp air and looked out the now empty port. The melted hole showed no lingering evidence of its grisly victim. All she could see was blue sky, and fleecy clouds.

There was an unnatural stillness, and Ripley suddenly felt like she was dissolving. The death of the Newborn had taken the very last remnants of her tattered strength. There was nothing left. She tottered on the verge of collapse.

But Call held her up. "You did it," the robot whispered. "You killed it."

"I did?" Ripley wondered dazedly.

"Yeah. You did it. It's dead. It's history."

"Great," the woman mumbled wearily. "That's really great."

Call looked up at her as she struggled to support the taller frame. "Maybe now we can both have good dreams, huh?"

Ripley tried to smile. "We made it. We're okay."

"Yeah," Call said with some amazement. "We are!"

Ripley heard the sound of an intercom flicking on. The hold was filled with Johner's whooping sounds of victory as Vriess, obviously laughing wildly in relief, called out, "Call? Ripley? You guys okay? We can see you, but—"

"We-we're okay," Call called back. She looked back at Ripley and really grinned now. "We're really okay back here."

Ripley nodded and tiredly rested her cheek against Call's head.

In the cockpit, both men howled with joy and relief. Johner lurched out of his chair, grabbing Vriess roughly around the head and kissed him hard on the mouth.

"Yeah!" Johner crowed. "We got this puppy by the danglies now! Let's put her down!"

Vriess nodded his head rapidly, grinning like a fool. Then he paused, glanced about the cockpit, and sobered. Glancing nervously at Johner, he asked quietly, "How *do* we put her down?"

EPILOGUE

Ripley stared out of the *Betty*'s viewport at the approaching Earth. She'd never seen a blue sky or real soil. At least, not in this incarnation. It was new to her, and she enjoyed the uniqueness of it.

She sensed Call standing quietly at her shoulder, and the robot's presence gave her a sense of comfort and companionship that she had never felt before.

The memories of Newt, and Amy, Hicks, and Bishop, and all the other people whose lives she'd touched no longer burned so painfully inside her. Now they made her feel warm. They made her feel human. She had loved and been loved. She had fought and protected and had died to save those she loved. She would do it again if need be. And again. And again. She was okay with it now.

The dream images that had so long flickered across her mind were no longer chaotic. The cold comfort of cryo-sleep. The driving need to protect her young. The strength and companionship of her own kind. The power of her own rage. The warmth and safety of the company of friends. The images were meaningful, sat-

isfying. *She recognized them on a level far beyond consciousness, far beyond learning. They were part of her, part of who she'd been, what she'd been. And now they were part of what she had become.*

She turned to smile at the smaller woman. Call was staring at their nearing landing site. "Earth," she said, as if only realizing it now herself.

Ripley nodded and almost smiled. "Earth."

"My first time," Call said quietly. "Ought to be plenty of places to get lost around here. I guess . . ." She paused, as if there were a whole battery of things she wanted to say, but couldn't find the words for.

That struck Ripley as funny. Call was a robot. She had the entire lexicon of language at her disposal, and she couldn't find the right words.

"What?" Ripley prodded, wanting to know.

"What do you think we should do? Where should we go?" Call was looking at her as if she had all the answers.

Ripley could only shake her head as she looked down over the planet. "I . . . I don't know!" She shook her head. "I really don't know, Call. I'm a stranger here myself."

The two women stood quietly, companionably, side by side, watching the distant lights of the nearest city. There was plenty of time to decide.